Sia Martinez AND THE Moonlit Beginning OF Everything

Sia Martinez

AND THE

Moonlit

Beginning

OF

Everything

RAQUEL VASQUEZ GILLILAND

SIMON PULSE

NEW YORK   LONDON   TORONTO   SYDNEY   NEW DELHI

SIMON PULSE

An imprint of Simon & Schuster Children's Publishing Division

1230 Avenue of the Americas, New York, New York 10020

First Simon Pulse hardcover edition August 2020

Text copyright © 2020 by Raquel Vasquez Gilliland

Cover illustration copyright © 2020 by Jeff Östberg

For information about special discounts for bulk purchases, please contact Simon & Schuster Special Sales at 1-866-506-1949 or business@simonandschuster.com.

The Simon & Schuster Speakers Bureau can bring authors to your live event. For more information or to book an event, contact the Simon & Schuster Speakers Bureau at 1-866-248-3049 or visit our website at www.simonspeakers.com.

Jacket designed by Laura Eckes

Interior designed by Jess LaGreca

The text of this book was set in Adobe Garamond Pro.

Manufactured in the United States of America

2 4 6 8 10 9 7 5 3 1

Library of Congress Cataloging-in-Publication Data

Names: Vasquez Gilliland, Raquel, author.

Title: Sia Martinez and the moonlit beginning of everything / by Raquel Vasquez Gilliland.

Description: First Simon Pulse hardcover edition. | New York : Simon Pulse, an imprint of Simon & Schuster Children's Publishing Division 2020. | Audience: Ages 12 and Up. | Audience: Grades 10–12. | Summary: Artemisia (Sia) Martinez's mother was deported to Mexico by ICE, and disappeared in the Sonoran Desert trying to make it back to her American family; Sia believes that she was as good as murdered by ICE and the sheriff in their small Arizona town on the edge of the national park, and wants revenge against him and his son, Jeremy—but her search for the truth will uncover many more secrets than she counted on.

Identifiers: LCCN 2019028330 (print) | LCCN 2019028331 (eBook) | ISBN 9781534448636 (hardcover) | ISBN 9781534448650 (eBook)

Subjects: LCSH: Mexican Americans—Juvenile fiction. | Post-traumatic stress disorder—Juvenile fiction. | Racism—Juvenile fiction. | Secrecy—Juvenile fiction. | Missing persons—Juvenile fiction. | Mothers—Juvenile fiction. | Fathers and daughters—Juvenile fiction. | Alien abduction—Juvenile fiction. | Science fiction. | CYAC: Science fiction. | Mexican Americans—Fiction. | Post-traumatic stress disorder—Fiction. | Racism—Fiction. | Secrets—Fiction. | Missing persons—Fiction. | Mothers—Fiction. | Fathers and daughters—Fiction. | Alien abduction—Fiction. | LCGFT: Science fiction.

Classification: LCC PZ7.1.V4 Si 2020 (print) | LCC PZ7.1.V4 (eBook) | DDC 813.6 [Fic]—dc23

LC record available at https://lccn.loc.gov/2019028330

LC eBook record available at https://lccn.loc.gov/2019028331

To Ansel.
You are my greatest dream come true.
I love you, I love you, I love you.

Please be aware that *Sia Martinez and the Moonlit Beginning of Everything* contains the following content:

Sexual Assault

PTSD

Physical Abuse

Parental Death

Racist Violence

Sia Martinez AND THE Moonlit Beginning OF Everything

IT'S BEEN SIX HUNDRED AND NINETEEN DAYS SINCE I found out Mom died. And only one until I get my revenge.

It's all thanks to Mrs. Tawn, my elderly English teacher.

"It would be such a blessing if we could all put this unfortunate incident behind us, for the school and the community." She smiles, displaying white teeth stained with peach lipstick.

I close my eyes and nod, though I can only think about how clean the words sound, *unfortunate incident*, as if renaming a murder could make it something that can be tucked away and forgotten, much like my trig homework.

"After all," she adds, raising her eyebrows, "forgiveness is an attribute of the strong."

I roll my eyes so hard, I can basically see my brain. Only old white people came to me and Dad after Mom died, going on about forgiveness. Even Rose's mom, with her rosaries and holy water, had the sense to never mention such an impossible act.

Mrs. Tawn takes way too long to stand and reach over her desk to place her translucent hand on mine. "Write a letter to Jeremy expressing humanity and grace."

I have no idea what that even means, but Mrs. Tawn beams as if she's revealing the universe's secrets. "You'll be the first to read in class. Does that sound alright, Sia?"

I snap my hand back. "Yeah. Sure. Whatever."

2

"WHAT THE HECK ARE YOU GOING TO WRITE?" ROSE asks as we drink milkshakes at Maude's after school.

"It's gonna be my revenge, Rose. So, the truth. Which is exactly what he deserves." I shrug. "Maybe then I can move past all this and become, like, I don't know. Normal?"

"Oh, heck yes. Revenge. Normal." She pauses. "But, like, write what, exactly?"

I twirl my straw. "How about, *Hey, Jeremy, you're a big jerk and your dad is a disgusting subhuman. Oh, and by the way, you're also both racist assholes, and I wish I could stomp on your ugly, freckled faces until you choke.*"

Rose's eyes are wide and she touches a finger to her lips.

Shit. The whole restaurant is way too quiet. My cheeks burn. Damn it, Sia. This is why no one sees you as anything beyond the Angsty Girl Whose Mom Died.

Rose changes the subject quickly. Nail polish or something. I can hardly listen till we get out to the parking lot, where I kick the sand. It settles in a cloud all over my shoe. "This town is too small."

"No one heard. Really."

"Rose." I sigh.

"Okay. Maybe they did hear some of it. But no one's going to make a big deal about it."

I just nod. God knows I want her to be right. She's not, but man, that would be nice.

3

I PASS MR. ALBARN ON HIS WAY OUT OF HOMEROOM AS
he mumbles something about not having enough copies. The second
he's out the door, Jeremy McAssHat sits on his desk and says, loud,
"Hey, Eric, wanna hear my draft for Tawn's letter?" He and Eric snicker.
And everyone in class leans in.

"Dear Sia Martinez." He makes an exaggerated effort to roll his r's,
but he still manages to sound, and look, like an especially ugly fish
pulled out of the water. "I heard you were talking shit about me at
Maude's yesterday. Fact of the matter is, everyone in town is on my side.
I got spies everywhere." He lowers his paper and stares at me. Well, not
at me. More like my hair. Coward. "My dad's the sheriff. Your dad's a
park prancer." He and Eric laugh like that was extra funny. "You got
nowhere to go and nowhere to hide." And that's when he makes his fatal
mistake. "Just like your mom."

There's an audible gasp in the classroom. Mostly people look horrified, but Jeremy and Eric take no notice as they laugh like apes.

I wish I could say this is the moment Mr. Albarn walks in and that's
why no one defends me. That they have no time to call Jeremy an ugly
horse-face. But it's three excruciating minutes before Albarn returns. No

one says a word as Jeremy points at me and says, "Aw, I was joking, doll. Don't gotta take everything so seriously."

I don't listen to a word of Mr. Albarn's lecture. Instead, I write my letter to Jeremy. After I sign my name, my hands don't shake anymore. I think that's a good thing.

4

Dear Jeremy,

Monday morning, you, yet again, called my dad a "park prancer." I don't know why you talk like my dad's job is an insult, because being a park ranger is awesome. Also, my dad has a PhD in biology from Stanford. He's literally the smartest person I know.

He met my mother when they were twentysomething. Long story short, she broke his nose and he fell in love. They ended up together and we moved here so my dad could study the species that rely on the cacti forest.

Three years ago, your father, a deputy sheriff, turned my mom over to ICE, who sent her to Mexico, a place she hadn't seen since she was six months old. She tried to come back to us a hundred times, but they didn't let her. Finally, she decided to cross the Sonoran. That was the last thing we heard from her.

Last June, my dad told me my mother was dead. I've hated summer since.

Maybe my father's a park prancer, if that's what you insist on calling it.

But at least he's not a murderer.

Sincerely,

Sia

5

THE SILENCE IN THE ROOM IS THICK. AS THOUGH YOU
can toss it over your shoulder, take it home, and cook it for dinner. But
Jeremy shatters it. He stands and shouts, "Who the hell do you think
you are?" He charges, while Eric and Tate hold him back. I want to
smirk and say, *Oh, doll, it was just a joke*, but things are way too loud
with the class erupting into shouts and hollers and Mrs. Tawn's coyote
screech trying to rise above chaos.

Eventually, I find myself outside the principal's office.

Dad runs down the hall. "Sia! What happened?"

I guess all they told him was I'd had an altercation with another student, no details, so he let his mind run with all the possible worst-case
scenarios. I explain it to him as he catches his breath.

Rose thinks my dad is handsome. I don't let her say what she's really
thinking—that he's hot, ugh—but when my dad gets all intense like
this, I can picture him in the men's Express catalog or something, looking off into the distance while wearing a polka-dotted skinny tie.

By the time I'm done speaking, Dad's eyes are narrow and his jaw is
tight, and I thank all the gods it's not me he's mad at.

We walk into the office where Jeremy sits with his dad. I always want to throw up when I see Tim McGhee, especially when he's in his too-tight-round-the-gut cop uniform. The principal, Mr. Savoy, dismisses them and they both glare at me as they leave. I wonder what they'd say if Mr. Savoy weren't here. They've both called me and Dad some pretty nasty names when there weren't any witnesses.

Dad speaks first. "I don't want that woman teaching my daughter anymore."

"Mr. Martinez, will you please have a seat?" Mr. Savoy pushes up his square, green-rimmed glasses.

"Not until I'm finished, sir. I want her transferred out of that class immediately."

"Your daughter provoked Mr. McGhee with callous and baseless accusations regarding, the, ah—" He coughs for a few seconds and I shake my head, biting back a grimace. He can't even say it.

"I don't give a damn what she did or didn't say. I want a good reason why I shouldn't sue your school for a *callous and baseless* assignment that triggered Sia's PTSD."

Mr. Savoy turns a deep shade of pink as my dad continues. "Do you routinely allow your teachers to interfere with the students' psychological processing of traumatic events?"

Mr. Savoy is now shuffling papers like he's looking for lost correspondence from the president.

I know people threaten to sue everyone all the time, but my dad has a lawyer and she's totally sued the Caraway Police Department for racial profiling anyone who's remotely brown with the hopes of deporting them. My dad's been searched a dozen times for "papers" in the last two years alone, even though he was freaking born in Oklahoma. Plus, this town is so small, everyone knows he's legal. Word got around about the lawsuit I guess, as it always does. And now he can get any petty man to tremble with the idea of their worst fear. Losing money.

"Let's not get carried away, now," Mr. Savoy says finally. "I'm sure we can work something out."

6

"WHY'D YOU DO IT, M'IJA?" DAD WON'T LOOK AT ME. "Why'd you call him a murderer?"

I glance out the window of his Chevy at the sky, so blue and cloudless it looks like someone draped a silk up there. "Revenge."

Dad sucks in a breath. "Was it worth it?"

"Yes."

When I glance at him, his eyes are closed. "Sia. We can't hold onto anger, to hatred like this. It makes us no better than them."

"Have you forgiven the sheriff, Dad?"

His eyes whip open and he stares at me for ten whole seconds. I can see myself in his pupils. The clench in my jaw. Finally, he blinks away and turns the car on.

Neither of us says anything on the way home.

7

IN THE END, I GET TRANSFERRED TO A NEW SCIENCE
and English class. Dad can't get me out of a three-day suspension. It's
not fair the true villain, Jeremy, doesn't have to deal with any punishment whatsoever. Just like his dad. But at least I don't have to see his
ugly pug face first thing in the morning anymore.

I hear Sheriff McGhee wants me kicked out. Not a surprise. He
wants every brown person kicked out of everywhere.

8

MY GRANDMOTHER LIANA HERNAN TOLD ME SHE SENT
spirits to help my mom survive the Sonoran. Up until the day she died,
Abuela was convinced Mami was still out there. "Ponte una flor en tu
cabello, Sia, your mamita might come back today." And it didn't matter
what anyone told her. She said, "M'ija vive." My daughter lives.

I can't believe that anymore, but I'm just as superstitious as that viejita.
Every new moon, I drive deep into the desert and light San Anthony's y
La Guadalupe's candles for one hour, to guide Mom home. Abuela used
to do it like clockwork. Moonwork, she'd call it, but now it's up to me.

Sometimes Rose joins me, but tonight she's at choir rehearsal.
Tonight it's me, Anthony, and la Madre, the blue-core flames, and a
river of saguaros, tall, arms stretched like a welcome. Or like an attack.

Once I looked up what it's like to bake to death in a desert. How in
only a matter of weeks, someone goes from alive to half-eaten by birds
and coyotes to bone, white and smooth against the taupe sand.

When I'm eighteen, I want to find my mother's skeleton. I want to
string it together and sing her alive, just like my grandmother said the
first curanderas did, their clay skin still wet from the fog of God's breath.

9

IT'S GETTING DARK. I PROMISED DAD I WOULDN'T BE out too late, so I snuff the candles with my fingertips and climb back into my rickety Jeep. As I turn the key, I stifle a gasp when headlights approach. They stop some thirty yards away.

I don't know what to think. I've never seen anyone else here in my spot before, between the two cacti that look particularly humanoid. The ones my grandmother said might've created the world.

The car stops and its headlights shut off. I wait a few minutes and press the gas. Screw it. I know I'm not supposed to be here, but what could happen?

I gulp, thinking what Sheriff McGhee would do to me out here, too far away for anyone to see.

I know he didn't pull the trigger on Mom. But I think he wouldn't mind at all if my skeleton joined hers.

I drive by, slowly, and exhale long and thick when I see it's just an old pickup truck, red and rusty. I can't see who's inside. I just make my way home.

10

NEW STUDENT ALERT, **ROSE TEXTS THE NEXT DAY. I CHECK**
my watch. She's at lunch.

Guy or girl? I text back.

Guy. Very much.

I raise my eyebrows. So you like him?

I didn't say that.

I chuckle. I can almost hear her, the playful tone in her voice.

Name'?

Noah.

Noah what?

Dunno.

I wait a minute. You're not gonna tell me how he looks?

Later. Gotta go. Class.

I roll my eyes and groan. Rose loves keeping things in suspense. I
know she's planning on giving me the details in person, stretching drop
by teeny drop like coconut syrup. I sigh and toss the phone on my bed.

11

I'VE READ SOME OF *THE HOUSE OF THE SPIRITS* BY Isabel Allende (one of Mom's books), had brunch, made tea, spent an hour scrolling aimlessly on social media, tossed dinner in the slow cooker, and organized our spice rack. I can't believe I still have six hours before Dad gets home from work.

Even though it's too damn hot to do anything outside but pant like a hare, I push my sunglasses on and wander into the light.

My abuela always had a reverence for maíz. She lined kernels on all her altars, small and dried like saved baby teeth. She said maíz es la madre, el padre, los hermanos y hermanas, y toda las familias. She said for all we knew, we came from pieces of corn at the beginning of everything. She spoke like that a lot, as if she wasn't sure about some things, like whether or not it was okay to go to church while bleeding. Or whether we are the descendants of plants.

She grew corn every year, until she was too old and rickety. Then Mami grew it. And now they're both gone, so I grow maíz. My corn patch is little, but it's always stuffed with stalks. I plant too many kernels and I can't bring myself to thin them out.

This year, I'm growing Oaxacan dent and a variety that's so red it looks like blood. I planted marigolds between them, to attract pollinators that will cross the corn.

I want to make something new. Make something that will mean living here is less painful.

The stalks reach up and up like they see something out there I can't, something they need to touch. I take a husk in my hand and give it a gentle squeeze. They're already bigger this year than the last.

Feed them coffee. My grandmother's voice is as thick and defined as the wind, and I roll my eyes. Always meddling, that vieja, even from the afterlife.

"Fine," I grumble, and go inside to boil the water for the French press.

When the cobs are all ripe, I'm going to pluck and dry and grind them in my molcajete. I'll mix them into a masa, thick, roll them in Abuela's old tortilla press. Cook with cheese and hot peppers, eggs on the side, diced avocado. Our own special, homegrown, coffee-fed corn tortillas. I think Dad would like that.

12

"GREEN EYES," ROSE ANNOUNCES AS SHE WALKS INTO my room this evening. She throws her backpack down and takes a seat in my desk chair, leaning back.

"Green eyes," I repeat.

"Yes." She stands and falls onto my bed, arm outstretched dramatically, as though she were reciting a monologue in a tragedy. "Just like Harry Potter."

Then it clicks. "Oh! You mean the new guy."

"You mean new . . ." She pauses. "Man."

"Ew. What do you mean by that?"

"He's tall. Broad shoulders. Dark hair. Tan."

"White boy tan, you mean?"

"Yeah." She lifts her head to look at me. "How'd you know he's white?"

"You said his name is Noah, remember?"

"Oh, yeah." She sighs, drops her head back down. "Noah DuPont. That's his whole white boy name."

"So he's French?"

"Dunno. Didn't speak to him. He's in our earth and space class, though."

Oh, right. I'd nearly forgotten about my schedule change.

"We also have a new earth and space teacher by the way."

"What?"

"Mrs. Presley went into early labor."

"Wow. Is she okay?"

"I guess so. She's on bed rest for the rest of her pregnancy."

I crawl to my headboard, lean back, and cross my legs. "So we have a new boy and a new teacher all in the same class."

"Yes, ma'am." Rose pushes up again. "How was the first day of your temporary exile?"

I shrug. "Kinda long, actually."

"Aha!" Rose reaches for her bag and pulls out a folder. Tosses it in my lap.

"What's this?"

"The cure for your boredom, my lady. All the assignments you'll miss for the whole three days."

"Really?" I open it and pull out a couple of worksheets. "This is un-freaking-believable!"

Rose cocks her head. "You okay?"

"Yeah, why?" I'm examining the list of assignments from trig class.

"I've never seen you so excited about anything before. Like, ever."

"Well, this," I say, holding up the papers, "isn't part of the terms of my punishment. I'm not supposed to be able to catch up."

Rose scoffs. "Really? That's ridiculous."

I hum in agreement, my eyes still on the papers. "So you walked up to all my teachers today, asking them for my work?"

"Nah, I'm not that good of a friend." She laughs. "Ms. Gerber gave it to me in art."

"Ah." My favorite teacher. Even though she has the hots for Dad.

"Guess you know they're all on your side." Rose gestures to the folder.

"Yeah." Goosebumps prick along my arms. This town is so tiny and close to the border, sometimes it feels like everyone thinks all the brown folks ought to be on the other side of a big, ludicrous wall. So I like being part of a secret revolution against Jeremy and Tim McGhee. It's like being on the side of Wonder Woman versus Ares. Or maybe God and Lucifer.

13

OUR NEW SCIENCE TEACHER WANTS HIS FIRST ASSIGNMENT submitted tonight, but he gives me until Saturday at noon, or so he writes in my notes. That's how I spend a weekend morning writing about my favorite astrological body.

My mother used to take me into the desert to watch the moonrise. She told me the moon used to shine full all month long but that extra light made the plants on Earth grow too much. The whole world was covered in vines and trees and shrubs that started to strangle one another. So the moon decided to birth her own body every month.

When she is new, she is so small, like a baby, we cannot see her. With the darkness of the moon's birth, the world became balanced again.

My mother said her mother told her this story, and her mother told her, and on and on back until the first woman, whom the moon told directly. (My mom's mom also said the first people were kernels of corn, so I take it all with a grain of salt.) Either way, I grew up thinking the moon told stories.

This is my favorite astrological body. The one I'd like to learn more about.

There were a lot of things I didn't write. Like, after I found out my mom was dead, I went out and begged the moon to tell me otherwise, to tell me it could see her, still breathing, tracking her way through the Sonoran. And how sometimes I wonder if the moonlight that touches me when I light saint candles in the night is the same moonlight that also touches my mami's bones. And if somehow, I'm connected to her through that light. Like I'm still touching a part of her.

But Mr. Woods says one page is enough.

AT THE END OF THE ASSIGNMENT, MR. WOODS WRITES,
What unusual question would you ask if you were getting to know someone better? (Points deducted for inappropriate content.)

I type, *Which plant are you a descendant of?*

15

SATURDAY NIGHT AT ROSE'S, I'M SURROUNDED BY BOTTLES
of oils and creams, salivating from the smell of her mom's cooking.
"When is dinner going to be ready?" I ask.

"Five minutes ago, it was in twenty minutes. You can do the math,
my lady." Rose grabs the extra-virgin cold-pressed olive oil. "Should I?"

"Rose, no. Remember, you made me memorize it two weeks ago:
olive oil makes your hair look like—"

"Seaweed, I know, I know. But I saw this adorable vlogger who
swears by it!"

"Rose."

She sighs. "Fine. Coconut oil it is." She mixes a few spoons into her
concoction. "What shows did you bring?"

"The library didn't have anything new. So don't get mad at me."

She rolls her eyes. "So our options are *Battlestar* and *Buffy* again?"

"Well, I found this VHS of *Pretty Woman* in the linen closet. With
Julia Roberts? Looks super old. Like, older-than-*Buffy* old."

She scrunches her nose. "Julie who? You know what, don't answer
that. *Buffy*, then. I need some Tara in my life right now."

"Mmm. Okay."

"Don't forget to lock the door. If Dad—"

"I know, I know." Rose's dad would probably die of a heart attack if he caught a glimpse of a vampire or bug monster or any non-Jesus creature on the show. I put the DVD in and search for a good Tara episode.

Rose's father thinks most things are the devil: pop and rock and country music, any movies rated above PG, boys, bright makeup, cleavage, long earrings. I'll stop there because it's quite a list. He's okay with only a few things, really: me, homework, and, well, that's about it. He likes my dad, I guess, but I think it's because he feels sorry for him.

We're not allowed to do almost anything at Rose's, but I try to get a couple meals a week there regardless. Her mom cooks food good enough to present to God in heaven. When Mrs. Damas calls that dinner is done, I run to the kitchen to fill my plate with red snapper and peppers, red beans, and rice alongside a pile of tostones. Mrs. Damas smiles. "What's your mix today?" She gestures to our heads.

"Oh, the usual," I say. "Coconut oil and honey."

"I'm trying that new deep conditioner Gram sent," Rose says, and Mrs. Damas's smile drops. She's not a big fan of her mother-in-law, apparently, and Rose tends to enjoy this. Mrs. Damas doesn't respond, though. Instead, she says, "Sia, Rose tells me you're helping with the First Communion prep this month."

Though it's hard, I refrain from groaning. I'd almost forgotten that Rose had guilted me into teaching the class with her. It's the last one before the First Communion mass, so it's always packed with energetic children who need to be chased and caught every five minutes. Literally. I have timed it. I swear, those little jerks are organized or something. But I do owe Rose. She's tutored me in trig all semester and I'm actually passing. "Yes," I say as Rose grins at me from behind her mom. "Looking forward to it!"

"We're always blessed to have you, Sia." Mrs. Damas touches the cross at her neck. It's gold and beautiful. I used to have one just like it, in silver. Before Mom died.

Mr. Damas clears his throat. "Grace." It's more of a command than a reminder.

Rose and I bow our heads and close our eyes, listening to his monotone recital. "May everything in our lives bring us closer to Christ, who suffered relentlessly despite our unworthiness. Keep these two young women away from the prying eyes and hands of the Devil, my Father." I raise an eyebrow at Rose, who bites her lips, trying not to laugh.

"O God, we are not worthy of this life, or of this food, and we thank you. Thank you for giving us the gift of Jesus, who died on the cross so that we may have eternal life."

"Amen," I say. Maybe a little too enthusiastically, because Mr. Damas raises an eyebrow. "Praise the Lord," I add. This appeases him, I guess, 'cause then he begrudgingly allows us to eat dinner in Rose's room like barbarians.

16

WHEN I GET IN MY CAR, MY HAIR IS SHINIER THAN A
new Mercedes. Rose begged me to stay over again. I told her I have to
finish all that homework, but she knew. Getting up Sunday morning at
the Damases' means I have to go to Mass. And I can't. Not for two years
now. I mean, I can barely handle chasing kids who are supposed to be
rehearsing their First Communion.

Before going home, I take a detour into the desert and park near the
humanoid cacti. I reach into the back, grab La Guadalupe's candle, light
it in my lap. The flame flickers back and forth with my breath.

When I was, like, eleven, my grandmother said there were countless
worlds in addition to ours. The underworld, the ghost world, the world
of beetles and bats and hummingbird moths. There's a world for war-
locks and brujas and one for coconut trees and even a world just for our
dreams. That one, she said, was always changing.

As soon as Abuela returned to the kitchen, I rolled my eyes at Mom.

"Oh, please," I said. "How can there be so many worlds if I can only
see one?"

"There are many ways to see," Mom said. She then closed her eyes
for a second, as though she were savoring the smell of bubbling fideo

de pollo. As though she could see something impossible under her lids. When she looked at me again, she just said, "Come on." She turned to the back door.

"What? Why?"

"I said come on, Artemisia."

I grumbled and stomped through the door behind her. The backyard of Abuela's trailer looked like the whole wide desert. It still does, I guess.

"Face me."

I turned, scoffing. Finally, I looked at her.

Mom smiled. "You remember what I told you about the saguaros? That—"

"They dance when no one's looking? Yes. And I actually believed it, you know." I glanced at the cacti, their arms and heads all traitorously stiff.

"Stare at me."

I dragged my gaze to her once more. "Yes?"

"Keep looking."

I looked and looked at Mami's brown-gold eyes, until my own watered.

"There," she said. "You see that?"

I didn't want to admit it, but yes. I did see it. The cacti all around us. They *shimmied*.

And then, so fast I almost missed it, one to my right side extended one green, prickly arm out to another. Like it was asking her to dance.

I stopped breathing for a few seconds, jerking my eyes right on their plant-bodies. But they were as still as the dry air.

"They—did you—Mom, did you see—"

"Muy bien," she said, grinning. "Come inside, m'ija. Tengo hambre."

She had to take my hand and pull me in, where we sat under braids of garlic and ate sopa con Abuela. Otherwise I think I would've stayed out there for hours, staring, waiting for those saguaros to spin and turn and dip like they were in love.

17

I GASP AS A RED TRUCK—*THE* RED TRUCK—PULLS IN close.

The sunset reaches across the sky. It's light enough that I can see the driver's face. He looks young. I pinch the flame, place La Guadalupe in my cup holder, and open the door. I walk quickly; the dry wind rattles against me as I approach his window. He jumps a bit as I rap it with my hand.

"Uh, hi?" he says as he rolls it down. He looks older than me, but not by much.

"What are you doing out here?" I ask. "Who are you?"

He furrows his brow. "Is there some law I'm breaking—"

Truthfully, we're both breaking the law, considering you can't drive off road here. "What is it, exactly, that you're doing?"

He picks up a notebook and waves it about. "I'm writing."

I stare at him. He's wearing a taupe linen button-down and jeans. I wonder if he's from Bloomington, the closest town to ours. "Why here?"

"Why not? It's fucking gorgeous." He gestures to the sky.

"This is my spot."

"Sorry, I didn't see a 'No Trespassing' sign." He tries to hide a smirk.

I fold my arms. "This," I sputter, pointing to the space between the two green humanoids. "This is the beginning of the world. And you're just mucking it all up with your weird, rusty truck."

"Your Jeep's got rust, too," he retorts, but he's smiling. I try to memorize the specifications of his features in case I run into him again. Dark hair. Hazel eyes.

"Whatever." I roll my eyes and huff back to my car.

"Who are you, anyway? What are you doing out here?"

I don't answer. He yells again as I slam the door shut and drive away. I think it's something like, "What do you mean, this is the beginning of the world?"

18

I SHOULDN'T HAVE YELLED AT SOME BOY LIKE THAT.
Especially some white boy. The last thing I need is for the sheriff to find
out about my spot and come here and arrest me or something. I'm sure
he'd love that.

My grandmother found that spot, after she moved here, to the States.
She had to up and leave everything, with nothing to her name but a few
pesos and a baby. I can't even imagine that. White people pretend they
can imagine it, but you really can't, not unless you've been there.

Abuela said she was just taking a walk, my mom tied to her back,
napping. It was early in the morning, the only time she felt any peace.
And just as the sun broke over the mountains, just as the sky shimmered
from blue to pink to bright, she saw them, the man and the woman
cacti, their arms stretching toward each other. Like she'd caught best
friends, or lovers, finding one another again, after a long, long sepa-
ration. In that watercolor morning light, she said she felt like she was
witnessing the beginning of the world all over again. She knew this
space was sacred.

And when Abuela found out Mom was lost and dead, she came out
here and said that she felt the indigo of the night sky, the line of hiplike

mountains, even the cacti themselves, she felt each one tell her Mami was still out there. And she reached into her old Buick and grabbed a candle, I don't remember which, but I want to say La Guadalupe. Abuela always loved her best, and she said most mothers of the faith did, because who else knew best about the heartache of motherhood? Jesus? And she would laugh and laugh about that.

So Abuela lit the Guadalupe candle and prayed that Mami, wherever she was, would sense it. That the flicker of light, soft as a lantern, would string itself to Mami's heart and pull her home.

That's why I have to protect that spot. From strangers. From rusty muck trucks.

I just hope I don't come to regret it.

19

BY TUESDAY MORNING, I'M ACHING TO GET BACK TO
school. Being alone like this has got me thinking too hard and too long
about my mom.

I leap out the door when I see Rose's text. "See ya, Dad," I yell. He's
in the middle of a gulp of coffee and waves.

Creedence is blazing as I open the passenger door. "Looking good,"
Rose says, winking. I smile. I'd decided to wear my biggest bell bottoms,
a gem I found on one of our trips to Phoenix's many vintage stores.

She's wearing a yellow sundress and denim jacket covered in red and
blue flower patches. "You're looking pretty hot, yourself." I buckle up.
"You're not all dressed up for the new guy, are you?"

"Sia." She gives me a sideways glance as she pulls out. "Everyone's
dressed up for the new guy. Even a couple of the fellas."

I laugh. "Well, if he's as hot as you say he is . . ."

"Even better. Smokin'. A total babe." I raise an eyebrow and she
looks right at it. "You'll see."

Rose and I met at St. Julian's Catholic Church when we were babies,
back when my dad still had that religious streak in his bones. We
became best friends in the sixth grade and have spent just about every
weekend together since. Even though we have our own cars, we always

ride everywhere together. There's no one else who will blare—and belt out—Stevie Nicks with me. No one.

In school, Rose grabs me as I near my old science class. "Wrong way, ma'am."

"Shit," I say. "Where's the new room again?"

"Over here."

Out of the corner of my eye, I see Jeremy at his locker, gawking at me and Rose. "Martinez," he yells.

"Don't look," Rose mutters, but I can't help it.

"Glad to be reunited with your girlfriend?" He gives a hearty laugh and flashes us an obscene gesture with his hand and mouth.

"Run along, McGhee," Rose calls. "Keep your wet dreams to yourself."

Jeremy's mouth drops open. Frankly, mine does too. Rose rarely talks shit to Jeremy and his goons, but damned if she doesn't drag him when she does. She rushes me into the classroom.

"I can't believe you just said that!" I gasp between giggles.

"Let's just hope it doesn't get to my mom." Rose smiles. "I don't need her to schedule another confession with Father John." She grabs my shoulder. "Oh! Sia! He's already here."

"What, the new guy?"

I turn as she whispers, "No, don't look!"

Too late. As soon as I see his face, I roll my eyes and sigh. "No freaking way."

"What? What is it?"

Before I can respond, Mr. Woods speaks. "Okay, let's begin, shall we?" He clasps his hands together and waits for everyone to settle down. He glances at me. "Miss Martinez, I assume?"

"Yes."

"Good. Then we're all here. Welcome back to earth and space science. Miss Listas," he says to a girl named Camille. "Pass these out, if you wouldn't mind." As she does so, Rose pushes her notebook close to me. I see she's written, *Why are you freaked out about the new guy?*

He's been loitering at my spot in the desert with his ugly red truck. I yelled at him a few days ago about it.

Are you serious?! she writes quickly, but Mr. Woods is talking again.

"I've divided you all into groups of two or three based on your responses to the essay prompt on the astrological body you'd like to learn more about. Please gather near your group as I list them off. First, Chana, Kendra, and Kinlee, who all picked various constellations. Next, MaKayla and Bryn for black holes. Lyra, Joshua, and Gustavo, if you'll gather over there . . ." He continues on. Rose, sadly, was matched with Samara Kingsley for nebulas. With a sudden dread, I realize I'm the only one left. Well, me and—

"And finally, for the moon, or moons, as one of you wrote, we have Artemisia and Noah. You may gather . . . ah, the back over there looks empty-ish."

Every single girl in the class flings arrows at me with her eyes. Well, all except for Rose, who silently cheers while mouthing, *You lucky duck!*

"If you'll notice, the packet in front of you contains a series of unusual questions. I want you all to get to know one another better, and truthfully, I'd like to get to know you, as well. So, your first assignment is to fill out this questionnaire for another person on your team, due next class. You may begin now."

I make my way to the back, where Noah leans against a desk chair, reading through the questions. He lowers the page as I walk up. "Ah.

If it isn't the girl who introduced me to the beginning of the universe."

"The world," I respond, not even blinking as I sit down.

"Come again?"

"The beginning of the world. The universe came from someplace else."

He grins. His cheer annoys me for some reason. "Where's that?"

I scowl. "We're wasting time." I rattle my packet. "Let's get this over with."

He holds out his hand. "Noah." I take it, briefly. It basically swallows mine.

"Sia."

"Not Artemisia?"

"Just Sia. And no comments on the musical artist of the same name. Please."

He gives a half smile. "You don't like Sia?"

"Not really."

"Ah. That's too bad." He smiles again. "So, why'd your parents name you Artemisia?"

"Uh." I don't think that's one of the questions, is it? "My mom picked it out, I guess."

He scans the paper once more, and I take a few seconds to examine him. Rose was right. He's a giant. His legs barely fit under the desk. Wide jaw. Freckles. But she got one thing wrong—his eyes. They're not green.

I realize I'm just staring like a creep or something when he clears his throat. "So, Sia. Where are you from?"

"That's not one of the questions."

"This is what I'm thinking, though." He straightens his back. "This is a getting-to-know-you exercise. But we've just met. So, why don't we go over the basics first?"

I glance at the clock. "Fine. I'm from here. This tiny, old town. No siblings. I live with my dad. The end."

The corners of his mouth quirk up a bit, which makes me scowl. Why is he so happy? "Well, I'm from Azules. And I also live with my dad." His mouth takes a firm, straight line and I can tell he hates his father.

"Azules, that's right next to the Sonoran, isn't it?" I can't help but ask it.

"Yeah, how'd you know? You ever been?"

"No reason," I say quickly. "Let's just start with the questions."

Over the next thirty minutes, I discover the weirdest thing Noah DuPont has ever eaten is raw tofu, he's been out of the country once, to Vancouver, and he could have grilled cheese for every meal forever.

"What's your forever meal?" he asks after I finish penciling in his response.

"Whatever Rose's mom is cooking."

"Who's Rose?"

I point her out. "The tall girl. Looks like a runway model. She's my best friend."

"What sort of cooking does her mom do?"

I shrug. "Haitian food."

"Really. I've never had. So it's good, huh?"

"Noah," I say. "You're doing it again."

He puts his hands up. "Right, right. Small talk makes you want to light yourself on fire on your way out the window."

"We have one last question and only five minutes of class left. So let's make it snappy." I glance down. "What plant are you descended from?"

He pauses. "Okay, so you know 'your spot' off the highway?" He makes quotations with his hands. "Well, there are two cactuses there. One looks like a man and one looks like a woman. It's really creepy, actually, but that's the first thing I thought of."

God, this is weird. "So, the saguaro." I keep my voice neutral.

"Yeah, I guess. What about you?"

"Corn," I say quickly.

"Really? Why corn?"

The bells chime and I shake my head. "See you later," I say.

"It was nice meeting you, Sia," he calls, but his voice is drowned out by the class as I make my way to Rose. When I look back at him, he's still watching me, a smile on his face, and I can feel my neck and cheeks heating up as I jerk my gaze away. God, why do I get so weird and hostile like this with boys? Well, actually, I know exactly why.

So I make a point to remind myself as I walk to my next class.

Noah isn't Justin. Noah isn't Justin.

20

MY GRANDMOTHER SAID THAT IN THE BEGINNING, there was nothing but the wide black nothing of space. She said this big nothing was a woman, and the woman longed to be touched. So this woman's belly grew big with longing, and soon she pushed out a baby. And when the baby ate from her breast, the milk that flowed became the whole universe.

Abuela said when she birthed all her babies, as they first latched to her chest, she could feel the prickly magic of that beginning. She could feel her own experience of touch continue the viento of creation.

So the universe came from milk and touch. I'm not sure I buy that, but it makes more sense to me than an old white man in the sky.

21

"WELL?" ROSE ASKS OVER MILKSHAKES.

"He's nice," I say. "And way too energetic. It's annoying."

Rose smiles and raises an eyebrow. "I heard some of your tone, Sia. It's a wonder he wasn't the one running away from you as the bell rang."

I groan and put my face in my hands. "Ugh. I know. I was rude to him. But I don't know how to act around guys anymore, you know?"

"Sure you do. You act fine around Manuel and Carter and—"

"You know what I mean."

"Uh, no, no I don't."

I shrug. "Flirts."

"He was flirting?!" Rose squeals but stops when she sees my face. "You still get freaked out, huh? Since . . . you know . . ."

"Yes, since Justin." I shrug. "It doesn't matter, anyway."

"So that means you didn't get Noah's number, then, huh?"

I scoff. "No way. We just exchanged emails. For class."

"I know, Sia. I'm kidding." She smiles. "So, I have some news."

"Oh?" I lick some of the whipped cream off my straw.

"I'm going to be spending the night at your place on Saturday."

"Cool."

She stares at me, waiting.

I give her a look. "What?"

"Aren't you going to ask why?"

"I mean, you stay over, like, once a month, right? It's not uncommon."

"We're going to Samara's spring break party."

"Uh, no, we're not."

"Sia! I've sewn a new wrap dress and everything!"

"I hate parties. And remember." I lower my voice to a whisper. "Jeremy McButtFace'll be there."

"And therein lies the kicker. I just talked with Samara, and McButtFace is going to be somewhere south this weekend. He's testifying in court or something."

"Why?" I ask. "Is he finally on trial for being a disgusting nematode?"

"Don't know. Don't care. Because we are going to that party."

I groan into my glass of mint chocolate foam. "Spring break isn't here yet."

"She's doing it early this year because that's when her mom will be out of town. So we are going and that is that, my friend." Rose winks triumphantly.

"Well, Dad just informed me we have practice on Saturday, too. So you should come over in the morning so we can make something super protein-y for breakfast."

Rose puts her hand on her head. "Oh, sweet Jesus. A new dress, a party, and close proximity to your dad. This literally just turned into the best weekend ever."

"Ew," I say, throwing a straw at her. "Stop that."

She tosses her curls to the side and smiles some more.

"Stop!" I say.

"What?"

"I know you're thinking something obscene about my dad."

"Sia, you know that's just about always true."

I roll my eyes. "Whatever."

"Sia, before I forget, I have to postpone trig tutoring this week. Samara and I have a ton to do on nebulas."

I frown. "Really? I have a test coming up. And it's on all those impossible little cosine and tangent and whatever graphs."

"Ooh. Yeah. You really are helpless with those."

"Hey." I throw an extra straw her way.

"Stop!" she shrieks. "Okay, I'll let Sam know. We'll adjust the schedule, okay?"

"Thank you," I say. "Thank you, thank you, thank you. I owe you."

"You do. Don't forget about First Communion, now, Sia." Rose is pointing at me with a french fry.

"I won't." I put a hand on my heart. "Even if all I want to do is forget about anything church-related, forever."

Rose pouts. "Hey. You're talking to the church choir assistant, remember?"

"Except for you," I amend.

We smile and I think how much worse everything would have been without Rose. But I shudder. I don't ever want to consider what a world like that would look like.

22

FRIDAY'S MY DAY TO GET ROSE FOR SCHOOL. I PUT THE
car in park and send her a text. Usually, she comes running out after a
minute, ready to model whatever groovy bit of fabulousness she's got on
that day, but today, five, seven minutes pass without a response. I'm about
to turn the car off and walk up when she finally comes out, head low.

She gets in. We don't say anything for a bit. Her eyes are red.

"What's up?" I finally ask.

"My dad." She flips the passenger's mirror down and fusses at her
makeup. "He almost murdered me this morning."

Most of the time, Rose and her dad fight about her appearance. I
glance at her outfit. She's wearing a floral-patterned baby doll top with
distressed bell bottoms covered in vintage patches. "Too much cleavage?" I guess.

"Nah. My hair."

When we reach a stop sign, I look over. I hadn't even noticed her
gorgeous and symmetrical Afro puffs. "Really?"

Rose sighs. "He's come to term with the curls, but he can't handle
any other style. Says he's going to make an appointment for a perm as
soon as possible. Like my mom would let him." She bites her lip. "And,

to top it off, he . . ." Tears river her face again. "He said the devil can hide in my hair now." Then she's laughing hysterically. I grab her hand. "I know it's ridiculous. But it still hurts."

"I'm sorry," I say. We're at the parking lot of the school, watching groups of kids talking.

"Everything he fears or hates is the working of the devil. Automatically." Rose snaps her fingers.

"Well," I say. "I think he should write a book. Since he's such a devil expert."

Rose snorts. "And call it what? *How to Avoid the Devil* by Cruz Damas. It would have one page, which would say, 'Stay at home and pray the rosary always. Oh, and perm your hair once every three months.'"

"Or how about, *The Devil is Hiding in Your Afro Puffs: How Perms Repel the Enemy of Jesus.*"

Rose laughs again, me along with her. I put a hand on hers. "Rose, your hair looks beautiful. You always look beautiful."

"I know," she says, smiling. She turns her palm over and squeezes my hand. "Thanks, Sia."

I glance at the clock. "We better get going."

"Yeah."

We stroll across the parking lot, her arm thrown over my shoulders. Before we walk into the homeroom building, Rose says, "We should light candles at the desert tonight. I haven't gone with you in forever."

"Sure. Wanna do dinner at Maude's beforehand?"

"Mmm. Can't push my dad like that. He's been in a bad mood all week. But I'll come over at dusk, okay?"

I smile. "Perfect."

23

"SO, EXPLAIN TO ME THESE SAINTS AGAIN?" ROSE LIFTS one of my candles.

"That's Saint Kateri. She was Mohawk. And something else, I think." Kateri's one of my favorites, because when I see paintings of her with her long hair and brown skin, she reminds me of my mother.

"Oh, right. She converted after smallpox killed her whole family, right?"

"Yeah. That's her."

Rose and I sit between the two humanesque saguaros, the wild sky open all around us. It's my favorite kind of night, with the weather so clear, it feels like you can see every star that was created. All draped and dazzling like silver and gold crystals on a cosmic Christmas tree.

"She must've had Stockholm syndrome," Rose says, placing the candle back between Saint Theresa and La Guadalupe. "I can't imagine willingly converting to a religion like that."

"Am I hearing this right?" I say. "Miss Church Choir Assistant Director thinks you need Stockholm syndrome to convert to Catholicism?"

Rose gives me a look. "Okay, Sia. You know I love Jesus. It's"—she makes a face—"all the other stuff. You know?"

I nod. "Right. The you're-not-and-will-never-be-worthy attitudes—"

"The confessions—"

"The million sacraments."

Rose snorts. "And the extra-credit bible studies—"

"Oh, you mean like that one we had to go to when Father John invited that medical examiner to go into vivid detail on the crucifixion injuries—"

"So we'd all know how hard Jesus suffered for us heathens. Yes." Rose takes a breath. "Plus, you know. All the 'hate the sin, love the sinner' talk."

I place a hand on her palm and she squeezes me and smiles before letting me go. It's a sad smile, tight on her eyes.

"She might still be out there, you know." Rose's voice is all soft.

I exhale slowly. She knows how I feel. That I can't believe that anymore. But Rose, like Abuela, has always refused to say that Mom is for real gone. And I don't know why, but knowing that Rose has that hope? It makes me think sometimes, only sometimes, like in the middle of the night, when all I can hear are the creaks of wood and crickets, when everything feels blue and fuzzy, like a dream. Then I think Rose might be right.

I don't say this, though. I just stare at the sky, trying to trace constellations, and Rose, her eyes closed, I think as she prays. I know coming out here is holy for her, too.

After a while, I glance at the candles. It's now so dark that all I can see are the flames, dancing like orange spirits, and the faint outline of Rose's legs.

"Maybe Kateri didn't have a choice," I say. *Like us back then, and like you now*, I don't say, but Rose nods like she hears anyway.

Out of the corner of my eye, there's a blue flame. At first I think a candle has thrown up a spark, but when I turn—

"Holy. Hell." I jump to my feet as three blue lights swerve in the sky, a zillion stars twinkling behind them like spilt quartz.

Rose jumps up next to me. "I've never seen a plane with lights like that."

"Me, either." We watch as the blue orbs do a little spiral. And then right before our eyes, they disappear. Like someone just decided to turn the lights out before bed or something.

I turn to see Rose crossing herself. "Lord have mercy," she says.

I cross myself, too, even though I haven't done the likes of it in years. Just to be safe. "Let's get outta here. Whatever that was, it gave me the creeps."

"Agreed."

24

AFTER I GET IN BED, I PULL MY RED QUILT TO MY CHIN
and angle my face toward the moon. It's waning, pulling the full of its
belly in and in and in until everything gets its much-needed break from
the light, just like Mom's story said.

When we first moved to this house, like, ten years ago, I'd insisted
this room should be mine. It's the one with the biggest windows, facing the succulent garden filled with plants you'd think should exist on
another planet. Thick, waxy leaves that spiral out in mint and pink
and violet, with names like "echeveria" and "houseleek" and "living
stone."

Mom sewed the curtains that hug the glass on either side. I was really
upset about leaving Abuela's house, and so I had requested some dark
colors for the curtains. Navy, burnt umber, black. "The night will be
dark enough," Mom said. "Let's go with something brighter."

We settled on the color of the ocean, but lighter, like it was mixed
with milk. "Teal," Mom called it, but it's more magical than that to me.
Like it should share a name with an otherworldly succulent. String of
sea pearls, maybe. The exact shade of turquoise in my grandmother's
rings, minus the cracks of brown and black. Mom chose thin linen, so

when it's afternoon, I can close them and my whole room looks like the inside of a raw aquamarine.

Now the night is dark as Mom promised, thick like paint. Our outside lamp lines the succulents with an edge of copper. The stars shimmer like glitter. It all reminds me of the woman in the sky who created the universe, of the gown she's wearing, inky with tiny silver sequins sewn in, shivering when she dances.

It's so unfair that the world ceased to be beautiful once Mom was gone.

As one star twinkles real bright for a moment, I think of the blue lights Rose and I saw. What in the world were they? I bet Mom would know. She always knew everything.

The last thing I remember before falling asleep is my mom's favorite Shakespeare line. *There are more things in heaven and earth, Horatio, than are dreamt of in your philosophy.*

25

I GIVE A BEWILDERED LOOK WHEN I SEE THE *THING*
Rose brings me to wear.

She crosses her arms. "I'm not going to be the only one all dolled up, Sia. And this isn't one of mine, so don't you start talking to me about your wide hips. It used to be my mom's. Like, it's legitimately from the seventies."

"But it's so, so . . ." I pause. "Bright."

"Emerald. A jewel tone. I keep telling you that you're a winter."

"And I keep telling you that I don't know what the hell that means."

"Look, you and Mom both have hips and tits. It's going to fit perfectly."

I sigh. "Fine," I say, tearing the dress from her hands and pulling it over my head.

I like that its sleeves are long and flare out, and that the skirt reaches my feet. A low-cut v-neck frames a modest amount of cleavage. "When the hell did your mom ever wear something so . . . so . . ."

"Sinful?" Rose suggests. "You know when. Before she met Dad."

I look in the mirror. Maura Damas has probably got a real good story about this dress, but I bet she'd never tell me about it.

Rose sits me down and pins up my hair. She rubs rouge on my cheekbones, brushes on red lipstick. "There," she says. "Now you look like Eva Mendes."

I scoff. "No one looks like Eva Mendes."

"She's foxy. And you're foxy."

"You are," I say and it's true. Her wrap dress is goldenrod and covers everything except a long slit to her mid-thigh. She's put gold shimmer all over her eyelids and the tops of her cheekbones, mahogany on her lips. She looks like she's ready for the cover of *Vogue*, not Samara Kingsley's annual spring breaker.

"Ready?" she says.

"Yeah." I nod. "Sure."

26

THE SKY LOOKED EXACTLY LIKE THIS THE LAST TIME I talked to my mom. Dark clouds all lined up like warriors against saltwater blue.

I was in the passenger's side, though. Dad handed me the cell as he drove.

"Hey, Sia." Mom's voice sounded choked.

"Hey."

"You doing alright? How's school?"

"Fine. It's whatever."

"Any new crushes?"

"Ew, Mom."

She laughed a bit, but it sounded forced. "Amor. Save that last tin of dulce de leche for me, eh?"

"Fine. Sure."

"Give the phone back to Papá, okay? I love you."

"Same."

I tuned out for a while, just counting the black wisps of clouds until Dad yelled, "No, Lena, don't you dare, you can't do it alone. Nadie cruce y vive. ¿Qué estás pensando? Lena, Lena, por favor." After a minute, he was calm. "Sí, sí. Te amo también."

As soon as he hung up the phone, he swerved off the road so hard the seat belt dug into my belly.

Before I could yell at him, though, he was banging his fists against the wheel. "Shit," he screamed. "Shit, shit, shit!"

The line of blood from a knuckle reached his wrist when he turned the car back on. We were supposed to go to the grocery store, but Dad just whipped the car around and we went back home.

I may as well have said nothing the last time I spoke to Mom. I didn't even tell her *I love you* in return.

Sometimes I wish I could go back and shake me.

27

"I'M SO HAPPY YOU TWO LADIES COULD MAKE IT,"
Samara says when we arrive. She sounds like she means it. "Come in!"

Samara's highlighted curls look brushed out, framing her face in a mag-
nificent cloud. Her dress is gold and short, nothing that would look good
on me, but on Sam it's effortless. She's switched out her nose stud for a
gold ring, too. "God, love the dresses. Groovy, right? Did I get that right?"

She and Rose talk for a while about sewing or something and I roam
around. There are too many people. Some god-awful song is on way too
loud. I think even my hair is vibrating. I make my way to the kitchen
and pour some ice water.

"Oh my God, do you see that, Sia?" Rose runs up, pointing dis-
creetly. "McKenna Carlson came with the new guy!"

"What?" I say, turning fast. Sure enough, Noah's in the corner,
talking to a bunch of people, McKenna hanging off his arm.

"Yeah, she literally pounced on him first chance she got," Samara says.

"Wasn't she dating Matthew Hemingway, like, yesterday?" I ask.

"Not anymore, I guess," Rose muses.

Samara shrugs. "She can date who she likes, right?" Rose and I
agree, but I don't know, I feel kind of weird about Noah being here

with her. But that makes no sense, so I keep the thought to myself.

Rose peeks into my cup. "Water, Sia? Really?"

"I don't feel like drinking. It makes me tired. Besides, I'm driving us home."

"I'm having one shot. With Samara." Sam's a few feet away now, pouring said shots, I assume.

"A shot of what?"

"Tequila."

"Girl," I say, shaking my head. "You're trouble tonight."

"I'm trouble every night." She punches my shoulder playfully.

Samara brings the shots over. "Sia's not drinking," Rose says. "She's the designated driver."

"That's valid," Sam says. She and Rose throw their glasses back and cough and scream.

"Looks like I'm missing out on a lot of fun," I say dryly.

"Hey," Sam says as the doors open. "Looks like the Chicanos are here."

I glance around and see Rita and all her brothers, Nacho, and Lupita, along with Manuel, Jonathan, and a few of their cousins pouring in. "Thank the Lord," I say.

Within minutes, some reggaeton/merengue mix is blazing on the speakers. "That's more like it," Rose yells.

Manuel approaches. "Baila conmigo," he says, gesturing to me.

"No," I say.

"For old time's sake, Artemisia?" He smiles.

I sigh. "Fine. But only because it's a good song." He takes my hand to what is now the dance floor and twirls me around.

Truthfully, the only reason I dance with Manuel is because we learned how—with a partner, I mean—together at the parties our moms used to throw. And because he's respectful, unlike his dick cousin Hector, whose hands always make their way to my ass.

"Aprendí un poco del tango," Manuel shouts over the music.

"Tango," I repeat. "Show me."

"Hold on." He goes to the music player. "We need a different song."

I nod. He puts on something slow and sultry and pulls me close to him, grabbing my hand. He slings his arm around my waist and I automatically place my hand on his shoulder.

"Damn, Manuel," I say. "Lay off the cologne, would you?"

He ignores me. "Camina," he says, and talks long strides forward. I follow his lead easily, stretching my legs back. He turns me suddenly and we switch directions. I lead now. "Straighten your back," he says. "You gotta look down on everyone. Like they're your servants." I lift my head and narrow my eyes. "There you go," he says.

"Now what?" I ask.

"Push your whole leg straight, to the side, like that. Now drag your heel in very slow." I do what he's saying, keeping my queenly posture.

"Muy bien. So, the song's gonna slow down in a few beats. I'm going to grab your leg up, and you need to lean back."

"Don't get handsy," I warn. He nods. I can hear the song about to slow, and he pulls my knee all the way up to the side of his torso. His hand is on my back and I bend backward to a few claps of a drum solo, holding my arm out. He lifts me fast, drops my leg. People clap and cheer for us and he grins.

"You like that?" he asks me as he gives a bow to our audience.

"Not bad," I say. He gestures to me and people whistle. I wave them off. Someone puts on a cumbia and we take our usual footwork as the dance floor fills.

"Rose still single?" he asks as he turns me around.

"Yep."

"Her papá still—"

"Religious? Yep."

He laughs. "Too bad. How's your papá?"

"He's good. Working a lot."

"I see him in the bosque de nopales when I'm driving out to Lupe's, tagging shit."

"Yeah. He's still studying that whole ecosystem out there."

Hector taps his back. "Can I cut in?"

I shake my head. "Hell, no, Hector."

"Aw, mami, you still mad about the last time? That was, what, over a year ago?"

I give him the finger. "Manuel, tell your mom I miss her."

I look for Rose, stopping when I see her and Samara snuggled in a corner. The way they're looking at each other, you know, in that way that a best friend ought to know about long before now, right? Maybe I'm just imagining it, though. Frowning, I cut out the back door.

28

WHEN MAMI TAUGHT ME TO DANCE, SHE DID IT WITH A
broom and a Selena CD. "You got to shake your hips like this, Sia. No, no, not like that. You look like you ate too much chile, woman!"

"You're asking me to do the impossible, Mom," I said, rolling my eyes. "If I moved my hips any harder, they'd fly off!"

Mom just sat me down for a minute while "Techno Cumbia" finished its last notes. "I think you need to grow hips," she said.

"Thanks, Mom."

"Oh, hush. You know what I mean." She leaned against the back of the sofa. Back then, we covered everything in bright tapestries, stuff Abuela picked up from Juárez. Our home looked like we let a rainbow Mexican unicorn decorate it. "Our ancestors, before the Spaniards came, I mean. We had rich dancing. Rico. It was the sort of dancing that made the seeds germinate, made the corn plump, made babies."

"It was the sort of dancing that made babies?" I scoffed. "That's disgusting."

"You know what I mean."

"I do, and it's gross."

She laughed and stood. "Again."

I spun in a circle until I got dizzy. "There, Mami, now the corn should be ready!" I spun again. "Oh, look, I'm pregnant!"

Mom laughed so hard, she cried. When Dad got home and he heard my jokes, he didn't find it so funny. "No puedes tener un bebé hasta que obtengas tu doctorado," he said, pointing his finger at my belly.

Mom was right, though. I couldn't move right until I grew hips, which didn't come until after she was gone. She never got to see.

29

IT'S COOL OUT, WHICH FEELS NICE AFTER ALL THAT tango. Only a handful of kids stand around smoking out. We're all lit with the dim glow of fairy lights strung up on the deck. I take a seat on a bench and stretch my legs out. I like the view. The light of the stars is like cake sugar.

"Can I sit here?"

I gasp, turning to glare at the Hulk-like form of Noah. "Sorry, didn't mean to scare you," he adds quickly.

I wave my hand at the bench and he sits. "How are you doing, Sia?"

"Not bad," I say. "It's not the worst party ever."

He nods. "You go to parties a lot?"

"Almost never, actually."

He nods again, randomly snapping his fingers, out of nervousness, maybe. "Where'd you learn to dance like that?"

I pause. "Which dance?"

"The slow one. Where that guy bent you really low—"

"Oh, that. He was teaching me that one just now."

He stares. "You just learned that? That thing with the leg? Tonight?"

"Well, Manuel's a good partner," I say. "He and I, we've been dancing forever, it seems."

"So he's your boyfriend, then."

I make a face. "I didn't say that, bro."

"You two seemed close."

I sigh. "He's not my boyfriend. He's a family friend. Not that it's any of your business."

He gives me a wild smile, the one that lights up his dimples. "So . . ." He rasps his fingers on his legs. "You don't have a boyfriend, then."

I glare at him. "Isn't McKenna looking for you?"

He shakes his head. "She's busy right now."

I inhale. "What are you doing out here? Besides disrupting my solitude?"

"Well." He takes a breath. "We have that assignment from Woods over spring break, remember?"

"Yes." I groan. "Let's just plan it over email."

"Well, I'm here now, and you're here now, so we could"—he snaps his fingers—"just do it now."

"Fine. When do you want to measure the moon or whatever?" I say it all monotone.

"How about tomorrow?"

I try to think of a good excuse, but it doesn't come fast enough. "Tomorrow it is, then." He says it with a smile. I grimace.

He stands, as though to go, but doesn't. "Yes?" I say.

His eyes are all twinkling. "I can dance, too, you know."

I snort. "That's a total lie."

"It's true."

"Prove it."

He moves his feet robotically, swinging his arms.

I raise an eyebrow. "The Charleston. That's impressive. Not like you could just learn it from a video game or anything."

"What about this one?" He starts snapping his fingers and convulsing his shoulders.

I can't help it. I snort and double over. I want to speak but I can't stop laughing.

He's staring at me now, flabbergasted. "What?" I say.

"I knew it."

"Knew what?"

He shrugs. "That you'd have a pretty smile." I open my mouth to tell him he's ruined everything, but Rose walks up to save the day.

"Okay, kids!" She sits, puts an arm around me. "We've got to get going, darling."

"Curfew already?"

"It's close."

"Hey, Rose," Noah says.

She smiles, twirls a curl with her finger. "Noah."

"Well, see you tomorrow, Sia." He nods as we stand up.

Rose opens the door and music flings itself out of it. I turn to Noah. "What time tomorrow? And where?"

"Eight. At the beginning of the world!"

30

I LOOK UP FROM *ARISTOTLE AND DANTE DISCOVER THE*
Secrets of the Universe by Benjamin Alire Sáenz and watch Rose text her
brother in my office chair for a few seconds. "You good?"

"Of course." She says it too fast and too cheerily.

"I'm just asking because you've been acting weird since we left."

"How so?"

"Well." I shut the book. "You're not jumping up and down in ecstasy
because we finally made it to a party. Or even—ugh, I can't believe
I'm going to say this—you didn't even say something gross and wrong
because my dad didn't have a shirt on when we walked in."

Rose sighs. "Alright." She drops her phone on my desk. "I don't want
you to get involved with Noah."

My mouth drops open. "What? Who says I have any plans to get
involved with him?"

She bites her bottom lip. "You guys were laughing when I walked
out to get you. I mean, you, Sia. Were laughing."

I scoff. "Did you not see the way he was dancing? I was laughing at
him, not with him."

"The boy likes you."

"I'm not even going to respond to that." I inhale deeply. "Anyway, your argument doesn't make any sense. You were so excited when he and I were assigned to be partners for the celestial project. Why do you hate his guts all of a sudden?"

"I don't hate his guts, Sia." She sighs. "I just . . ."

"What, Rose? What is it?"

"Okay. Sia. Okay. I was just driving with Mom to get groceries over the weekend, and I saw Sheriff McGhee in the parking lot."

"And?"

"And there was a guy with him who looked a lot like Noah." Rose grimaces. "And McGhee put his hand on Maybe-Noah's shoulder. Like they were buds or something."

I shake my head. "Okay."

She blinks. "You don't think that's a little suspicious?"

I raise my hands and drop them again. "What is? That the sheriff knows a guy who looks a little like Noah?"

Rose drops her head back like she's praying for strength. When she looks at me again, she is resigned. "I'm not going to argue with you. I know it was probably nothing." She puts a hand on my forearm. "I just want you to be careful. Don't go falling for a guy until you know what he's about."

I sigh. "You know I don't date anymore, anyway. I don't know why we're discussing this."

"Just be careful. That's it. End of message." She brightens a bit. "You know, I've always thought it's wild how your dad lets you date and you refuse, and how mine would rather invite the devil over for dinner when—"

hen you'd have a hot date every night."

smiles. "Well, at least we're dateless together."

I smile. "We should start a club."

Rose laughs. "The Dateless Losers."

"Or, the Hot Dateless Girls Who Could Date if They Wanted but Are a Little Too Busy Being Awesome?"

Rose snorts. "That's one really long way to frame it." She pauses. "Sia, I forgot to tell you what Sam and I learned on the nebula project. It's amazing. You'll love it. Hold on." She scrolls through her phone. "Okay, here it is. Some nebulae are hundreds of light-years large. Hundreds of light-years. Can you even imagine?"

I'm smiling. "No way."

"Oh! This is the part you'll like. Some kinds, they're where stars are born. Isn't that miraculous?"

I do like that. So much that a flicker of gooseflesh glides along the back of my neck. "That's amazing. I'm jealous. That is so much cooler than the moon."

"It's inspired a new fic."

I straighten my back. "You started a new one? Awesome, Rose!"

Rose started writing Harry Potter fanfiction last summer. And she's incredible at it. Her stories get hundreds of followers. "Is it another Drarry one?"

"Not really. It's actually for Buffy."

"What?" I smile. "That is exciting!"

"It's a Buffy and Faith pairing. Do you think that's kind of weird?"

"No, of course not," I say. "Faith is so sensitive on the inside. Buffy's sensitive on the outside. They're a lot alike because of it.

They're like matching puzzle pieces when it comes to their emotions."

Rose smiles. "I knew you'd get it. I'm sending you the draft this weekend, okay?"

"Yes! I'm ready for it."

And then she yawns. "Let's get ready for bed, huh? I'm tired."

"Yeah. Same." And when we turn the lights out, I look at the stars out the window, wondering about how old they are. Do they fall in and out of love, do they tell stories? And which nebulae are their mothers, and do they long for their mothers so much, they feel like their hearts are breaking at every moment, even when things are supposed to be normal and happy?

I don't get answers, though. Not even in my dreams.

31

I'D JUST TURNED SIXTEEN WHEN I WENT ON MY FIRST date. The guy's name was Justin; he was visiting town for the summer, staying with an older sister. He's still alive and out there, I suppose.

He'd just parked the car on the side of a gas station—we were about to pick up a bag of caramel chocolate popcorn to hide in my purse for the movies. And he looked at me with his steel gray eyes with their thick, pale lashes and told me how pretty I looked. We kissed. And then, out of nowhere, he put my hand on his dick.

It made me gasp, but he mistook it for a good reaction. "Big, right?" he said, grinning. Then he grabbed my neck and pulled my face into his lap.

I yelled and opened the car door, but he grabbed my arm so hard, pain shot into my neck. I screamed and screamed into the open sliver of car, and some cowboy filling up his tractor came running over. Justin let me go.

My dad wanted to press charges. I begged him not to. The last thing I wanted was Sheriff McGhee to know. He'd assume it was my fault and then his darling son would let the whole school know what an out-of-control skank whore I was. Dad tried to guilt trip me, saying some other girl could get hurt. He dropped it when I pointed out Justin would never face any punishment, not in one hundred thousand years. Nothing would happen to him, just like nothing happened to Sheriff McGhee, just like nothing happened to Jeremy.

For two weeks, I had to cover a hand-shaped bruise on my arm while at school. I felt Dad's eyes on it constantly when I took my cardigan off at home. When it turned to faded lime, he decided I needed to learn self-defense. And ever since, he's been teaching me and Rose how to kick ass.

32

SOMETIMES, WHEN I'M IN THE DESERT, I PRAY FOR
any girl who happens to get near Justin. That her hair will stand up,
that some part of her wild animal body will know he's a predator. And
that she will run fast and far away, away from all the boys who think
they deserve to be sucked off just because they have dicks.

33

"COME ON, ARTEMISIA. I KNOW YOU'RE STRONGER
than that."

I groan and kick a rock. "I can't do it, Dad."

"So, you're just going to quit, that it? If you ever get attacked from
behind, you're just going to—"

I scream and lunge at him. First, I aim for his shoulder, but he blocks
it. I aim for the other side, but as he's on the defense. I turn and kick his
leg in from the back. He stumbles forward and I jump and kick off his
hips like he's a trampoline. He flies back as I hit the dirt.

He stands and dusts himself off. "Your reflexes are improving, m'ija."

"I know." I lick the salt of sweat off my lip. Rose jogs up to me and
grabs my hand.

"That was amazing, Sia. You looked just like Rogue and Storm
and—"

"Supergirl?" Dad supplies. Rose and I both wrinkle our noses.

"Catwoman, maybe," I say.

"Well, Catwoman, then, needs to master the back attack. Rose's
been able to do it for two months now."

"Well, I'm a lot taller," Rose supplies.

I sigh. "Please, Dad. I obviously can't do it."

He narrows his eyes as he tosses us water bottles. "Work on leg tosses for the next two weeks. And do some running. Two Saturdays from now, you're gonna throw me."

I let out a gasp after gulping down too much water. "Whatever," I choke out.

He ignores me and shakes our hands like he always does at the end of each session. "Thank you, Mr. Martinez," Rose says as Dad heads inside for a shower.

We collapse on the patio chairs and Rose checks her phone. "Crap," she says. "We've been at it for almost three hours."

"Ugh," I say. "No wonder I'm starved."

"Smoothies?" she asks.

"I'm kinda feeling cheeseburgers, actually."

"Oh, heck yes." And then Rose pauses. "I can't be too long, though. I have to shower and go bowling with Samara this afternoon."

"Really?" I say. "I didn't know you were into bowling." Which is a lie, because I know Rose used to bowl with her brother before he moved to Haiti. I guess what I'm really saying, on the inside, is *I didn't know you were into doing things without me.* That's a little too pathetic, though, but it's almost like Rose hears it anyway.

"You could come. We'd love to have you."

"Who's all going?"

"Me. And Sam."

I think of them next to each other at the party, smiling so big, fireworks may as well have been going off all around them. "Wait, is it, like, a date?"

Rose laughs. "Of course not. Remember?" She points to herself. "President of the Dateless Losers Club?"

I shake my head and smile. I must be really stressed out or something. Everything is getting to me lately, even Rose. "Sorry, I didn't mean to interrogate you. I thought I sensed something between you guys. But no, I think I'm going to stay in and read."

"What about later tonight?" Rose asks. "We can take some of my mom's cooking to the desert. Have a picnic with the candles."

"Can't. Noah and I are going out. To work on our project," I add quickly, before Rose can explain the suspicious look on her face.

"Oh, well. It's spring break. We've got all next week, right?" We both sit in a weird silence for a couple of seconds before Rose stands up really fast and touches my arm. "Come on, Sia. I'm starving! And those cheeseburgers aren't going to eat themselves!"

34

I WASN'T THERE WHEN THEY TOOK HER. I WASN'T THERE, so I can imagine the worst. See, there, her brown hands, clenched and spinning; her screams, high and shattered. There are skid marks on the sidewalk where she dug in her boots and said, *No, no, no, what about my family, what about my daughter? ¿Qué va pasar con mi esposo, y mi bebé, qué va ser de mi vida?*

All I knew is she didn't come to pick me up from school. I was thirteen, standing outside of school by myself like some kind of loser, and I was pissed that she didn't answer any of my calls. I'm so mad at myself for being angry, but I didn't know. I swear, I didn't know.

An hour after it happened, as I sat at the school pickup line, counting weeds, Dad pulled up in the Jeep that would be mine in two and a half years. His eyes were red.

"Sia," he said. "Something happened."

I thought that was the worst day of my life.

I was so fucking wrong.

35

DAD HAD INSISTED ON MEETING NOAH BEFORE "hooliganing it up" (Dad's words, ugh), so Noah arrives at about a quarter till eight. I'm loading the dishwasher, and before I can even start to peel my rubber gloves off, Dad reaches the front door.

"Mr. Martinez? I'm Noah DuPont."

I'm sure Dad's shaking his hand forcefully as he says, "I know who you are, son. So you plan on taking my daughter out to the desert. Alone. Just the two of you."

I slam the dishwasher shut and yell, "Dad! Stop it!"

"Are you sure this is for school?" Dad asks me as I approach. Noah's ears are bright red, and it almost makes me giggle. Instead, I glare at my father.

"Dad," I say slowly. "Lo estás asustando."

"Good," Dad says victoriously.

"Did you just tell him you're gonna kill me out there?" Noah asks, his eyes wide.

"Of course not. Come on." I grab his hand and pull him around my looming father. "I'm going to make tea to bring." I've got the kettle going already. "Do you want any?"

"Uh, sure." Noah's taken a seat on a dining chair, but he's eyeing my dad, who cracks his knuckles in the foyer.

"What kind?"

He gives me a noncommittal shrug as he looks around warily. I decide on a calming blend. Lemon balm and tulsi, dried from my winter herb garden.

"Sugar? Honey?"

"Honey, sugar." He winks, then gives me a wide smile. I grimace at him, turn, and see my dad watching us like a creeper.

"Dad, don't you have anything to do?"

"I'm seeing you off, m'ija."

"Ugh." I drizzle some honey and pop the lids on the thermoses. "Let's get out of here."

To Noah's horror, my father walks us to the door. "Be home by nine," Dad says.

"What? It's eight fifteen now!"

"Nine thirty."

"Ten."

"Quarter till."

We shake on it and I usher Noah out the door.

36

I'M SKETCHING THE MOON INTO MY NOTEBOOK AS NOAH determines its size. We work quietly. I can only hear pencils scratching paper and the occasional drumming of his fingers against the passenger door.

"Okay, I think I've got it," he says.

"Let me see." I take his notebook and survey his work.

"No, look," I say. "The depth of it is incorrect. You see? You've inversed the shadow and the light parts." I cross out a few of his calculations and write some of my own. "There. Now it's right."

"Let me see that." He narrows his eyes playfully, then looks down at the notebook. "Okay, yeah. Yeah, that's right."

"Do you need me to explain it?" I ask.

"No, no," he says, still looking at the page. "I see it."

We're done with our work. I'm about to turn the car on when I stop and turn to him. "Hey," I say. "This might sound kind of random, but do you know the sheriff in town? Timothy McGhee?"

Noah furrows his brow. "No, can't say I do." He gives a half smile. "Why, are you in trouble with the law or something?"

I smile a little. "No, I'm just being weird. And random." The relief is all thick in my voice. The relief that I'm not currently spending time with one of the jerk sheriff's cohorts.

I turn to the ignition again when he asks, "So. Why do you light candles out here?"

I freeze, my keys in the air. "It's personal. It's a family thing."

"Cool. Like a ceremony or something? That's cool."

I don't say anything for a few seconds, but he doesn't add anything else. I finally put my keys in the ignition and pause. "Okay. This has been bugging me for a while. How do you know about the cacti that look like people here, in this spot? Who told you about it?" I ask.

Now he's the one who looks unsettled. "Well, it's kind of a long story."

"We have twenty minutes until we have to head back."

"Yeah. Okay. Well, I used to live here, in Caraway, when I was little. And my mom took me here all the time." He points. "She said that cactus was Adam, and that one was Eve. And it stuck with me, you know? When we moved back, I made her show me where they were." He looks out the window. "I guess I come here to feel close to her."

"Is your mom Mexican or something?"

"No. She's French and Italian and Greek and, uh, something else, I think. Why?"

"No, it's just that's sort of why I come out here, too. My grandma told me that those two cacti created the world."

"Ah, so that's what you meant by that. And wow, yeah. That's a weird coincidence."

I furrow my brow. "I don't believe in coincidence."

"So, like, what do you believe in? Fate? Or whatever?"

I don't answer him. Instead, I touch the rim of St. Anthony's candle in my cup holder. "Why'd you move here with your dad?"

He swallows, looks down. "My mom got another DUI a couple months ago, and well, they don't see her fit to raise me anymore. She's fighting it in court and all that. But I'm stuck with my dad in the meantime."

I want to ask him why he hates his dad so much, but I figure I've pried enough. My hands reach for my keys again, but I stop. "My mom's dead." He doesn't look surprised. I guess he's probably heard by now. "She was deported. Got lost in the desert trying to get back. I light candles to guide her home."

To his credit, he says nothing. Then he reaches over and wraps his hand around mine. It's warm and calloused.

"So where'd the universe come from, Sia?"

I look at the night sky, indigo on one side with a cornflower glow on the other. A few bright stars dot it with their yellow glimmer. Right there, between the moon and that wispy cloud the shape of a Pegasus, that's where Rose and I saw those freaky blue lights a couple days ago. It feels like a dream now. Like Rose and I just imagined it.

And then I remember Noah's question.

"It came from a woman who wanted to be touched." I say it without thinking, but as soon as the words come out, it's like electricity has been charged in our bodies. His hand sears mine. He stares at me and his eyes look like the night ocean or black diamonds or something equally embarrassing.

I pull my hand away, and like a machine being unplugged, the hum of whatever is between us dulls and stops. "We've got to get going." I turn on the car, hard, and drive us back.

When I get in the house, I text Rose. I asked. Noah's never heard of the sheriff.

She writes back right away. Lucky him.

37

I'M SUPPOSED TO BE READING ROSE'S BUFFY/FAITH
story, but when I stare at my computer screen, the words are just meaningless. They are animals darting on each landscape line and I can't catch them. Not a single one.

I hate days like these. The kind where all I can think about is Mami.

If only she had just stayed in Mexico. Even next to homeless. Even not knowing anybody. Even weeping her guts out every moment we weren't together. If only she'd stayed. Brokenhearted and hungry and so lonely, her chest aching like a part of her flesh was still pinned to me and Dad and Abuela here in Arizona, aching as though she were dying, dying, but not actually dying, not completely.

That's better than dead, right?

38

BEFORE SHE DIED, ABUELA TOLD ME THAT BEFORE WE had trees and clouds and tomatoes, before even this earthly world, there was una familia. The mother had many children, but they were wicked and wanted dominion over all the worlds. They gathered each world and stuffed them in their pockets like they were pieces of carved jadeite.

You can't just do that with a world. It's like snapping off a yam-orange marigold and expecting to be able to lord over all the flowers now. Things don't work that way.

The mother's youngest son knew each world was most perfect, most needed, where it had grown its roots. While his siblings slept, the youngest took the worlds from their pockets and placed them gently back in the dirt. Back where they came from.

When the siblings discovered what had happened, they whipped out their weapons. A bow, a dagger, an arrow, a sword.

The mother screamed so loudly, she became the moon. The boy became the sun. And all the wicked older siblings turned into the wild things that live in the forests and deserts and sea.

This is why wild animals so often sniff the dirt. They're still searching for worlds to steal.

I know that the bad guys in the story, the siblings, became animals as a punishment. But ever since Abuela told me this tale, I've been jealous of them. Like, there are so many days when I want each part of my body to become something else. Not like the moon or sun, not bigger and more important.

I want my arm to become a wren with a line of brown on the corner of its eye. My feet, a smooth, gold puma, my hair, a coarse-furred wolf. My hands, two stretching hares, my hips, round river rocks. My nose, a bee, drenched in pollen. My cells, bits of plankton that swim as though they are all one smooth body.

Just whenever I need a break from being me all the time.

And if I come across a world like carved jadeite, I'd peek to see if Mom existed within it. And maybe I'd just step inside, the way we tip-toe toward el santuario at church.

39

HEY, **I TEXT ROSE.** WHERE ARE YOU?

I've been waiting for her for ten minutes at the library. The little, falling-apart Caraway Public Library. Literally, like, a dust storm once toppled and broke one of the outdoor iron tables and someone just put caution tape around it. Left it like that for years now.

This is where Rose and I meet for tutoring every couple of weeks, before a test or quiz or whatever. We've tried doing it at one of our houses, but we kept getting distracted by shiny things like the TV and the Internet and a kitchen full of Little Debbie Zebra Cakes and plantain chips. So after I almost failed two tests in a row, Rose had the idea to do it here instead.

What do you mean? she writes back. And then, a second later: Crap, Sia! I'm so so so so sorry. I completely forgot. Completely. But Sam and I are in Starbucks rn. Can we meet up at your place after?

I let out a wheezing breath that makes the old man next to me give a sharp look. I don't know if I've annoyed him or if he thinks I'm dying. It doesn't matter, though. All I can focus on is the feeling like Rose has reached inside my stomach and pulled out all the vital organs. Because she forgot. She just forgot.

Or maybe she just likes Samara more than me now.

I swallow and respond. Not tonight. Dad wants to talk about . . . I think for a second. What sounds important? . . . colleges and stuff. I'll let you know when's a good time to reschedule. To reschedule me. The best friend since sixth grade.

It's a full five minutes before she writes back. Okay. That's it. That's all I get.

I want to cry, but I don't. I'm an expert at keeping the tears inside now. Instead, I open up the textbook and pretend like I know exactly what I'm looking at until I can't stand it anymore.

40

"HOW'S THE MAÍZ DOING, M'IJA?"

Dad and I are drinking hot cocoa on the back porch. As though it knows we're talking about it, the corn patch shivers with wind.

"Good," I say. "I keep finding these weird red bugs on it, but I think they're just munching on the leaves for a quick snack. I'll make some garlic spray if they get outta control."

He leans back and smiles. "Your mamá loved growing maíz, didn't she?"

I bite my lip so hard, it stings. I hate it when he talks about her. But I just nod.

"She loved it so much, I told her I'd string the kernels and make her a necklace, a bracelet, some earrings. And I thought she'd get mad at me for making fun of her, but she loved that idea. She said maybe for our anniversary." He starts to speak again, but trails off, staring at the stalks rustling their leaves.

See, that's why I hate this. No matter how happy the memory, we can't escape the fact that she's gone now.

"You know, they have gemstone corn," I say finally. "It looks like jewels, the maíz, you know? Every color, even azul."

"Imagine that." He sounds cheerful but the lines around his eyes look very deep.

41

I DON'T REALLY REMEMBER WHEN I FIRST NOTICED what Abuela called the kitchen spirits. Once, alone while making tea, I turned on Fleetwood Mac's *Greatest Hits* and totally lost myself in a book. When I finally jumped up and ran to the stove, I found the burner had been turned off with a millimeter of water in the saucepan.

Okay, though. Maybe I turned it off without thinking about it. Not like that hasn't happened before.

But then there were the papitas I fried one morning for breakfast. The oil sizzled so hot and the potatoes cooked too fast, their skins turning brown-black. I shoved the cast-iron skillet across the stovetop to get it away from the flames, and a bunch of grease sloshed on my hand.

I ran to the sink and rinsed and rinsed, convinced my skin was going to bubble up and peel off. Pero nada. My hand didn't even turn pink.

Last year, I decided to make me and Dad baked potatoes with dinner. I turned on the oven to preheat and within minutes I smelled something weird. I opened the oven door and found two foil-wrapped potatoes, already cooked. Like, I hadn't even pulled the papas from the pantry yet, and there they were, too hot to touch.

We covered them in butter-fried peppers and queso fresco. They were delicious.

About a year ago, though, I told the spirits to stay the fuck away.

Spirits didn't save Mami. Spirits didn't warn her when ICE stalked her down the streets like a coyote con una liebre. And they're not gonna bring her back.

When I told my grandmother about it, she just shook her head. "Los espíritus did save her, Sia."

"Yeah?" I said. "Where the hell is she, then?"

Abuela just smiled and did what all grandmothers do. She fed me, pushed tea into my hands. She grabbed her rosary to pray over my head, my heart, from my shoulder to my other shoulder. "Spirits," she finally said. "They work on their own time."

Whatever. I still don't want them in my kitchen. Even if it wasn't their foolish decision to walk the whole wide Sonoran alone like a star speck, with no one around for light years, no one to hear you cry or stumble or curse or slowly become nothing but bones.

42

MY TRIG TEACHER IS ONE OF THOSE SUPER COOL,
efficient sorts who grades quizzes right there in front of you, so you can
feel the judgment emanating from his eyes like lasers. And then I get
the confirmation of those hateful eye-lasers when he slides the paper
onto my desk and it's got D+ written on it so large and so red, I think
the whole class is glowing in its reflective color. I stare at it for so long,
it seems to start pulsating.

I know. I should've rescheduled the study session with Rose. But.
I really wanted to see if she'd remember. In case it wasn't obvious, she
didn't. At all.

When she drives me home, I barely say anything to her. And she
doesn't ask what's the matter. Doesn't even think to ask, it seems.

Instead she says, "Did you read the fic yet?" She sounds excited; her
cheeks are pink, and she looks beautiful in her fuchsia rose-embroidered
white linen dress.

"Sorry, I've been so busy," I respond. My voice is flat. And then Rose
says nothing. Actually, both of us say nothing the rest of the way home.
Nothing, nothing, nothing at all.

43

ONE OF ROSE'S BEST QUALITIES IS THAT SHE SEES
miracles in everything. Which used to make no sense to me. If everything is a miracle, then nothing is actually as special as a miracle's supposed to be, right?

When I first planted corn, and those little sprouts and roots started
pushing out of the seeds, listening to whatever magic was in the water
and dirt and warmth that told them, *now is the time to be born*, Rose
came over and gasped. "Sia! It's a miracle."

She said the same thing when we both saw our first shooting star
while hanging out in her parents' backyard. I wasn't even sure what I
was seeing, but Rose knew. A miracle.

When Rose went to see her baby niece and nephew for the first time,
back before her brother and his family moved to Haiti, she made me
go with her. "I'm scared," she said. "I don't know how to hold a baby."

And I laughed and said, "Like I do?" But on the way, I looked it up
on my phone. "Support the head," I announced. "You always support
the head."

But when Abel brought us the twins, I stopped worrying about
the right way to hold them, because all I could do was marvel at how

much they looked like dolls, so tiny and smooth and perfect.

I held Mary and Rose held David. I put my finger in Mary's grasp. Her nails were so small, as tiny as we must've seemed to that shooting star, I'll bet.

"Aren't they both miracles, Sia?" Rose whispered. That's how we talked around the babies, like even their ears were too holy for normal-toned voices.

And I had to admit, yes. Yes, they were. And Rose was the one who made me see it, you know, that everything being a miracle doesn't negate the power of miracles. It means that everything is extraordinary, just as it is. The cracking of seeds to roots, the burning of a star in the sky, the two most perfect angelic babies in our arms. All of them. Extraordinary.

I keep thinking about this, even when I'm frustrated with Rose. She taught me to see miracles everywhere. And even though whatever it is we're going through is so annoying, I won't lose her. I can't. I refuse. I'm just going to keep looking at all the miracles around me instead. The wind rustling the fingers of the Joshua trees. The ancient stones lining the garden path, ones my father found stacked in the desert. And all of us, little humans falling in and out of love, breaking and repairing hearts, on this spinning, watery, salty planet. Miracles. All of them.

44

HEY, **I TEXT ROSE.** WHAT ARE YOU DOING TODAY?

Shopping with Samara. She's looking for a dress for her cousin's quince.

Ugh. Rose knows the only kind of shopping I like is the thrift store sort, where we laugh at the absolute weirdest finds, and sometimes score amazing vintage pieces. Still, I wait for an invite. After, like, eight minutes of nothing, I write back, Isn't this the third day in a row of y'all hanging out?

Yeah. Why?

Weird. Does she mean for that to come off as defensive? God. I can't figure it out. So I write, No reason. But we're still on for Maude's, right?

Rose and I go to Maude's every single week. Same day, same time, if we can. Because when we were littler, it was a ritual my mother invented with us. Girl time, she'd call it. Sometimes Rose's mom would come, too. And we'd eat greasy food and milkshakes and giggle about boys and stress out about grades and anything else going on in our lives. It was the best day of the week for me. It still is, because Rose and I kept the tradition. There are a few unsaid rules. It's always just us, always at the same booth, our booth, ordering the same milkshakes. Mint chocolate for me, coconut caramel marshmallow for Rose.

She writes, Of course. Wouldn't miss it for the world. & we're still on for First Communion, right?

Ughhh. First freaking Communion. Is it already here? Crap. But I just write back, Wouldn't miss it for the world. With a dozen upside-down happy face emojis.

I feel kind of like a fool for actually going there in my mind, but I kind of think Rose might be lying. Like, I think she would skip our Maude's ritual not only for the world, but specifically, especially, for Samara Kingsley. I keep thinking I'm being too sensitive, but the feeling prickles in my belly, like an annoying little bug. So when Noah emails me and asks if I want to meet up to do more work on our project, I don't put up that much of a fight.

He knocks on the door softly and looks relieved when I open it. "Is your dad home?" he asks.

"No, he's working."

"Ah." He's smiling now. "No offense, of course, but—"

"I know. He's intimidating."

"He's just . . . so ripped, you know? Like I know he could tear my head off with his bare hands."

I guide him to the kitchen table, where we set up our laptops. "You're taller than him, though."

"Yeah, but, but, his freaking biceps . . ."

I laugh, because honestly, he's starting to sound like Rose. "My dad's really into capoeira and martial arts. So, yeah, he can kick just about anyone's ass."

Noah nods. "I believe it."

I wait for my computer to warm up.

Noah clears his throat. "So, do you know capoeira, too?"

"Yeah," I say. "My dad's been training Rose and me for almost a year now. But he combines it with a lot of basic and advanced, I guess, regular old self-defense moves."

"Really? So you can do, like, flips and high kicks and stuff?"

"Uh." I type in my password. "Yeah. I'm not as good on the flips as Rose, though."

"Do you think you could teach me sometime?" He gives me one of his wide, dimpled grins and winks.

Is he flirting with me? The idea makes warm butterflies flutter around in my belly and chest and throat. I cough. "I'm not any good at teaching, Noah. If you want to learn properly, you'll have to ask my dad."

He shudders. "I think I'll pass."

The end goal of our project is to convince the whole class that the moon is better than any other celestial system. I'm thinking Mr. Woods is trying to make us care about this way more than normal, because we're going to vote on it and everything, and the winners get movie tickets.

Noah says that we need to find really unusual facts on the moon, stuff that might even freak people out during the presentation. "Shock value," he calls it. I have no idea how anything about the moon can be exciting to anyone except for, like, astronomers and astrologers, but we're going to try, I guess.

"Oh, here's one," he says. "The moon has earthquakes! Only they're called . . ." He drums his fingers for suspense. "Moonquakes."

"Moonquakes," I repeat. "That sounds like a box of cereal."

"So it's not shocking then?"

I shake my head without blinking. We return to searching.

"Moon dust smells like gunpowder," he announces ten minutes later.

"That's not shocking. That's not even sexy."

He raises his eyebrows and begins reading again. "Whoa, look at this," he says. I come around the table. "This site has photos of all these weird structures folks have spotted on the moon. Like, this tower and this, I don't know, building thing."

"It looks like a big nothing, though," I say. "Blurry spots anyone could call anything. I'm sure Woods would disapprove of alien conspiracy theory."

"Yeah, I know," Noah says. "But it's the most shocking thing I've spotted so far."

I wrinkle my nose. "Well, maybe we can do a portion of our presentation on conspiracy theory. Just letting Woods know that we know it's pseudoscience."

"Sure." Noah nods. "Yeah, that works. We can make the moon very mysterious. And sexy." He wags his eyebrows and I smack his shoulder.

He grabs my hand for a second before I pull it back, and I pretend I don't feel any tingles where his fingers touched mine. "For real, though." He turns his body toward me. "You don't believe in aliens or anything like that?"

I pause, glancing out the window at my corn, then finally give him a shrug. "If there were any out there, we'd know by now, wouldn't we?"

Noah tilts his head. "Some people might know that they're out there. Depends on who you ask."

I can tell that Noah wants me to jump up and say, *Yes, aliens are freaking real!* But not even my grandmother, who knew the beginnings of everything, could give me a straight answer on aliens. "Ay, Sia," she'd say. "All I know is there are spirits. Spirits and men."

And then I remember the blue lights Rose and I saw in the desert, between the cacti with arms and fingers reaching toward one another. What if . . .

"It's fine," Noah says finally. "There's just a lot of interesting information out there. I could fill you in sometime, yeah?"

"Sure. Maybe later." I return to my computer. I pause. Gosh, I hope I don't regret bringing this up. "So, if someone were to have a UFO sighting? Let's say, in the remote desert."

"Go on," Noah says.

"That's something you'd like to hear about, right?"

Noah's eyes are wide. "Uh, yeah!"

I smile and bite my lip. "Okay. Rose and I saw some weird lights a couple weeks ago."

"Really? Like, how weird? What shape was it? Were they blinking?"

I can't help but laugh at his enthusiasm. "Oh my gosh."

"What?"

"You're so nerdy."

Noah's face kind of falls, so I put my hand on his forearm. "It's not a bad thing."

"It's not?"

I shake my head and he grins again, his eyes crinkling, his hand going in his hair, mussing it all up. My knees feel weak even though I'm sitting.

"That's so awesome that you saw a UFO," he's saying. I am very distracted by a freckle on the line of his bottom lip. God. I need to stop staring.

Looking down, I clear my throat. "So, Rose is going to some outlet mall with Samara. And my dad's working late."

Noah gives me a weird look. "That sucks," he says.

I hope I don't regret this, either. "Do you want to stay for dinner?"

"What? Me? Really?" He jumps up and snaps his fingers so fast, his hands are blurs.

"Dude, have a seat. You're acting like I just performed a miracle."

"Well, someone did," Noah mumbles as he sits back down.

I hide my smile. I mean, he's so strange and dorky and lanky but he's sweet and shy, you know? Sweet and shy guys are so rare. I don't know what Rose's real problem with Noah is. All I know is I'm suddenly really looking forward to dinner.

45

WE'RE SITTING ON THE BACK PORCH, FINISHING OFF
Japanese takeout.

"What's with the corn?" Noah says.

I shrug. "It's something the women in my family do. Grow corn."

"Is it, like, that GMO stuff?"

"God, no. No way. These are heirlooms."

"Oh, like heirloom tomatoes?"

"Yeah. It's actually really cool if you think about it. These plants were considered so precious that their seeds were passed on and on for decades. Or even thousands of years in some cases." I take a sip of my tulsi tea.

He's smiling so goofily at me, I want to slap it off his face. "Yeah, that is cool. Or groovy." He nods at my bell bottoms. "So, what's up with that, anyway?"

"What's up with what?"

He shrugs. "You know. All those old-sounding bands you guys play all the time. I mean, they're good!" He holds up his hands when I glare. "But they're . . . old, you know?"

I stare. "How do you know anything about our playlist?"

"You guys play your music, like, really loud." He winks. "I can hear it all the way across the senior parking lot."

I sigh. "The seventies, alright? The most awesome decade."

"It's just so random, though. Lots of decades were cool. Take the 1870s. Everyone wore hats. Oh! And what about the 1470s, when dudes wore corsets and two-feet long shoes, and, like, your standard market bread could make you high?"

I roll my eyes. "Oh my God, fine." I take a long sip of tea. "My mom had these older cousins that were big hippies. She thought they were so cool when she was little. Their dresses and, like . . ." I make a swirling motion with my hand.

"All the love, peace, and harmony?"

"Yeah. That. And they all worshipped Stevie Nicks." I shrug. "Anyway, it totally influenced Mom's style. Even though she grew up in the eighties."

Noah nods, turning his gaze back on the maíz. I'm glad he doesn't ask for any more details.

My phone buzzes. It's Rose. Hey, Sam and I finished up early. Buffy marathon? My place?

I write back, Can't. Studying with Noah. I turn my phone on silent and put it away. When I turn to Noah, he's looking at me intently.

"What?"

He blinks and shakes his head a little. "Sorry. It's nothing."

"Really? You looked really serious for a minute."

He shrugs. "Yeah, I was just thinking about the sheriff. . . . You know, that guy, McGhee?"

My hands want to clench, but I try to keep them still. "Yeah, what about him?"

"I, uh, heard about what he did. To your mom." Noah turns to me. "And I'm really sorry."

"Oh, it's okay." I start to wave it off, but then stop. "Actually, no, it's not okay. But we can't do anything about it, I guess." Not without a time machine, at least.

"He just, he seems like a such an asshole."

I nod. "Oh my God, he is. And do you know Jeremy McGhee?" Noah's not looking at me, but he furrows his brow. "Well, that's his son. They're both such—" I groan. "You know, once the sheriff started suspecting Mom's status, he started following her. Like, he'd slowly drive by our house at dinnertime, or he'd show up at the corner store as she was leaving and stare her down. And the worst part was, she couldn't do anything about it. He was trying to get her to retaliate, I think, so he could arrest her and send her off."

Noah grimaces. "That's so shitty."

"And Jeremy, my God. He just taunted me at school. He followed me, too, come to think of it. Saying things like, *your mom's days are numbered*. And when I'd walk by his friends, he'd start talking super loud, things like, *we need to round them up, all those lazy ass illegals, and put them behind a big, beautiful wall*. It was disgusting. Or, he was disgusting. They both—" I stop talking when I see Noah's face. He looks almost like he's in pain, staring off in the distance. "Hey, is everything okay?"

"What? Yeah. Yeah, sure, I mean, I just hate to hear this crap, you know? What they've done to your family."

I nod. "I get it. I hate to talk about it." I straighten my back. "So let's change the subject."

He relaxes back into his chair and takes a deep breath. "Sure. To what?"

"What are you into, Noah?"

He blinks, looking back at me. "What do you mean?"

"Like Rose. She's obsessed with Harry Potter and fashion and comics and physics. And I like my garden . . . and that's about it. So what do you like? I mean, besides the 1470s."

He laughs. "I like writing."

"What, like stories?"

"Sometimes. Sometimes I write poetry."

I groan. "I freaking hate poetry."

"Okay, seriously," he says. "What poets have you read?"

"Uh—" I pause while he smirks. "Whatever, man. I've read stuff for school. Just because I can't remember the names doesn't mean I don't know what I'm talking about."

"Well, how many, then?"

I shrug. "Ten."

"See? That's just ten. That's the tip of the iceberg. No, that's a scratch on the surface on the tip of the iceberg."

"Is that one of your poems?" I ask.

"I'm gonna find a poem that you're gonna love." He's pointing with one hand, his tea mug in the other.

I snort. "Good freaking luck."

He smiles and we watch my corn for a bit. When I look back at him, his lips are pursed as if he's thinking, probably of some poem to convert me to his special brand of weird.

But I keep looking at them. His lips. The top is a little fuller than the bottom. He's got a wide mouth, which makes sense. It's why all his smiles are so wicked.

I freeze when I realize what I'm doing. I mean, what am I thinking? I'm just leering at his lips, for heaven's sake. And what for? There's no reason to leer at anyone's lips ever. Unless . . .

"You should go." I stand. "My dad's going to be home soon."

46

IT KIND OF FREAKS ME OUT THAT I MIGHT WANT TO

kiss Noah.

47

"HOW LONG HAS IT BEEN?" ROSE ASKS, BREATHING HARD.

I look at my phone. "Fifteen minutes."

She puts her hands on her head. "Jesus help me."

"You want to stop?" I'm all for it, honestly. Running is the worst of our drills.

"No way."

I make a face.

"Hey," she says. "You're the one always wondering how I outperform you in almost all our moves. This is how. You never push yourself."

"Yeah, yeah, I know." I pop in my ear buds and we take off.

"You doing anything tonight?" she asks when the thirty is up. I'm doubled over, trying to catch my breath. "I'm thinking of trying this new argan oil masque my auntie sent," she continues.

"Can't. Working on moon project." I'm still choking down air.

She frowns. "I thought you guys already did your old-school measuring technique?"

"We're working on the presentation right now. The moon sucks, apparently. We have to find an edge."

She takes a long drink of water. Her jaw is clenched a little tight. "Sia. Remember what I told you."

I turn my head and roll my eyes. "Rose, please."

"Please what?"

"Stop treating me like I'm a child when it comes to Noah."

"Whoa." She holds her hands up. "I didn't think that's what I was doing. I just want you—"

"To be careful. Believe me, I remember."

She sighs. "Okay, Sia. I'll stop. I'm sorry. I know you can handle it."

I nod. "Thanks. And I'm sorry I just blew up at you. I just . . . with Noah. I think he's cool."

"You think he's cool?"

"Yeah."

The tension is back. But she's not saying what she's thinking, at least. So I try to change the subject. "But I really want to hang out, Rose. I miss you. It feels like we haven't done something fun in forever. Maybe tomorrow?"

"Can't. Got plans with Samara." Her answer comes out really fast.

"I thought you were video-calling Abel." She chats with them twice a week, at least, since he and the family moved to Haiti.

"After that."

I wait for her to tell me when she's free, but she says nothing. "We have practice on Saturday. Will you make it, or are you going to the mall with Sam again?" There's definite contempt in my tone at that last bit.

"We'll see." Her voice is cool.

I fight the urge to roll my eyes again.

"Are you ready?" she asks, standing.

"No. I need to run some more." I take off before she can respond. I push my legs to keep up well after they feel like they're on fire. I slow to a walk when I can't take it anymore and look back. Rose is watching, but she squints. Like she can't even see me.

48

WHEN I GET HOME, I WANT TO PUNCH SOMETHING. I
go into the garage and put on Dad's old kickboxing gloves. And then I
hit at his punching bag until the backs of my hands feel numb.

In my room, the first thing I see is that giant D+ glowing on my quiz
paper. And I don't even hesitate. I grab my phone and text Rose. Can't
make the First Communion thing on Sunday. Dad's going to
help me with trig. And Rose will know it's kind of a bullshit excuse,
since the only sort of math Dad can help with is the kind with concrete
calculations. He's always transforming my assigned problems into field
research so he can get it better. Which takes forever.

But then again, if Rose isn't going to help, I kind of have to rely on
him now.

After absolute ages, Rose texts, okay. Great. Another fucking *okay*.

49

IN THE BEGINNING, I USED TO CRY A LOT. OUT OF
nowhere, the tears would poke at my eyes and like the arrival of a rainstorm, I'd have to run for cover. It was the worst at school. Restrooms were my go-to for spells of tears, but one day I walked in and saw Charlotte Gawland, the first person to call my mom a wetback to my face.

So I ran to the nearest supply closet and wept over tubes of paint and pads of newsprint. I could hardly breathe. But then the door flew open and I froze, staring right in the face of Jeremy McGhee.

For a long moment, after the shock? I swear to all the gods, Jeremy looked like he actually felt bad. That must sound so astonishing, I mean, it's Jeremy fucking McGhee, after all. But then his face hardened into its usual mode of vile-shaped stone and he snarled.

"You shouldn't be in here," he said, snatching a roll of paper. "And your mother shouldn't have walked that fucking desert."

He waited for me to say something, but when I just sniffed, he slammed the door, leaving me in the dark.

I never told anyone this, not even Rose. But the reason why I didn't say anything is because for the first and only time, I agreed with Jeremy about something.

50

AS ANNOYED AS I'VE BEEN LATELY, I HATE THAT I
haven't heard from Rose today. The fact that I care about this at all is doubly annoying, in fact. She's always the one to text first in the mornings, usually with a What's up, buttercup?

I make it through practice with my dad, checking my messages every ten minutes, even though he yells at me that I could've died eleven times, facing a perpetrator with my face in my phone like that. Finally, after Dad gives up on me, I sit in the kitchen with my water bottle and write, We haven't been to Maude's at all this week. You said you wouldn't miss it for the world.

Let's meet there at one.

What? Why? I wrinkle my nose and stare at her words for another minute. Rose and I haven't met up anywhere in . . . well, ever. We always catch rides together. Even when it makes no sense.

Sam and I are on the other side of town.

Of course. I debate responding. Instead, I grab garden shears and head outside.

51

ROSE IS INSIDE OF MAUDE'S. IN OUR SPOT. WITH Samara. *In our spot.*

I watch like a complete creep though a clear spot in the dusty windows. They're laughing. Sam's hair is in twists and pinned up, and she's wearing a black dress with soft fringe on the edges, her long arms covered in spirally turquoise jewelry. Rose has on a baby doll dress that reaches her knees, the lavender fabric covered in a pattern of pink peonies. Probably something she made herself.

I glance down at my ripped jeans, black Chucks, and brown tank top, everything faded and covered in garden dirt. I sigh and make my way inside.

52

SAMARA IS REALLY SWEET, AS USUAL. SHE COMPLIMENTS
my hair, how it turns bronze in the sun, and then I have to tell her how
in love with her jewelry I am, and we all start gossiping about classmates
and laughing. I begin to forget what I was even worried about when
Sam gasps and says, "Sia, can you believe that Gustavo asked Rose's
dad's permission to take her to the spring dance?"

I almost choke on a chocolate chip. "Gustavo did *what*?" I stare at
Rose hard, but she just glares right back at me. "When?"

"He just came over," Rose says, "with bouquets of lilies for Mom and
me." She rolls her eyes. "I think that made it worse, to be honest."

I snort. "So your dad killed him, then, right? Like, there's a body we
need to hide now, huh?"

Sam laughs, but Rose sort of half-smiles and half-grimaces. I guess she's
really, really pissed at me for flaking on the First Communion prep. But
all I have to do is remember my D+ and voilà, my guilt vanishes. Magic.

There's a silence that goes on for too long, until Samara finally says
to Rose, "Did you finish your chapter yet?"

"Not yet. Maybe tonight." The smiles she gives Samara are
real-looking.

"For the fic?" I ask. "The new one?"

"Oh God, it's amazing, isn't it, Sia?" Samara says.

"Everything Rose writes is amazing."

Rose tilts her head. "But you didn't really answer her question."

"What?"

"Did you think the new one is amazing? Or have you still not read it yet?"

I guess my face says it all because Rose lifts her eyebrows and just sighs. There's another awkward conversation break. Samara tries to save us once again.

"So, Sia, what's going on with you and the new guy?" She and Rose glance at each other and it pisses me off that they've talked about this, about me and Noah, something I can't even bring up to Rose without her losing her mind.

But I just wink and say, "Oh, you know, the usual. I'm pregnant with his triplets, we're engaged to be married, moving to Paris in the summer."

Sam laughs again, but Rose, of course, doesn't, and I, once again, feel out of place. So I smile a real sweet smile and put my chin on my hand. "Samara, did you know that Rose and I used to come here with my mom every weekend? Right here, this table. It was ours. But then the thing with my mom happened, and to cheer me up, Rose said we should keep doing it. Our tradition." I glance right at Rose before turning back to Sam. "And then, for the longest time, it belonged to just me and Rose. It was sacred, you know?"

"Wow. I didn't know that," Samara says. She looks confused and helpless and Rose looks like she wants to stick her straw in my eye socket.

"Anyway, I'm going now," I say, standing. I grab money from my pocket and toss it on the table. The bills are all wadded up, so someone will have to smooth them out by hand. It's a dick move, but I feel like being a dick right now. "Thanks for inviting me to our spot."

Samara says a cheery goodbye, but I don't even look at Rose. Instead, outside, I resume my spot in front of the window and peek in.

And Sam and Rose, under the table, are holding hands. It's probably nothing, but then Samara runs her finger up Rose's arm, and Rose gives her a shy smile, her eyes twinkling as though she and I aren't having the biggest fight in our entire history of knowing each other. And that's it. I'm done. I just stomp into my car and drive away, the tires squealing like chickens.

53

"I THINK I HAVE THE POEM ALMOST READY FOR YOU," Noah announces. "It's not official yet, but"—he snaps his fingers—"I'm close."

"Cool story, bro," I say.

"You watch. You're going to love it." He pushes open another one of the pile of moon books he brought.

We're sitting in the bed of his ugly truck, wrapped in the lilac-smelling blankets he laid out. Noah suggested that being in moonlight in the desert might inspire us to find what we're looking for. I was pretty skeptical of the idea, but my dad? He definitely didn't believe it. I reminded him that he was acting like Cruz Damas. And Dad let me go with a slightly stricter curfew than normal.

"Okay, so the moon is in what's called a synchronous rotation with the Earth. That means we always see its same side. And we never see its far side."

"*The Dark Side of the Moon* is Pink Floyd's best selling album," I say.

"Is that a fact? Are you finally offering a fact?" He looks giddy.

"No." I scowl. "It's just a conversation."

"Good. 'Cause that one kinda sucked." He grins as I smack his forearm.

We read for a while.

"McKenna asked me to the movies Friday night," he blurts suddenly.

I blink a couple times. "Okay."

"What do you think? Should I go?"

He's watching me very carefully.

"I guess," I say. "She's nice."

I want to tell him McKenna's an awful, vindictive bitch and he should stay away. Or something like that. But I can't. I don't know her. She probably is nice. I decide to change the subject instead.

"This is weird." I point at the book in my lap. "The moon is drifting away from the Earth. Almost four centimeters every year."

"Whoa. Does that mean it'll eventually spiral off?"

"No, they think it'll stop in"—I slide my finger down the sentence—"fifty billion years." I frown. "By then, it'll take forty-seven days for it to orbit the Earth. I don't like that."

"How come?"

I take a breath, gazing at the Adam and Eve cacti a few yards ahead. The lines of their skin in the moonlight look like muscle and bone. "Look," I say to him, gesturing at the humanoids. "Doesn't it seem like they're reaching for each other?"

He turns and cocks his head ever so slightly. "Yeah. Yeah, it does."

"That's why."

"I—I'm sorry. I don't get it."

"I've always seen the moon as belonging to the Earth. You know? Like it's Earth's great love. I don't like that it's edging away."

"I always thought the ancient myths paired the moon and sun."

I stick out my tongue. "Blah. That's old news. So predictable."

"You ever think, Sia, that maybe the moon belongs to itself?" He's quirking up his lips and I want to touch them, so I shift all the way to the other side of the bed, pretending I need to stretch my legs.

"Mayb—" I break off as a blue light shoots off in the distance. "Hey, that's—"

"Shit," Noah says. We both follow the lights with our eyes. They zoom back and forth in a long figure eight. There's three of them.

I gasp. "Those are the same creepy lights Rose and I saw the other day. You think it's some kind of drone?"

"It's *way* too big to be a drone."

It passes in front of some clouds lit gray by the moon and I gasp. It's shaped like a triangle, and God, it's huge.

"My hair is standing up," Noah says, holding his arm out. Mine is, too.

"Look." Noah points. "You see, there, on its right side? Looks like it's on fire."

The spot of starlike glow near its tail does look like a flame. I shiver a little, thinking of all the saint and Guadalupe candles I've lit out here, guiding Mami home. Is that bit of fire there, on that freaking UFO, is that what my candles would look like to her? If she were still alive, I mean, walking all the way up from the other side of this desert? No, no, I'm just being ridiculous right now.

The craft releases a little puff of smoke. "Shit," I say as it dives down like a water bird grabbing some fish. And just like that, it's gone. Nothing but a spiral of gray fog where it'd been.

"Did you see where it went?" Noah asks, looking around.

"No. God. It just disappeared."

"What the hell was that?" he asks.

I feel strange. Like way more alive than normal. I look at Noah, whose eyes are still wide on the landscape and I just keep thinking, I don't want to be so fucked up about what I want anymore. So I crawl over to him. He realizes how close I am and there's a sharp intake of air when I put my hands on his face.

"Do you want to kiss?" I say.

He pushes his lips onto mine instantly, before I can even finish the question. His arms wrap around my waist and he tugs me forward, until I'm on top of him, legs on either side of his. At first everything is slow and soft, but when I put my tongue in his mouth, a wild volt of electricity blasts open between us, and it's like we can't kiss fast or deep enough. My hands, somehow, make their way under his shirt, along his stomach. And he freezes, groaning in his throat before running his hands on my belly, back, hips, thighs. I pull back and we both breathe hard.

"God," he says. He's looking at me very intently.

"What?" I feel like I did something wrong.

"You're fucking gorgeous."

My cheeks heat up and I thank the gods it's dark and he can't see. I glance around and see the time on my phone.

"We should leave," I say.

"Okay," he says quickly, but he looks super dazed for a long while. I have to fling a book at him so we can go.

54

ROSE'S CAR IS IN THE DRIVEWAY WHEN WE GET HOME.

"That's weird," I say.

Noah gives me a quizzical look.

"She just said she had plans tonight." With Samara. Naturally.

We pause. "Do you want me to walk you to do the door?" he asks.

"That's a little absurd," I respond. "Why would you do that?"

"Oh, uh, I, I don't know." Even though we're only lit by the windows of my home, I can see the pink in his neck and cheeks.

I shake my head and smile. "I'll see you soon, okay?"

"Soon? Like, tomorrow?"

"Maybe," I say. "I'll let you know."

"Cool," he says. "Cool, cool." He drums his fingers on the dashboard.

"Later," I call as I shut the car door.

Something's off. My stomach performs tiny flips as I step into the threshold.

"Rose?" I call.

"She's in your bedroom, amor," Dad says from the kitchen. He steps out and his eyes reveal concern.

"Is everyone okay?"

"Everyone's okay," he says. "Go talk to her, though. She needs you."

I fling open my door and find her lying on my bed, watching Buffy. "What happened?"

"Your dad didn't tell you?" She grabs the remote and pauses the show. "My brother got into a car accident."

"Shit, Rose," I say, dropping my bag. "How is he?"

"He's—he's—" She chokes up a little. I jump on the bed and wrap my arms around her. "He's gonna be okay. A few broken bones, a punctured lung. Meena's got a concussion and some scrapes."

"And the kids?"

"They weren't with them, thank God."

I hug her for a while longer and she leans into it. I let go and flip my legs over until we're side by side.

"My mom's flying out this weekend, to help with the kids while Abel and Meena recover. I might go with her. I don't know, though. She'll be gone a whole week."

"If you need to go, you should go. It's spring break. You could email the teachers for homework so you don't get behind for the day or two you might miss."

My phone starts chirping and buzzing wildly. "That would be all my texts and calls in the last two hours, probably," Rose says.

"God, I'm so sorry," I say, grabbing my phone. "We were in the desert."

"How are things with you and Noah?" She adds, "You know, besides the triplets and the wedding." The room feels very small, even as she jokes.

"Things are, you know. He's a weird kid," I say without glancing up.

She straightens her back. "What happened with you two?"

"Don't know what you're talking about."

"Come on, Sia. I know you."

"Fine," I say. "But please don't get mad. I want you to be happy for me, okay?"

"Shit," she says and I blink because Rose almost never curses out loud. She nods slowly. "Okay."

I shake my head softly. God. How do I even start? I decide to just cut to the chase. "Tonight . . . I sort of . . . kissed Noah."

The only thing she does is sigh. And then silence.

"Rose? What is it?"

"Sia." She lifts a hand. "I told you to be careful with him. I told you to not go falling for him and that's exactly what you did."

I literally cannot believe what I'm hearing. "Are you serious right now? I told you Noah said he didn't know McGhee. At all."

"There's something up with him, Sia. Something off." She makes it sound really cryptic.

"Okay. I'll bite. What is the big secret now?"

Rose straightens her back. "Do you remember when we went to Sam's party? How Jeremy couldn't go because he went to court?"

"Yeah?"

"Well, you know how Amy Bowers spends her free period volunteering in the front office?"

" . . . Yeah?"

"Well, she heard the sheriff talking to Ms. Parker about the court case. And then Amy told Trina Nichols who told Samara that Jeremy went to testify for a lady who's last name is DuPont."

I swallow. "DuPont isn't that rare of a name, Rose."

"Sia, you said that Noah's mom is fighting a DUI in court. Don't you think that's a really weird coincidence? Almost too coincidental?"

I stand and cross my arms. "Noah doesn't have anything to do with the McGhees. He already told me. He hadn't even heard of the sheriff before. And you know what? If you really thought this was a big deal, then why am I hearing about it just now?"

"Samara thought I should wait—"

I snort. "Are you kidding me? You're letting Samara dictate the information you're allowed to share with me?"

"It's not like that, Sia."

"Oh, really? Because it sounds to me like you're talking shit about me behind my back."

"Sia, you were a total jerk to Samara at Maude's. Don't even pretend like you've got a high horse to get on." Rose nods her head at my phone in my hand. "Call him. Ask him about the DuPont lady Jeremy testified for."

I scoff. "I'm not doing that."

"If he has nothing to hide—"

"He doesn't. He told me he doesn't know the sheriff, Rose. And that's it. I believe him."

Rose crosses her arms. "He's lying."

"Whatever." I throw up an arm. "I know what this is about, Rose." I narrow my eyes. "You're just angry that I was a jerk to you and Samara. Which, okay, I was. But—"

"I am trying to protect you, Sia, from getting hurt. This guy is a liar and connected to the McGhees and God knows what else. And yes, frankly, I am pissed. You have been spending all your time with him, and it's turned you into a crappy friend. There. I said it."

"Oh, that's rich, Rose, coming from you."

Now Rose is standing, hands on her hips. "And what's that supposed to mean?"

"Samara Kingsley is what I mean, Rose."

Rose scoffs. "I'm only hanging out with her because you're too busy t—"

I throw my arms up. "Are you joking? You starting choosing Sam over me way before this whole thing with Noah started. And you know it."

Rose huffs. "The only reason I started hanging out with Samara more is the first time you decided to believe some guy you barely know over me. I know it was him in that parking lot with the sheriff. But you're too ignorant to face the truth."

"You didn't even see if it was Noah for sure, Rose! You said it yourself! You said, and I quote, *It was probably nothing.*"

She acts like I didn't speak at all. "And you're doing it again, with this information on the DuPont woman. You're believing him over me." She's pleading with her eyes. "Can't you see how messed up that is?"

I scoff. "You know what? You haven't given me a lot of confidence in your word lately, Rose. Thanks for that D+ in trig, by the way."

"Sia." Rose puts a hand on her eyes. "I'm sorry. I am. Even when I haven't yet received an apology from you for leaving me to teach First Communion all by myself. Or for completely neglecting to read my Buffy story."

"Fine. Sorry." I bark it out, then stop and take a deep breath. "I would have understood if you had told me the real reason why you keep choosing Sam. Which is what you're supposed to do. You're supposed to tell your best friend if you start falling for someone, not leave me to flail and guess! I want to be happy for you. Even if all you do is spend your time with her." My eyes are stinging and I will the tears back inside.

Rose laughs. "Oh, like you let me know about you falling for Noah."

"That's because you freaked out every time I mentioned his name!"

Rose sighs again. "Sam and I aren't the point."

"You sure about that? Because she is your whole social life now. And when I'm with you, we don't have fun anymore. All you do is criticize me for liking Noah!"

"Oh, now you admit you like him."

I ignore that. "And you took Samara to our spot at the diner, Rose. Our. Spot."

Rose waves me off. Her cheeks are turning pink. "You know what, Sia? No one owns that booth at Maude's. We didn't own it when your mom was alive, and we don't own it now that she's dead."

My mouth opens and closes for a second as she backtracks.

"I mean—Sia. You know what I—"

I push down that ache in my chest, the one that tells me my heart is about to crack like an egg for the hundredth time. "You know what? Yeah. I think we've both been shitty friends. And maybe we need to stop. Being friends, I mean."

I may as well have slapped her. She's looking at me with eyes shining like jewels and I want to take it back, to pull the words right into my mouth like a string of bitter berries. But I don't know how. Inexplicably, I think of my grandmother. Like she's nearby. Not now, viejita.

"Okay. You're going to throw away five-and-a-half years of best friendship over a guy?" Her voice is cracking.

"Why not? You've already thrown it away over a girl." I shrug like this is nothing. Like my heart isn't audibly cracking like paper-thin glass.

"I'm going to Les Cayes with my mom," Rose says, standing up. "I need a break from all this."

I close my eyes. I keep them closed as she slams the door.

I DREAM OF MY GRANDMOTHER. WE'RE SITTING IN HER kitchen, drinking teas from her garden herbs. The light coming in the window is all gold, like when a lightning storm clears just before dusk. She's got her hair braided and pinned up and she's wearing blackberry lipstick. And she says the same thing she always does.

"Artemisia. Your mama's coming home soon."

56

I SPEND THURSDAY EATING ARROZ CON LECHE AND watching *Battlestar Galactica*. After the last bite of pudding, I still feel my grandmother around. I decide to make some tea and confront her.

"Why are you bothering me?" I say to the photo of her on the fridge. "Why can't you help me with something real? Mami esta muerta. Even when *you're* dead, you can't accept that."

I swirl the tea with my spoon. The steam overflows out of the mug like it's a witch's cauldron. "Tell me what to do about Rose. Tell me what to do about this boy, Wela. They're both making me confused in the exact opposite ways. La luna y el sol. Eso es lo que son."

After a minute, I sigh. "You know what? Never mind. Talking to dead people, that's your thing. I'm focusing on the living." I stomp to the sink and dump the tea.

AFTER DINNER WITH DAD, I WRITE NOAH AGAIN. HEY. Don't know if you're taking McKenna to the movies, but you can come over tomorrow if you're not busy. Dad's working late again.

I get his response ten minutes later. I'll be there.

58

"WHAT'S GOING ON WITH YOU AND ROSE?" DAD ASKS as I pour our coffee.

"Nothing," I say.

"It didn't look like nothing when she stomped out of here last night."

I pour the cream in my mug, trying to make the white spiral on the surface last as long as possible. "She's jealous I'm spending time with Noah."

I know it's just half the truth, but it's the best I can do right now. I really, really don't want to get into details. I mean, what could I say? *Well, Dad, you see, it's like this. I believed Noah over her, so she put Samara before me, and then the passive-aggressive tension and comments and flake-outs built and built and built until last night we basically ended our freakin' five-plus-year friendship. Oh, and I'm probably gonna fail trig, too.* Definitely not.

Dad's fine with my lack of explanation, luckily. "Is she going to Haiti con Maura?"

"Yeah."

"You tell her to travel safe for me. Tell her we'll miss her."

"Fine."

Dad stares at me as he sips from his mug. "What's going on with you and that white boy, anyway?"

I shrug. "I kissed him."

"You *what?*"

I stare at him because I know he heard me. He shakes his head. "I'm sorry, m'ija. I just wasn't expecting that." He pauses. "What kind of kiss?"

I roll my eyes. "Dad."

"I just want you to be careful, Sia. You're a smart girl. I don't want you getting pregnant until you've got your PhD."

"A kiss doesn't get a girl pregnant, Dad. You should know that from experience."

"I know where kissing leads, Artemisia. From experience." He has a faraway look in his eyes and I groan.

"You're being gross," I say.

"Kissing is fine. Just make sure he keeps his hands to himself," Dad continues. "You remember what I taught you?"

I nod. Yup. I can basically neuter a guy with a fist chop. It's, like, the first thing Dad showed me.

"Good." He grabs the paper and retreats to the back porch.

I reach for my phone. Please have a safe trip, I write. We will miss you.

Rose doesn't respond.

59

SOMETIMES, WHEN I HAVE NOTHING TO DO, I PLOP IN
bed and think about all the bullshit people have said to me since Mom
was deported. I imagine what I should've said to them instead of nothing.

She shouldn't have broken the law.

Can't say how many times I've heard that one. I want to scream now,
that my mom was a baby when she got here, that this land, this sand,
this moon under this dry sky is all she's known.

She should've done it legally.

She tried, assbrain. She tried. Both before and after ICE dragged her
away just outside my school.

Her parents shouldn't have broken the law, then.

First of all, I thought when Jesus came, we stopped punishing people
for the sins of their parents.

Secondly, my abuela brought my mom here because she had nothing
but a husband who beat her. When he lost his job and they were down
to one cup of arroz, she decided she'd rather slip into this country to be
with her brother's familia than watch her baby starve to death.

If you had to become an undocumented immigrant to feed your
children, wouldn't you?

Wouldn't you?

There had to be another way.

White people—guys especially—always imagine another way because their paths have always been saturated with forks. For Abuela and mi mamá, there was no fork. No other way.

Sometimes, in the desert, alone with my back in the dirt, I draw lines with my fingers in the sky. I imagine the path my mother took in the Sonoran, her size-eight footprints in the searing sand. And I give her another way. A fork at the end of her trail.

I give her a thousand ways home, like I can go back in time and save her, over and over again.

60

THERE'S A KNOCK AT THE DOOR AT AROUND THREE. I
open it and Noah's there, smiling so big, both dimples are deep. "Hey,"
he says.

I can't help but smile, too. "Hey." I move to let him inside.

I can feel the electricity crackling between us as we walk to the sofa.
It's like our bodies keep thinking of kissing. And other things.

"You're not going to believe this," he says, pulling out his computer.
He sets it on the coffee table and opens it up. "That spacecraft we saw?
It flew into town yesterday evening. There were dozens of witnesses. I
saw it in the *Sentinel* this morning."

"Holy hell." My spine feels funny, like it wants to shiver.

"Look." He points and I sit next to him, so close that our legs touch.
I can tell he notices because he leans at a weird angle, like he's not sure
what to do with his arms.

I read the headline. *Officials State Unidentified Object Is Weather
Balloon.*

"That's what they always say when they're hiding something real.
Anyone who's ever watched the *The X-Files* knows that," I say.

"You like the *The X-Files*?" he asks me.

"I've seen a few episodes."

"It's me and my mom's favorite."

You're my favorite, I want to say. *Kissing you is my favorite. We should definitely kiss again.*

Instead, I lean over his computer, where he's pointing. There's a fuzzy picture taken with a cell phone. "That doesn't even show how huge and angled it is," I say. "Everyone reading this is gonna believe that it's nothing."

"I'm sure they did that on purpose," Noah says.

I lean back. "So what does this mean? Is, like, an extraterrestrial visiting us?"

He shrugs. "Maybe the government is flying some secret advanced craft of their own."

"They're doing a shit job if they're trying to keep it a secret."

"Yeah." He drums his hands on the coffee table for a bit. And I wonder for a moment, what's it going to take to get Noah to kiss me?

I straighten my back. "Let's do some research on those conspiracy websites. See if we can find something that looks like what we saw." And then I stand. "It's way cozier in my room. We should move there."

Noah gives me the absolute shyest smile. "Uh, wow. Yeah. Great idea."

61

"SO TRIANGLE-SHAPED UFOS HAVE THEIR OWN TYPE of classification," I say.

"Yeah, I saw that. Here, it says that there's some mythic Aurora aircraft rumored to have been developed in the eighties. But the government denies it ever existed. See, here, though. It's got the right shape."

I lean over and my bed creaks. We're both sitting against the headboard, computers in our laps.

"Hmm," I say. "But here, it says that the Aurora project comes from reverse engineering."

"What's that?"

"Okay, I know this from my mom. She's got—I mean, she had a degree in computer science. Robotics. So, yeah, reverse engineering is when you look at a machine or something and you figure out how it works by studying it. Then you apply that to something else. So here, it says that reverse engineering is a huge thing with extraterrestrial spacecrafts. All the government is interested in is gaining technological knowledge. And making new stuff from it."

Noah narrows his eyes. "So maybe the human-made Aurora craft comes from studying a similar UFO craft?"

I shrug. "That's what this site says."

"Whoa," he says, pointing at his screen. "There's only been one good photo taken of one of these. By a British guy, I guess. Take a look."

I lean again. Goosebumps run along my flesh. "Holy shit, Noah. That's it. That's exactly what we saw." Triangle, blue lights on the corners. The proportions are exact.

I lean back. "What on earth is it doing here?"

He gazes at me and his lips quirk up ever so slightly as he shrugs.

62

I CAN'T HELP IT. I KISS NOAH AGAIN. SURPRISE, RIGHT?
It's like we're magnets or something. Or he is the sun, expanding, and I, la tierra, want nothing more than his heat. Whatever metaphor I can come up with isn't quite accurate, really. All I know is he's on top of me, his hands cup my face, my fingers slide along his back. And I can feel all of him all over all of me.

I want to be okay with my body.

I want to be okay with his body.

I want to undo everything that's been done to me.

I pull back and look at him, at the olive and gold spots in his eyes. "I want you."

His eyes widen. "What? You mean . . ."

"Yes."

He looks completely stunned. "Okay, Sia. I need, I mean, I . . . I need you to be very specific with what you mean by that. Because I'm not sure—"

"I want to have sex," I say.

"Now?" he says. "Are you sure?"

I nod.

He glances around. "I—I didn't bring a condom or anything."

"I have one. From health class."

He kisses me again, then lowers his lips to my neck. One of his giant hands eases under my shirt. He lets out a low groan when I reach for his belt buckle.

63

THERE'S SO MUCH SKIN CONTACT, EVEN THOUGH WE both still have our underwear on. I love that he's taut, that he has a farmer's tan. I love the sharp indentations at his hips. When I touch him there, he shudders.

And then I feel it. It. On my leg.

I can't move. Or breathe.

"Hey, hey," he says, pushing his torso up. "Are you okay?"

"Your penis."

He looks down. "Uh—"

"Put it away."

Now he looks confused. "Put your fucking pants back on, Noah," I grit out, and he jumps up. When he's got the button worked in, I let out a long, shaky breath.

"I'm sorry," he says. When I don't respond, he goes on. "I knew it was too soon. I should've never agreed . . ." He trails off when he sees my tears. "Shit, Sia. Can I—is it okay if I sit here?"

I nod and he puts his arms around me. I lean into him and weep.

When I can speak again, I tell him about a mean boy pushing my face to his ugly dick. About how dicks have freaked me out ever since and I wanted to be fixed, fixed so badly, I want the thousands of pieces of me to be sewn back together again, but without seams, like I was before, before Rose and I fought, before Justin, before the McGhees. Before my mother became bones in the desert.

And he doesn't say anything; he holds me, he holds me, he holds me until the light coming through the windows turns dusk blue.

64

"I'M SORRY YOU AND ROSE FOUGHT BECAUSE OF ME,"
he says.

"It's not your fault." I sigh. "I just. I can't remember when we've ever
been this mad at each other. I'm still so mad at her. And even though it
makes no sense, I miss her."

"Tell me about how you guys became friends." Noah's stroking my
hair and it's making me calmer. Almost lazy.

"It was the first day of middle school. I'd gotten a new backpack. Those
sporty ones, you know, made of mesh? I thought they were so cool."

Noah laughs a little. "Yeah, I know what you're talking about."

"*So* middle school right?"

"So middle school." He kisses my hand. Even with me feeling like
crap, his lips leave little shivers on my skin.

"Anyway, what's not advertised with those kinds of book bags is they
don't have good support. By the end of the day, my bag was full of
textbooks, and I was walking by the bus loop, where it seemed like the
whole school population was hanging out."

"Uh huh . . ."

"And the zipper just ripped open. Right then and there. And my books, pens, pencils, every piece of paper in the world, everything, it all came out like an avalanche. I turned and everyone was watching me. And, this part was like in slow motion, everyone started pointing and laughing. One by one. My face was so red. I almost burst into tears right then and there."

"But something happened, right? Something stopped those tears."

"Someone. Rose." I swallow. "She came running out, saying, *Oh, my gosh, are you okay?* And then she bent down and helped me pick everything up. And she was like, *You go to St. Julian's right? My dad is the music director there.* And she walked home with me, because her brother was running late, and we ate plantain chips with French onion dip and watched *Hannah Montana* reruns until Abel came and got her." I pause. "And that's how Rose has always been. She's so kind. She's the best person I know. That's why I can hardly understand how we got in this mess to begin with."

"You'll be friends again soon," Noah says.

I'm crying again. "You sure about that?" I say. "I said some pretty mean stuff last time I saw her."

"You guys, you care about each other. And you said Rose is kind, and you're kind, too, Sia. Trust me. It's going to be okay."

"Yeah. I hope so." I sigh and dry my tears on Noah's shirt. I love that he doesn't mind at all.

65

"MY DAD HIT MY MOM," HE SAYS. "THAT'S WHY WE LEFT him, this place."

I look at him. "But you're back living with him? That's so messed up. Does he hurt you?"

He shakes his head. "No. I think he only likes to hit women for some reason." He pauses. "For a long time, she was scared to go places, even the grocery store. She had this fear that she'd see him and he would— he'd kill her this time."

I put my hand on his. He entwines our fingers.

"But eventually, she was okay. Happy, even. She could go out, be with people. Go grocery shopping." He turns to me. "You're . . . God, Sia. You're perfect. Not broken. Perfect."

He pulls me into his chest. "And soon, this thing you're scared of?"

"You can say it, Noah. I'm scared of penises."

"Yes. That fear. The penis fear." I smile as he continues. "It'll pass, Sia. It will."

66

WE'RE KISSING AGAIN. I WANT HIM SO BADLY, NOT JUST because I want to be fixed. But also because I feel something tingly and devastating pulsing through my body when I touch him and it feels like I can't get enough, like nothing in the whole world can be enough.

When I tell him this, he smiles and lowers himself down the bed. He slides his lips over my hip and I gasp. "I think I can help you with that," he says. "If you're okay with it, I mean."

67

NOW I KNOW HOW THE UNIVERSE WAS CREATED BY touch. Now I know. Now I understand. That woman out there, what she desperately wanted was not a baby. That came later. First there was someone who knew how to make her feel so good, planets and their teal rings and full moons and nebulas and nothing and everything came from her, from her hips and hair and the tips of her fingers. Later, there was a baby, and yes, her milk made the stars. But first, there was this. Me, my legs shaking, pulling Noah's mouth closer. Closer.

68

WHEN DAD GETS HOME, NOAH AND I ARE EATING PIZZA
on the couch, watching *The X-Files*.

"M'ija," he says. "No debes estar sola en casa con un muchacho que
has estado besando." I huff, but he continues. "New rule. Noah's not
allowed over unless I'm here."

"I'm sorry, sir," Noah stammers.

Dad stares at him and a smile spreads across his face. "Noah, you
busy tomorrow?"

"Oh, no," I say.

"Oh, yes," Dad says. "Come over in the morning. We'll do a little
practice."

"Oh, your fighting practice? Sure, I'll be here. Looking forward to it,
sir." Noah looks a little sick.

"You don't have to come," I tell him as Dad saunters to the kitchen.
"He's just teasing you."

"If I don't come, he'll think I'm a coward," Noah whispers.

"Suit yourself," I say. "But I know my father. He's going to make me
kick the shit out of you."

"I'd rather you than him."

I shrug. "Okay, then."

69

"WILD," NOAH SAYS, LEANING BACK AGAINST THE SOFA.
I've just sat down with another bowl of brown butter popcorn, remote in my hand.

"What it is?" I ask, scrolling through season four. We've just finished Noah's favorite episode, "Max," about a really nerdy alien abductee living in a trailer. Now it's my turn to choose.

"Look at this." He angles the computer screen toward me.

"'The Truth About Everything They Don't Want You to Know,'" I read aloud. "'Proceed with caution, because Big Brother is watching.'" I snort. It's a blog or something, its background black and lit with twinkling stars, the headings of each entry in a Ransom font.

"He's from Bloomington. Been tracking the blue lights in the desert based on tips. Says there have been sixteen more sightings than what's been reported by the paper."

"Okay." I furrow my brow. "That's interesting, I guess."

"He says it's escaped from some top government alien baby facility? In . . ." He scrolls a bit, tapping his fingers on the computer in a little beat. "Colorado?"

"Come on. That's entirely made up."

"What, you don't believe there's a human and extraterrestrial breeding program in Denver?" He smiles and winks.

"Noah." I roll my eyes. "I'm not going to humor a blog by a guy named, what was it . . ." I lean over, placing a hand on his thigh, ignoring the way he immediately stiffens and clears his throat. "Are you freaking kidding me? He calls himself Sabertooth?"

"Maybe he's an *X-Men* fan."

"No way. He spelled it all wrong."

Noah shrugs. "Okay, he says he has to remain anonymous, or—"

"Oh, let me guess. Or else men in black will bang down his door, take him away to *breed* with little green women?"

Noah shrugs, smiling. "I know. It sounds bananas. I just think it's fascinating."

I nod. "It is fascinating that there are people out there who actually believe this crap."

"Alright, alright," Dad says, appearing in the doorway. I pull my hand back from Noah's leg when Dad narrows his eyes at me. "It's almost ten. Noah's gotta go."

"Dad! One more episode," I say, waving the remote around for emphasis. "The one with la Chupacabra? Please."

Dad scoffs and folds his arms. "Fine. But only because that's a good one." He plops down next to me, swiping the popcorn bowl. Noah begins drumming on his laptop like a madman.

"Oh my god," I say to Dad. "*What* are you doing?"

"Good popcorn," Dad says, grabbing the remote. "Let's start it, then."

70

NEXT DAY, DAD HAS US WARM UP WITH SOME PUSH-UPS.
Noah's not bad—he says he's worked up some endurance from biking. He
can even do a few more than me, but I've always been weaker up top.

"Now some high kicks," Dad says. He has me go first. I start low but
get higher and higher until we do a few jump-kick combos.

"Looks good, Sia," Noah says. "Good form, good posture."

"You don't even know what you're saying," I say, waving him off.
"Here, your turn. Kick."

I begin laughing immediately. He looks like a fawn trying to stand
for the first time. "You can't even stretch your leg out, can you?"

"I can," he says. "When I'm sitting down."

"Man, you need to work on your flexibility. Yoga or something."

"Let's just focus on lower kicks for now, Noah," Dad says. I stretch
my arms and back away as they complete their drill.

"Can you do any flips?" Dad asks Noah.

"I can flip into a pool," Noah supplies.

My dad doesn't look impressed. "Sia, let's practice some off the house."

I run as fast as I can, climbing the wall a couple strides before throwing myself backward on my feet.

"Holy shit," Noah says.

"Again," Dad orders. I repeat a few more times until I feel too dizzy. I drink water as Noah gives it a go. He takes a breath, runs, but doesn't go high enough. He breaks mid-flip and falls.

"Not bad," I say, helping him up. "Way better than my first try."

He tries about four more times until he finally lands on his feet. He's wobbly, but it's a huge improvement in a short amount of time.

"Well," Dad says. "You're not as bad as you look."

"Dad!"

"Ah, I'm just playing. Let's work on sparring."

"Uh—what now?" Noah asks.

Dad goes over a few basic steps with him, and then turns to me. We block each other's punches and kicks for a bit. But then I see Noah watching, his lovely lips pursed, and it distracts me for one second too long—Dad's got his hand around my throat. "If someone got you here, what's your next move?" I go to knee him in the groin, stopping just short. "Good." He releases me. "Next, Artemisia. You know what we need to do."

I groan. "Fine."

"Noah," my dad says. "Attack her from behind."

"Attack her?" Noah says. "You mean, like—"

"Just run up and grab my arms or something. Don't go easy on me," I say.

"Don't go easy on *him*," Dad says, pointing at me, then Noah.

Noah does what he's told, and to his credit, he's strong. I can't wriggle away. "Now," my father commands.

I throw my head back against Noah's chin. "Ow, Jesus—" Whip my elbow back and strike his shoulder, then do the same on the other. "Christ!" Take a deep breath and stomp on his feet. "Holy—" Rake my heel over his shin. "Shit!" His arms have loosened, so I throw them over one shoulder, bend my knees, and use all my weight and strength to flip him over my back. He hits the ground with a thud, all sprawled in a daze, looking like he can't believe what just happened.

"Qué bien, Sia!" Dad runs over, whooping, picking me up with a hug and twirling me around like I'm a little kid.

"Dad, calm down. You're the one who said you knew I could do it."

"I did," Dad said. "And you can. Though Noah es muy flaco. You need to try on someone bigger next time."

"Oh, shut it." I roll my eyes.

"Uh," Noah croaks. "Some help, please?"

71

AFTER SHOWERING, I WALK INTO MY BEDROOM, WHERE
Noah's at my desk with his computer.

"Don't shut the door," he says. "Your dad just gave me another lecture. On us not being alone and stuff."

"Oh God." I plop on my bed. "He didn't threaten you or anything, did he?"

"Nah. I mean, he did make a comment on how skinny I am and how you could kill me with your bare hands, but other than that . . ."

I laugh, grabbing my hair to braid it. "I was expecting worse, honestly." We're silent for a few seconds as Noah watches my fingers in my hair.

"Hey," he says, snapping out of it. "You know that conspiracy theory guy, Sabertooth?"

"How could I forget?" I respond, whipping my braid over my shoulder. "I mean, you discovered his weirdness just yesterday."

"Right. Well, I, uh, kinda emailed him about what we saw the other night. In the desert? When you asked me to . . . and for the first time, you know, we—"

"Kissed?" I lean back against my headboard.

I can practically hear the peach blush appearing on Noah's cheekbones. He coughs. "Um. Yeah. That."

I'm smiling before I can stop myself, but then I scoff. "So what about this loser, Sabertooth?"

"Well, he wants to meet us. Tomorrow. At the diner?"

"No."

"Please, Sia."

"No."

"I'll buy you pie, yeah?"

I shake my head. "Why do you want me to meet him so badly?"

There are several moments of silence. I mean, I can't even hear us breathing. Finally, he speaks. "Because you're my, uh, gir—friend. You're my friend. And it seems like it's going to be a weird and creepy experience. And I want to share it with you. If nothing else, we could totally laugh at him afterward."

I nod slowly. "Fine. We'll give him one hour of our time. And you need to buy me a mint chocolate chip milkshake. Not pie."

"Mint chocolate chip. Not pie. Got it." He smiles. "Thanks, Sia."

"Yeah, yeah." I smile, even though it kind of scares me that all Noah has to do is give me an adorable speech and I turn into such a pushover. I'm basically the texture of melted butter.

But that's probably not all that bad, right? It's okay to trust when you like someone this much. It's okay to begin to trust again.

BEFORE HE LEAVES, NOAH HANDS ME A FOLDED-UP paper. "It's the poem," he tells me. "But promise me something. Wait until you feel like you need to read it before you actually, you know. Read it."

"I never feel like I need to read a poem, Noah."

"Good," he says. "It'll be a significant moment in your life, then."

I roll my eyes, but when he kisses me, I wrap my arms around his neck and pull him in deep.

73

I HAVE ALWAYS BELIEVED THERE'S A SPIRIT IN EVERYTHING.
It's the one thing that set me apart from the cosmologies of my mother
and grandmother. Mom was convinced mosquitoes were soulless; with
Abuela, it was mice. Like some things are too small and annoying to
house a spirit.

But there are these creatures, right? Microscopic. They're called tardi-
grades, but I like the common name best. Water bears. And they've been
here for hundreds of millions of years. They've watched whole ages come
and go. They've seen, with their plump bodies and black-hole mouths,
actual saber-tooth tigers, armadillos the size of cars, the asteroids that
scraped the Earth. They watched the very beginnings of us, even. They
know the moment when we became human. We don't even know that.

It's easy to believe, I think, that elephants have souls. They cry over
their dead loved ones, cover their bodies in palm leaves as though they had
their own personal rituals to say goodbye. And dolphins actually give one
another names. And bees decorate their homes with dried flower petals,
until their little houses look like brand-new red and blue and violet blooms.

But at the ends of all the worlds, water bears will be the ones that
survive. And I've always thought the old, lasting things, no matter how
small, are the most deserving of spirits.

"HE'S LATE," I SAY, NODDING AS THE SERVER BRINGS our order.

"Two minutes." Noah shrugs. "That's not, like, full-on late, you know?"

"One second past our designated meeting time is legitimately late." I swirl my straw in my shake, rolling my eyes.

"Excuse me?"

Noah and I both glance over at a woman who's examining us like we're long lost brethren or something. She doesn't look all that much older than us, but she's dressed super grown-up, in dark-washed jeans with a red blazer over a thin white tee. Her hair is incredible, mahogany and in a full twist-out. I want to text Rose about it, since she's been dying to try the style once her father gives her permission, but my hand freezes over my phone. As if Rose would even read a message from me. Much less respond.

"Are you two here to meet Omar?" the woman asks.

"Who?" Noah's eyebrows are all scrunched up.

"Average height? Black Pakistani American? Glasses. Kinda goofy-looking. Like you." She gestures to Noah. I bite my lips so I don't smile. I like this person already.

When we don't respond, she sighs. "Christ. He didn't tell me you hadn't met him yet. Acting like you all were his pals or something." She slides into the booth across from us. "I'll take an espresso," she tells the server as he walks by. "So you only know him as Sabertooth, huh?"

I snort. The way she says it, it seems like she and I both feel the same about the code name.

"Yeah," Noah says. "I mean, yeah. I found his blog. The Truth About—"

She waves him off. "He couldn't have chosen a more corny name, could he?" She chuckles.

"So, who are you?" I ask.

She holds out her hand. "Imani Clarke. I'm a student at Arizona State, but I also intern at the *Sentinel*. And Omar assures me that you two have a story I need to hear."

"Wow, for real?" Noah's eyebrows are, like, basically at his hairline as he shakes her hand. "So you, I mean, you actually believe him? All this conspiracy stuff?"

She scowls. "Look, my job is to humor the boy. He wants to be a journalist, or so he says. And I want to convince him aliens and armies made of robotic lizards aren't ever going to help him on that career path. Or any career path." She adds a packet of brown sugar to her espresso. "No offense."

"Don't include me in all that," I say. "I don't believe a word of it."

"That makes two of us, then." Imani raises her head, glancing behind us. "Well, speaking of our sabertooth."

Noah and I both turn. I almost laugh, because Omar's a freakin' parody of a cliché conspiracy theorist. Dressed in all black and gray, he looks back and forth before pushing open the glass door—and looks both ways again once inside. Despite the black Ray-Bans he refuses to take off, he spots us immediately and makes his way over.

"And who do you think you are with that?" Imani waves her hand over his face when he approaches. "You should've called yourself the Terminator."

"Very funny." Omar looks at Noah and me. "Imani, these are, uh, Noah and, damn it, I swear I didn't forget—"

"Sia," I say. "And it's fine, we've already introduced ourselves."

"Right. Well, I"—he slides his glasses off, and, tossing his head to the side just a touch, finishes with—"am Sabertooth." He drops the shades on the table as though they are a microphone.

75

"I'VE ALREADY TOLD THEM YOUR NAME." I CAN TELL Imani's trying really hard not to laugh. "The real one."

"What?" Omar says, his voice jumping up a few octaves. "Imani, we don't know if we can trust them yet."

She huffs and pulls out her phone. "I'm not playing, Omar. Just tell me what I'm doing here."

He rolls his eyes. "These," Omar says, pointing to Noah and me, "are your primary witnesses for the faulty UFO spotted in the desert two days ago."

"Faulty," Noah says, sounding just a touch devastated. "I thought you said it's legit?"

"The craft, though, man," Omar says. "Lit up? With smoke? Like it was broken or some shit, right?"

"Wait a minute," I say to Imani. "You're actually doing a story on it? But I thought you didn't believe this stuff."

Imani shakes her head. "Look, I'm just the 'Outlandish Oddities' blogger. My editor's interested in these sightings, but he also regularly cuts my pieces for Internet kitten fashion shows. There's no telling if this will see the light of day." She shrugs. "Omar said I just had to hear your story. And, well, he's family." She says the last bit with a hint of regret.

"Imani's an unbeliever," Omar says darkly. His voice is all husky, and he slides his sunglasses back on, leaning on the torn pleather of the booth back. "Doesn't even accept the obvious source of last month's dust storm."

"Omar, for the last time, the governor did not cause that storm." She knocks his glasses right off as she says it.

Omar scowls. "The government has been manipulating the weather since 1968. Everyone knows it!"

"Uh," I say. "Sorry, but that's news to me."

"You never heard of chemtrails?" Noah asks.

I just stare. "Are you serious right now?"

Omar is still grinning. "Seriously, Sia, wake up and smell the burrito bowls."

Now I'm scowling. "Seriously, no self-respecting Mexican even eats burrito bowls, Omar."

Imani closes her eyes for a couple of seconds, placing a hand on her head. "I'm just gonna ignore that whole exchange."

"Sounds good to me." I cross my arms.

She clicks her phone on and turns to Noah and me. "So, ah, why don't you just tell me what you saw."

76

"SO THE CRAFT WAS ON FIRE." IMANI'S VOICE IS FLAT.

"That's what I told you," Omar cuts in before I can take a breath. "And you know what I did as soon as Noah emailed me?"

Imani lifts a hand. "You called the Lone Gunmen."

"Ha!" Noah says, grinning. "We know that reference, right, Sia?" He winks at me.

I mean, anyone who's seen *The X-Files* would know, but it's kind of cute how Noah wants this to be our inside joke or something. I just smile and roll my eyes, landing them on Omar. "What did you do, Sabertooth?" My voice is even flatter than Imani's at this point.

Omar totally puffs up his chest at his code name, which is so not what I'd intended. "I went out there." His face is so smug, I have to fight hard at the urge to smack him.

"You what? How?" Noah asks.

"I borrowed my dad's car and found that desert spot you mentioned, between those weird cacti with the heads and hips and shit? And I drove straight out at latitude 33.2899 degrees."

"And how did you measure that?" Imani asks.

"I just put it in my GPS!"

"And how hard did your daddy beat your behind when he found out you took his Lexus off road?" Imani asks.

Omar's cheeks are the color of La Guadalupe's collection of roses at her feet. "Imani." It's a half whine, half whisper. Her eyebrow remains raised.

"Okay," I say. "You drove out there. So what?"

A smirk crawls across Omar's face again as he pulls open his book bag and slams something on the table. It's a piece of metal, the color of stained steel, and it clanks like a broken bell.

"That's what."

77

"SO LET ME GET THIS STRAIGHT," IMANI SAYS. "YOU found that piece of crap in the desert and decided it must belong to a ship from outer space. That was your first conclusion." She turns off her phone and slips it into her purse. "What am I talking about? Of course it was your first conclusion."

"It was right where the sighting was!" Omar points to some scratches etched in the surface. "Those marks? They change, you guys. They didn't look like that this morning."

And now I've lost it. I bury my face in Noah's shoulder as I laugh. When I come up for air, Imani is slow-blinking at Omar.

"What am I going to do with you?" It's hardly a question, the way she says it as she zips up her purse. "I really shouldn't have to say this, but there's no way I'm reporting on this shit."

Just like that, his smirk is wiped away. "Imani, no! This is real." He lifts the piece of metal and drops it again, pointing right at her face. "This is seriously real, I'm telling you. Don't let it all go to hell just because you're an unbeliever."

Imani shakes her head. "You know what's turned to hell, is this so-called mentorship. I know I told your dad I'd help you out, but come on. Real journalists don't insist this garbage"—she points at the metal—"*is seriously real.*"

Omar's mouth is tight. "Oh, so now you're a real journalist? Reporting on the real important stuff, like cupcake shops and shit?"

Imani sighs, edging him off the bench so she can stand. "I know my internship is bullshit, Omar. But writing about this? That's not going to get me where I want to go." She snorts. "Like they would even print it to begin with." She ruffles Omar's hair, but he pushes her hand away. "I'm off." She hands Omar a twenty, which he stuffs into his pocket, scowling the whole while.

"So, Ms. Clarke," Noah says as she dusts off her jeans. "What would it take? For you to believe in, like, aliens? If you don't mind me asking."

She doesn't even hesitate. "Land an extraterrestrial craft in front of the *Sentinel* headquarters." Her heels thump on the linoleum as she walks away. "Then we'll talk!"

78

"SIA, DID YOU SEE THAT?" NOAH POINTS AT THE METAL piece, which still sits on the table.

"No." I scoff.

But Omar looks elated. "It happened again, didn't it?" he says. "The shapes changed!"

"I don't think that circle was there before." Noah's examining the piece. It looks like folded-up tinfoil in his monster hands.

"Don't tell me you actually think—" I pause, catching the eye of a woman at the counter. Silver hair, dark skin. She's wearing a white suit, which stands out a lot in a town where tucking in your T-shirt is practically considered formalwear. The weirdest part about her, though, is the half smile on her face as she sips coffee. It's creepy as shit because she won't stop staring at us.

I force my attention back to Noah and Omar, who are now theorizing what the metal's shapes mean. "Maybe it's a whole new language, you know? Like, this is a communications device. Like—"

"Their way of texting," Omar finishes.

"Exactly." Noah snaps his fingers, like, a hundred times in two seconds.

I shake my head. "I can't believe I'm a part of a conversation about alien texting."

Omar glances around. "Keep it down, Sia, will you? You never know."

I snort. "Anyone ever tell you you're paranoid?"

Noah gives me a grin. "Just because you're paranoid—"

"Doesn't mean they're not out to get you! Fox Mulder! My dude!" Omar's reached his hand out to Noah and now they're sharing what I assume to be some extra-dorky *X-Files* fanatic handshake.

Omar calls me an unbeliever or something, but I'm not listening again because I let my eyes wander back to Creeper Lady. And yeah. She's still watching us.

"Do either of you guys know that woman—" But then something explodes outside. Like, whatever it is straight up shakes the table and the booths. I gasp and jump, Noah and Omar along with me.

We all look out the windows, where there's a car smoking in the parking lot. "Ted," someone yells. "Looks like your truck just popped!"

"God almighty." The man, Ted, presumably, runs out the door, cursing all the while. "What the hell. Trucks don't just pop!"

"God, that scared me," I say. Noah's hand finds mine under the table. I intertwine our fingers.

"Wait!" Omar yelps. "Where is it?"

"Where's what?" Noah says, squeezing my fingers.

"The, the UFO part! It was just here!" He glares up. "Which one of you took it?"

Noah and I look at each other, eyes wide. "I know you're not accusing us of stealing your foil paper," I finally say.

Omar bites his lips, then nods slowly. "It was them. They set up that, that car explosion. So we wouldn't be looking—"

"Oh my God," I say. "We were sitting here the whole time, Omar."

"But we were all just looking out the window," Noah points out.

"That's right! That was on purpose! It was a distraction!" Omar's jumped up now, pulling on his book bag. "I gotta go. I need to tell my, uh, associates about this immediately."

"Is that code for writing a blog entry?" I call, but Omar's already out the door.

I jerk my head back, looking for Ms. Creeper Lady again. Weird. It's been what, two minutes? But she's totally gone now.

As Noah walks me to my car, I scan for her, the silver-haired woman in white. But there's no one around, nothing moving except for the smoke still rising from Ted's charred car.

79

TONIGHT, IN BED, AS I WATCH THE SILVER SILT OF clouds outside my bedroom, I can't help but think of what Omar said, about the governor controlling the weather. And about my grandmother's knife.

One day after we'd sowed corn seeds, half the sky turned black, clouds thick and sinewy, like they were riding in on wild horses. We'd been eating baked yam empanadas on her porch, which was comprised of pine planks and a turquoise tarp.

"That storm will wash the seeds away," Abuela said. And she stood and stomped into the house, her brown leather sandals click-clicking on the ground like wooden spoons.

When she returned, she had a cuchillo in her hand, big and glittering like, well. Like that piece of metal Omar dropped on the table today.

"What's that for?" I said, but by then, she'd already taken her knife to the sky.

"By the power of el padre," she said, swooping it this way. "By the power of la madre, el hermano, la hermana." Swoop that way. "By the power in me, given by La Guadalupe en un dream en 1976. ¡Vete!"

And you know what? By the time she was done, the clouds were gone. Those big, black horse-drawn monsters, thicker than cream, fat with rain and lightning, were just gone. It was as if they'd never been there.

So this is what makes me think maybe, just maybe, Omar is onto something. I'm not saying that lizards run the world or anything like that. I'm just saying that I've seen a woman change the weather. And if she could, maybe others can, too.

80

NOAH EMAILS ME THE NEXT DAY. WE'D PLANNED ON
going to the desert tonight, but he can't make it because his truck's
broken and he's got loads of homework. That's fine. I kind of need to
go by myself, anyway.

Weird, he adds. *I got an email from "62499@903.com." They said to
stop talking to reporters about UFO sightings . . . if I knew what was good
for me. (The last bit implied.)*

I sigh and begin typing. *Probably just our totally awesome friend
Sabertooth trying to convince us his alien/government conspiracy theory is
totally not fake. Fail.*

As I send the email, I try not to think about the woman in white. In
and out of Maude's like some kind of bruja.

81

IT'S A LITTLE LATER THAN I NORMALLY GET INTO THE
desert. I grab a new Saint Kateri candle and walk a bit, past Adam and
Eve, past the boulders that reminded me of bears when I was little.

When the sky's all clear like this, with the moon wide and bright, I
like to stretch out in the dirt and stare up. Eventually, I feel like I'm not
even real. Like I'm just a little part of that big forever out there.

"Mami," I whisper eventually. "You there?"

I never feel her around like I feel Abuela. I know Abuela would say
it's 'cause Mom's alive, but I don't know. Maybe it's because she never
got a proper burial or something.

"I met a boy," I tell her. "I like him. I think you would, too. And
Rose hates me right now. But I miss her and I miss you, too."

The candle next to me flickers real low. I feel my grandmother
approach and settle next to me. We say nothing for a long while. Then
I feel her fingers on my arm. "Mira," she whispers.

I push up and look. There, a single blue light. Before I can take a
breath, it's gone. And now I'm not sure if it was ever there.

82

IT FEELS ALL EMPTY DRIVING TO SCHOOL WITHOUT
Rose.

I sit for a few minutes in the parking lot, blaring "Dreams" by
Fleetwood Mac.

Jeremy McGhee pulls up in the distance. I groan. Of all the days I
don't need to see his face first thing.

But then Noah gets out of the passenger side.

All of a sudden, things feel a lot worse than empty.

83

I'M HERE EARLY BECAUSE NOAH WANTED TO HANG before school. But I can't get out. I stay in my car, frozen like beads of dew on some cold desert morning, counting my breaths until the first bell rings. I can't get out until the late bell.

School drones on. I feel numb. I ignore Noah all day.

When my last class is dismissed, I walk real slow to my locker and drop off my books. I can feel Noah's eyes on me as he approaches.

"Hey, Sia," he says. "Are you okay? You weren't at the steps this morning, and . . ."

He stops when I slam my locker shut. "Why'd you get a ride from him today?"

His eyes are wide. "Shit. This is what I wanted to talk to you about."

"I can't believe it." I huff. "Rose was right. Rose was right and you lied to my face about it. Twice. I defended you and lost my best friend because I didn't want to believe that you were lying to me." Noah tries to cut in, but I won't let him. "I can't believe you, Noah. You know what he is. What he's done. What his father—"

"We're brothers." His voice breaks like he's twelve or something, and he swallows hard.

I just stare. My jaw seems to be locked open.

"Well, half brothers, really. I'm one year older, but I was held back when my mom left . . . and we moved around a lot. Jeremy's mom, when she left, she didn't take him. So he was raised by our . . . father." His voice breaks again on that word.

My hands shake. "What? Are you fucking telling me that that bad hombre is your fucking dad? The man who—who—" The rest of the sentence breaks in my mouth, so I reach for another. "No, that can't be true. Why doesn't anyone know?"

Noah takes a shaky breath. "They don't like me much. Jeremy didn't want anyone to know for as long as possible. And I was happy to comply because I don't like him, either."

"Why didn't you tell me?"

He can't look at my face. "You know why, Sia."

"Let's go," Jeremy shouts from down the hall. I jump when I hear his voice. Jeremy's now looking at us funny. "Wait a minute," he says, taking long strides toward us. He points to me. "Is this a joke?" he asks Noah.

"Don't," Noah warns, but Jeremy McGhee, I've long known by now, never obeys the laws of decency.

"Oh, Dad's gonna love this. You've been gone all spring break because you've been with her?" Noah's jaw is clenched as Jeremy laughs. "Dad's gonna love this. You know he hates spic bitches, bro. And he really hates *that* spic b—"

The loud slap of Noah's fist on Jeremy's face interrupts the sentence. It echoes down the hallway and catches the attention of a handful of students still around. Jeremy touches the red on his cheekbone as he lifts his torso back up. "You're gonna fucking regret that." And he charges.

They wrestle back and forth for a minute while some people run over to tear them apart. "You can't fucking beat me!" Jeremy screams. "You're fucking weak and pathetic, just like your cunt mother!" Noah breaks away from the arms holding him and lays Jeremy another on the chin. Jeremy snatches his arms forward and jumps on Noah like a cat. Then he pounds at his face, not even stopping to take a breath.

I'm frozen. "Shit," Samara says, touching my arm. I didn't realize she'd run up next to me. "I'm gonna get a teacher." Then she's off.

That snaps me out of it. I stomp over to them and kick Jeremy off of Noah. He flies back a few feet, then glances up to see me. "Oh, you've got to be fucking kidding me." He stands and sees me glowering. "Get outta my way, spic."

I crack my knuckles. "You seriously don't have any idea how long I've wanted to do this."

He makes to shove me away, but I kick him in the stomach. While he's doubled over, I get my momentum with a couple turns, then knock him right the fuck down with my boot. He pushes himself up, snarling like a wild beast.

He's gonna kill me.

Not if I kill him first, though.

But by then, a half-dozen teachers surround us. They escort us to Savoy's office like we're criminals.

84

WE'RE ALL SUSPENDED. NOAH AND I GET A WEEK.
Jeremy gets two for provoking the violence. The teachers corroborated Samara's witness account, even though I don't remember them being around from the beginning.

I want to write them all thank-you cards. Thank you for being on the side of the righteous.

85

BEFORE DAD ARRIVES, MR. SAVOY TAKES ME ASIDE. "IF
I hear of any disruptions from you, and I mean anything—cheating,
tardiness, loitering—anything, Ms. Martinez, and you're done."

I smile and grab my phone. "Mr. Savoy, could you repeat that for the
record? I'm sure my dad's lawyer would appreciate it."

He leaves without a word.

86

DAD IS SO HAPPY I'VE KICKED JEREMY'S ASS, HE TAKES
me to a fancy fondue restaurant dinner to celebrate. Even though the
food is delicious, I can't really focus.

"Just so we're clear," Dad says. "We're here because I'm proud you
defended yourself."

"Okay."

"This doesn't mean violence is the answer, you know?"

"Dad."

"Just humor me, Artemisia. Tell me you understand that ninety-nine
percent of the time, violence is not the answer."

It's so hard to not roll my eyes. So hard. But somehow I say it with a
straight face. "I get it, Dad. Violence isn't the answer most of the time."

He seems satisfied with this, but then he starts fidgeting a little.
Breaking up a piece of bread into two hundred pieces; organizing his
silverware. I have no idea what's coming, but before I can demand it out
of him, he starts talking.

"Sia. You know my grant is almost up."

"Yup," I say, dipping a sausage bite into a pond of cheese.

"I was thinking after that. About making a big change. And I wasn't sure before, but after your abuelita joined the Lord, and after today, I just . . ." He shakes his head. "There's nothing good for us here. I thought we might make it until you graduate, pero . . ."

"You want to move?" I'm holding the sausage in midair. A drop of cheese hits the table.

"Yeah. Anywhere we want. Anywhere I can get a job."

"Anywhere," I repeat.

"Phoenix, Portland, Seattle, Los Angeles." He rattles off a few more cities while counting with his fingers.

The food finally makes it into my mouth. I swallow. "What about Rose?"

"Rose tiene su familia. And she can visit whenever. She'd like that. She's an adventurous girl."

"I don't know if her dad will let her."

"Cruz can't do nothing once that girl is eighteen. Which is when, a year and a half?"

"¿Y Noah?"

My dad scoffs. "There'll be a thousand skinny white boys for you to choose from in Portland or Seattle or wherever we end up."

He doesn't know about Noah's parentage. He arrived a little too late to see him leave with the McGhees.

I shrug. "I don't know, Dad. I mean, today was especially sucky. That's true. But I don't think I'm ready to leave yet." Not ready to leave our home with Mom, my spot in the desert. Not ready to leave Rose.

Dad puts a hand on mine. "We don't have to make a decision now, Sia. It's just something to think about. That's all."

87

MR. WOODS WRITES ME AN EMAIL ON TUESDAY. *I'M SURE you've heard that Mr. Savoy is taking extra precautions this suspension with your grades.*

I had heard, actually. Ms. Gerber had told me, when she came to see me last night (a ploy to flirt with my dad as much as to check on me), that she can't let me make up anything for this week because Savoy insists on checking the grade book to make sure I fail all the assignments.

She just assigned extra credit. She says that's what they'll all do.

But I want to extend a helping hand. This Friday, there will be a partial lunar eclipse fairly early in the evening. If you and Noah could document it, write a little something about your experience, then that will more than make up the quizzes and readings you miss this week.

I want to tell Mr. Woods that there's no way I'm working with Noah anymore, that he's lied to me for as long as he's known me, and that I'd rather snort a serrano pepper whole than listen to him lie some more, but my fingers stop on the keyboard when I remember Mr. Savoy's threat. I wonder if switching partners in the middle of the biggest project of the semester counts as a disruption.

It sure sounds like one to me.

After a minute, I write back. *Sounds good. Thank you.*

I grab my phone and write one more message. I finally kicked the crap out of Jeremy McShitFace. God, it felt so good. When do you get back? I have so much to tell you.

But Rose doesn't text back. At all.

88

NOAH AND I MAKE ARRANGEMENTS FOR FRIDAY. I'M
going to pick him up at Maude's since I refuse to go near Sheriff McGhee
or Jeremy if I can help it.

I know we could do it separately. The assignment. But I want to confront him. I want to hit him. I want to make him see how much I hate
him before the week's through. Because, you know what, Mom never
got to do that with the jerk sheriff. And right now I have the chance
to say how I really freaking feel, and I'm not going to let it pass me by.

I'm in a foul mood after that email interaction, and so I make my
way to the corn patch. And here is where I encounter my abuela.

Rose asked me recently how I know my grandmother's around.
It's hard to explain. Usually, I can just feel it. Her. The blue-and-red-
flowered handkerchiefs she ties in her hair. The embroidered skirts,
sometimes so long they drag in the sand. Sometimes it's the smell of her
perfume: desert flowers and oak.

I told Rose the women in our family have always been able speak to
the dead. It's very simple. God made many pathways into heaven. He
pierced holes where the light leaks back down to Earth. We see these
and call them stars.

Taking walks in the starlight makes our senses raw. And we can hear and see and feel our ancestors. They're always among us, traveling back and forth by starlight. It's a kind of magic, my madre told me.

Star magic is the oldest sort. It's how humans became something a little different from animals. But that's another whole story.

Most people don't talk to the dead anymore. They can't. They don't get out enough in the stars.

Before I can ask her what she's doing here, Abuela is gone. Sometimes she does that. I think she just wants me to remember she's near.

89

ROSE ALWAYS GOES FOR THE LOVE STORIES WITH HER
Harry Potter fanfiction. She's written, like, a dozen Drarry short stories
in the last year alone. Drarry means a Draco and Harry pairing, which
at first makes no sense because they spent the bulk of the series being
enemies, you know? But then there are cracks open in Draco, in which
we see he isn't all bad, and then cracks in Harry, in which we see there's
some bad in him. Flaws, which everyone has. Some more than others.
"They match each other," Rose told me when I expressed my skepticism
at first.

But Rose convinced me with her words. Harry and Draco fighting,
but, like, going out of their way to argue with each other. And then
one of them slipping, you know, and with affection—Harry's hand on
Draco's shoulder. Draco sliding a lock of Harry's hair behind his ear.
And how slowly, so slowly, they realize something's there. A spark. And
when I was begging her to let them kiss, she'd drag it out just a little
longer. Enough to drive all her readers wild with impatience. So when
they finally did kiss, it was so satisfying. I swear, the first fic of hers I
read, I spent a whole week with hearts in my eyes.

And this story is no different. Well, a little different, because it's

Faith and Buffy, totally different characters, a totally different universe. But she dives into the narrative perfectly. They run into each other, they become friends, they fight vampires, they fight each other, they make up. But Rose hasn't finished it. Buffy has just realized she'd rather spend her time arguing with Faith than hanging out with anyone else. I can tell, this is where it starts to get really good, but then it just ends, unfinished.

And I look at the time and haven't even realized two hours have gone by, and all I want to do is read more. Rose's writing is like that. Makes you greedy.

I'm weeping again. And I get out my phone and just wring out my heart over its little keyboard.

I'm sorry. I'm sorry. You were right, Rose. About Noah. And I just keep thinking about how shitty I had to be to not see it, to not believe you. And I'm sorry I hurt you. And I wish you felt like you could tell me about Sam. She's nice and sweet and perfect for you, if she's who you want, she's just perfect. And I miss you. I keep thinking about what it's like, being your best friend. How you write the most perfect stories (yes, I read the story, amazing as always, but please I need more ASAP!!!!) and how when we met Mary and David for the first time, you said, I can't believe my brother's a dad, and then we held them and you said, Look, Sia, they are miracles. And how amazing that you always see miracles in everything, like when you kept telling me my mom was alive because Abuela said so. And I hope it doesn't take a miracle for you to forgive me, but even if you don't, I'm sorry.

After a minute, just one, short, miraculous minute, she writes, I'm sorry, too, Sia. I'm sorry I missed tutoring and I'm sorry for going to Sam even when I knew you were feeling left out. Can't write too much rn. At the hospital. But we'll be back Friday. Let's catch up Sunday. I miss you. I love you. And after a second, And I'm sorry about what I said about your mom. It wasn't what I really feel. Believe me, Sia. I think she still could be out there. Just like your grandmother said.

I cry so hard. So, so hard. Because I haven't lost everything, you know? And what a feeling that is. When I can breathe normally again, I write back, Yes. Sunday. Love you too.

90

NOAH AND I ARE ON OUR WAY TO THE BEGINNING OF the world.

He wants to speak but I told him not yet. I need to talk first. But the words are spinning all around me like brittle leaves and I can't catch them. It doesn't help that Noah won't stop freaking drumming on every surface in my car.

I pull into the space between Adam and Eve and turn the car off. The sunset to one side pulling all the clouds into it like a lover. Everything tinged in romantic peach and pink. Todavía no hay luna.

I turn to Noah. He's not looking at me, but his spine tenses.

"I can't believe you touched me," I say. He winces, eyes cast downward. "Your dad is the reason why my life is shit. Why, every day, my heart breaks open over and over and over again. And you knew this and you touched me."

I wait for him. He's still looking down, jaw flexed.

"Do you have anything to say to that?"

"I'm sorry." His voice is raw. "I didn't know at first. But when I found out it was you, that you were the girl with the mom. I didn't tell you because I liked you so much." He looks up at me. The bruises on his face are green on the edges. "I hate my dad. I like you. I'm sorry. That's all I can say."

I let out a slow, shaky breath and rest my head on the steering wheel. Out my window, the clouds are getting thicker. Darker.

"Well, I can say more, actually," Noah continues. I don't move. "I still want to be friends with you."

I turn my head. "Sorry," I say. "That's not going to happen." And I laugh just a little, because, the audacity, you know? "Rose and I had the biggest fight because of you. I almost lost a good friend, my best friend, because of you, but you still want to be friends?"

His face falls, but he nods. And then he swallows. "It was so shitty of me to let you and Rose fight like that. I was scared to lose you, Sia. You're, uh. Jesus." He is facing the window, but I think he's wiping his eyes. "You're an amazing girl. And I hope you don't hate me forever." His voice is crackling, but I think he's trying to cover it up by going deeper, louder.

I groan. He's the jerk, here. Why do I feel guilty about this?

Porque él no es su padre.

I groan again after the air gets thick with oak and prickly pear. Why can't that old lady ever mind her own business?

Noah sniffs. "Did you just spray perfume or something?"

"No," I say, rolling my eyes. "That's my grandma."

"She puts air freshener in your car?"

"Something like that."

Abuela continues to speak. God, that woman! Finally, I shake my head and yell, "Shut up, anciana!" Which is literally the worst thing you can say to a Mexican elder. Abuela's presence becomes thunderous, thick around us like steel, and then it's gone. Fast as a flame pinch. Christ.

I glance at Noah, who's looking at me as though I've pulled my brain out of my head and just presented it to him on a platter. I start to explain myself, but stop. Why do I care what he thinks? He's just another son of a racist prick.

When we reach the spot, *my* spot, I press the brakes a little hard, and Noah gives a yelp as the seat belt cuts into him. "We're here," I say, like an ass, because obviously we're here. But before he says anything in response, I open the door and fling myself out.

91

WE WALK A BIT. THE SHADOWS OF THE SAGUAROS ARE
long, like they're trying to pin their spines on us. The wind smacks itself
back and forth, and my hair keeps getting in my face. I tuck it into my
jacket and pull my hood up.

I can't stand the silence any longer. Neither can Noah, apparently.

"So." He snaps his fingers together in a quick beat. "Hey." He points.
"Remember that weird email I got from that collection of numbers?
That said, *Don't talk to reporters or else?*"

I don't respond.

"Well, I talked to Omar about it, and he got one, too. The same day.
Same minute, even. He said his cousin also got one. That's the wild part.
All three, the same exact moment."

I roll my eyes. "He's lying."

"But what if—"

"Noah. He's a liar." I sharpen my voice. "That must be why you two
get along so well."

That slaps us right back to silence. Even the wind quiets down, like
it's eavesdropping or something.

I look at Noah, and he looks back at me so devastatingly, I know he's sorry. But I just can't deal with the fact of his lies right now. "So Jeremy did go and testify for your mom, huh?"

Noah whistles out a sigh and nods. "Yeah. Uh, he went in there to confirm my father's history of abuse." He runs a hand through his hair. "Things aren't looking that great for her case at the moment, though. With him being a sheriff and all. He's got a lot of officer buddies who can confirm what a great, jolly fellow he is."

I snort and then there's silence for a long while.

Everything's numb. I can't even feel where I end and the air begins. But then my shoe snags a rock, and I trip, just about to face-plant, and Noah's arms are around me, long and warm, helping me up.

"Thanks." And then I feel so dense for saying it, to him, this liar, this asshole, who thought he could fool me. And fuck, he did. That's what I hate most about it. I'm supposed to be smarter than that. And I guess thinking about this has made me even denser than dense, because I trip again, my hands clutching at Noah's chest without my permission. I dust myself off and step back once I'm upright again. Meanwhile, Noah grimaces and clutches his ribs.

"Jesus," I say. "I didn't grab you that hard."

But Noah's not paying attention to me anymore. In fact, he looks like he's seen a spirit or something. He grabs my arm and points. I turn.

The blue lights are back.

The hairs on my neck stand straight up.

Noah's looking through the binoculars he brought for moon-gazing. "Yeah," he says. "It's that Aurora thing, alright." He hands them to me.

I put the prismáticos to my face. The craft; it's made of something really shiny. The moon glints off it. I think there might be letters or something carved into the sides.

I realize I'm seeing a lot more detail than I should, even with binoculars. I lower them as Noah says, "Uh, Sia?"

It's, like, only two freaking miles away. And it's getting closer, angling toward us. Like *we're* the destination.

"This is really a weird coincidence," Noah remarks, panic creeping into his voice.

"I don't believe in coincidences." I say it low, almost just to myself.

"What?" Noah asks, but we jump when the craft starts to rattle. Watching it choke in the sky, I realize how smooth it normally slides in the air, as though it were part goose or swan, not mechanical. Not made from any human hands.

But now it sputters and coughs. The blue lights blink haphazardly, as though signaling something like, *Someone fucking help, please.*

And about a mile or so away, it sinks into the ground, throwing up dust like a snarling bull before it charges. I glance at Noah, who's holding up his phone, filming. "Jesus," he whispers.

It slides closer with a smatter of red sparks, giving a low, long howl that sounds . . . God. It sounds unearthly.

Goosebumps glide along my arms and chest so strong it hurts.

The thing finally stops moving, the desert sand all around it like a fog.

Noah and I look at each other for a moment before we run to my car, fling the doors open, and dive inside. I turn the key before I can even settle into my seat and I press the gas so hard, we screech forward with a jerk, into the moonlit smoke that now surrounds us.

92

I STOP THE CAR ABOUT TWENTY FEET AWAY FROM THE
thing. Madre de Dios. It's the size of my whole house. Granted, it's not
a big house. But shit.

As I plummet out of the car, this weird buzzing fills me. It's a long
bass note, vibrating from my chest and head and hands. I guess it's coming from the craft. I make my way toward it.

"Careful," Noah shouts. "Might be hot. Make sure your shoes aren't
melting or anything!"

My Converse look fine. And anyway, this thing, this area, it's not
hot. It's freaking freezing.

Noah's next to it, taking photos of something with his phone. I join
him and see the inscriptions on the surface of the metal. They look like
they're scratched on with an old nail. The letters, or whatever they are,
they're beautiful. They're made up of spirals and triangles and discs.
They're a little more distinct than Omar's piece of metal. More purpose-
ful or something.

But it's weird; if I blink at them, it almost seems like they're
changing—but maybe it's the clouds moving over the moon.

I take a step closer. Shit. They *are* changing. Just like Omar said.

My heart beats loudly as a spiral turns into an *o*, as a circle turns into a *t*.

I gasp when it's finished. There's only two words pulsing in front of me.

THEY'RE COMING.

93

I JUMP BACK AND ALMOST KNOCK NOAH OVER. "DO you see that?" I say to him, pointing at the script.

"I know, it's incredible," he says, holding up his phone. "It's fucking glyphs, Sia. Like some ancient Mayan shit." He gives me a long look before turning back to his phone. "It looks just like the thing Omar brought us."

Guess Omar's not a liar after all hangs around us, unsaid. But I'm too freaked to engage inaudible words when there are ones carving themselves into metal right in front of my face. "No, I mean . . ." I trail off as I gesture to the letters. The English words are gone, replaced by spirals and scratches.

"Some weird shit is going on here, Noah," I say with panic rising in my voice. "I think we should get outta here."

We freeze as we hear a muffled groan.

"Jesus," Noah says. "There's someone in there."

"Of course there's someone in there. Someone's gotta be manning this thing."

"I thought it might be controlled remotely," Noah says, walking around the perimeter. "I mean, that's where all aircraft tech is going, and this seems really advanced—" He's rounded the corner. I can't see or hear him anymore.

I give the glyphs one last glance before I run after him.

"Sia!" he yells.

I run harder and see his silhouette, crouched over a huge gash in the craft. I get closer and my blood, my bones, my everything feels like stone when I see the line of a figure in front of him, crawling out.

I stop. My breath is fast and won't slow down.

"Sia," he says, motioning for me to come. "She needs help!"

"She?" My voice sounds funny, all high and shaky.

"Sia, come on!"

I nod and slowly walk.

The features of her are getting clearer, but it's still hard to see. She looks human. That's good. I think.

When I see her face, though, everything turns into slow motion.

I can't breathe. I can't breathe.

He's pulling her up, but she can't walk that well. He says something, but my ears are ringing—from what, I'm not sure—the bass note, panic, maybe my heartbeat. Maybe all three.

Finally, I can speak.

"Noah, that's my mom."

94

NOAH'S FACE WHITENS. "WHAT DID YOU SAY?"

"That's my mom."

"Jesus, that's what I thought you said, but—"

She's there, in his arms, all woozy, in and out of consciousness. When she sees me, her eyes widen and she grabs my arm and pulls me close.

"M'ija," she whispers. "We've got to get somewhere safe." She coughs and looks into our eyes. "Ellos vienen."

They're coming.

The way she says it. Something in my spine pays attention and yells at my limbs to move. She's passed out again, so I get under her other arm and we take her to my car.

95

I'M DRIVING ON THE HIGHWAY, AND THIS BOY I ALMOST
had sex with last week whose dad caused the death of my mother is sitting in the back seat with my mom's head in his lap. And she's not dead. My mom's not dead.

"I think she's concussed, Sia," he says. "We should take her to the hospital."

"No hospitals," she yells and I jump. "No hospitals, no police stations, not our home, either, Artemisia, no nada. That's where they'll be. We need to go somewhere. . . ."

I check my rearview mirror. Looks like she's passed out again.

"Shit," I say. "Where in the world am I supposed to go?"

Noah doesn't respond.

Where the fuck am I supposed to go?

96

MY GRANDMOTHER CARRIED CRYSTALS EVERYWHERE.
Nothing pretty and polished like you'd see in a New Age store. Her crystals looked like dusty rocks. I'm convinced half of them were actually just dirty desert glass, all matte smooth and pale pink under the sticky sand.

She put them all in a little leather satchel and tied the whole thing to her belt. During long desert walks, she'd pull one or two out and hold them to the sun, as if, somehow, the light through the stones told her where her next steps should be.

It didn't matter how far we went when Abuela took me to gather herbs and flowers, didn't matter whether or not we could see her shiny tin trailer on the line of the horizon. We always made it back home.

I have one of her crystals on my rearview mirror, hung with a hemp string. It's light yellow and chipped. Feo.

Right now, though, at a stop, I hold it in my fingertips, angling it toward the red light. I try to convey to the ghost of my grandmother how sorry I am that I told her to shut up.

Please, I beg. *Orient me.*

97

WHEN I TURN OFF THE CAR, WE'RE IN FRONT OF ROSE'S house. There are still a few lights on inside.

"Stay here," I tell Noah as I open the door. "Make sure she doesn't . . ." Doesn't what? I don't know. Die again? I don't know. I shut the door and walk up.

Mrs. Damas answers. "Sia?" she says, peering out at me in her pink pajamas.

I open my mouth to explain myself, but nothing comes out. I swallow.

Mrs. Damas takes a step closer, puts her hand on my arm. "Did something happen?"

I nod.

"What is it, is it your father?"

I shake my head, turning as I hear footsteps behind me. Noah's helping my mom walk up. "She, she wanted to come," he says sheepishly.

"Who's there?" Mrs. Damas steps out of the threshold. Rose is just behind her.

"Sia, that you?" Rose says. "What the heck is going on out h—"

She's cut off by the shriek of her mother. Mrs. Damas's arms are wrapped around Mom.

"Sia." Rose is startled. I'm not sure whether we're good yet, good enough to hug, good enough for me to cry on her shoulder. Rose looks unsure, too. "Who is that?" she says, looking past me.

"It's my mom."

"What? Are you serious? She came back?"

I nod, even though it's the understatement of the millennium. "Yeah. She came back."

Rose swoops right next to me and grabs my hand. She's whispering. I think I'm the only one who can hear it. "It's a miracle."

98

THEY HAVE MY MOM ON THE RECLINER AND SHE'S
sleeping or something. Before I can finish my thoughts, Rose's dad asks
us repeat our story. Again. For the thousandth time. I sigh.

"Are you sure you mean a spacecraft?" he says to me and Noah.

"The same one, Mr. Damas, that was spotted downtown last week,"
Noah says. "It was in the *Sentinel*."

"Are you sure it wasn't a, a truck? Or a mirage!"

"Oh!" Noah jumps up. "I have it here, on my phone, you can see."

"Who are you, anyway?" Mrs. Damas asks Noah as he taps on his
phone.

"I'm—uh. My name's Noah."

Both of Rose's parents eye the bruises on his face.

"He's my partner for a science project," I say. "And a fucking asshole," I mutter under my breath. Mrs. Damas frowns at me. Great.

I point at Noah's phone to remind him of the task at hand. "Right,"
he says. He plays the video and Cruz Damas's face turns green. He starts
pacing and speaking to Mrs. Damas in Creole.

Rose rolls her eyes. "Dad, please. Please."

"Is he saying my mom's the devil?" I ask, and both Cruz and Maura
Damas stop to stare at me.

"Since when do you know Creole?" Mr. Damas demands.

"I don't," I say.

He looks skeptical and glances at Rose, who shakes her head.

I sigh. "It's just that, anytime something freaks you out, you always say it's the devil. I hope I'm not stepping out of bounds when I say that you're very predictable, Mr. Damas."

"The *Lord* is predictable," he retorts.

"Sure," I say, nodding. "But that—that's my mom. I know my mom. That is my mother."

"How do you know?"

I blink in surprise at Noah.

He holds his hands up. "Look, I'm not saying she's the, uh, devil or anything." He gives a wary glance toward Mr. and Mrs. Damas. "But, uh, Sia. She fell out of a freaking spacecraft that crashed in the desert. What if she's a clone? Or a robot? Or a shape-shifting extraterrestrial?"

"You've been watching too much *X-Files*," I say.

"That's it," Mr. Damas says. "I'm calling the cops."

I stand. "Please don't do that."

"You brought this evil into my house. It's up to me to get it out."

I swallow. "You're calling the cops, though? You're calling Sheriff McGhee?"

This actually gives him pause. "Why don't you take her home," he says, his voice almost at a shout. "Take her to Luis."

Noah shakes his head. "She won't let us. Says that's where they'll look for her." He shrinks under the glare of Cruz Damas. "Erm, with all due respect, of course."

Thank the Lord Mrs. Damas steps in. "Your mother, what she keeps saying . . . They're coming. She's probably talking about Border Patrol."

I think of the letters on the craft. Is that what that thing was warning us about? Immigration officials?

"We should take her to the church," Mrs. Damas continues. Mr. Damas looks like he's going to explode, but she touches his arm gently. "If there's something sinister here, she shouldn't be able to walk into God's house. And there, she's also protected from ICE."

"That's right," Noah says slowly. "They can't take her from a house of worship."

Everyone looks at Mr. Damas. "Fine," he spits out. "But my daughter's staying right here."

"Dad!" Rose says, but he silences her with a look.

"I'll go," Mrs. Damas says. "Give me the keys and I'll let her into the safe house."

"Don't worry, Mr. Damas," I say. "We'll test her first. We'll put her by the altar and make sure she doesn't burst into flames, okay?"

He narrows his eyes at me. He always thinks I *might* be fucking with him, but whatever I'm saying always makes too much sense, I guess. He waves me off.

"Let's go," I say. I don't need to be around this guy a moment longer.

99

THERE'S A SAFE HOUSE NEXT TO THE PRIESTS' RESIDENCES
where parishioners can stay for a little while if they're down and out
for whatever reason. Mom stayed here when we first heard Sheriff
McGhee was pissed that her part-time mechanic work was putting Pat
Lorrington's shop out of business (a total lie, as Lorrington ran his garage
into the ground without help from anyone). But the sheriff sicced ICE
on her the second we thought we could return to our normal lives.

Lorrington's business still burnt out.

We put Mom in the twin bed and I sit on the edge for a few minutes. She's asleep, having woken up a few times on the road to say some
creepy shit like, *They cut into my blood* and *I'm the only one it didn't kill.*

When Noah's grabbing some water, Mom looks at me for a moment
and says, "You're next, Sia." And she's out again.

I decide not to tell Noah about that one.

The only things I got from my dad are my black eyes. Everything else
is from Mami—deep olive skin, wide fingernails, hair the color of buck-
wheat. She looks thinner, and she's in a weird, oversized gray uniform.
But otherwise, she's perfect. Right here, in front of me, eyes closed,
taking long, deep breaths, her hand curled around mine.

How can this be?

100

AFTER THE DEPORTATION, AFTER ALMOST A YEAR IN Mexico, trying to get back in legally. And after she gave up on that and slipped into the Sonoran. After all this, Dad told me Mom was missing. And that she'd been missing for so long, there was only one explanation.

I couldn't leave the house, not for days. Not without feeling like the desert out there, the wide-mouth sky, and its smooth, pointed boulders, were crushing me. Sometime after that Father John came over.

"Sia," he said, straightening the white stole at his neck. "You haven't been to church in several weeks. Is everything alright?"

I couldn't bear to say it, so Dad filled him in. The father expressed his condolences and put his hand on my shoulder. "We don't know why God allows some things to happen the way they do," he said. "We just know they happen for a reason."

I wished I'd just thrown the bastard out. Or at least asked him to please explain the reason my mother had to die, alone, in the Sonoran. While the McGhees get their free mile-high chocolate pie at Maude's every Officer Appreciation Day.

"Yeah," I said to him, wondering if he could tell I was fantasizing about beheading him. "Thanks."

I never went back to church. Dad hadn't gone in ages but that was my last straw.

"Good," Abuela said when I told her my decision. "Maybe now you'll believe me."

101

NOAH TAKES A SEAT NEXT TO ME AFTER A BIT. "WHOA."

"What?" I whisper it, gesturing for him to quiet down.

"All those cuts on her arm. Look. They're gone now."

I'd barely registered that she was cut up, but now that he says it, I can see the image of her, stepping away from the craft, scrapes deep in her forearm.

And he's right. They're gone now. Her skin is smooth, and if it weren't for the spots of dried blood, I might've thought I just imagined it.

"Don't tell your father," Mom mumbles. "I want to tell him. Let me . . ." She drifts off again.

Noah and I stare at each other for a few moments. We jump when Mrs. Damas calls my name.

She steps inside, my phone in her hand. "Your father's been calling."

"Shit," I say, then I realize who I'm talking to. "I mean, crap. I mean, I'm sorry, Mrs. Damas. It's way past curfew."

The phone lights up and buzzes. "Let me," she says, putting it to her ear. "Luis? Yes, this is Maura. . . . Fine, thank you. There was an emergency at the church . . . No, everyone is fine."

"Don't tell him yet," I whisper to her, Mom's request still ringing in my ears.

Mrs. Damas nods. "Yes, Luis. We had Sia help us out. Uh . . ." She glances at me again. "I think I'll let her fill you in about it. Yes. Okay. I'll let her know. You, too. Bye."

If it were any other day, I think I'd have done a backflip out of pure shock from Maura Damas covering for me. But now, the best I can do is say "Thanks."

"You should go home," she says.

"But—I can't just leave her. She just got back!" I don't say that I know Mrs. Damas can't stay, either, because I know she's not allowed by the awesome person she's married to. And Mom might need something.

"I'll stay." Noah stands. "I'll sleep on the sofa." We just stare at him as he shrugs. "I've been sleeping in my truck, anyway. Ever since my dad . . ." He trails off.

"Ever since your dad what, Noah?" I ask.

His face gets hard and he shakes his head. "Nothing. It's nothing."

Well, I didn't want to hear another word about the sheriff anyway. Fuckers, the both of them. "You know what? Fine. Stay," I say to Noah. "You owe me."

"I don't know—" Mrs. Damas begins, but I turn to her.

"Mrs. Damas. If you can't stay, someone has to. Even if it has to be him. I can't let—" My eyes fill with tears. "It's my mom, you know?"

"And you trust him?"

I glance at Noah. "No," I say. His face falls. "But I know he won't hurt her." And I do. Noah might be a little shit and a little liar, but he's never been malicious, you know? Plus, I feel like he actually does care about me, in some weird, warped way.

She nods, slowly at first. "Okay, Sia."

"If anything happens to her . . . ," I say to Noah.

"I won't let anything happen," he says. "I promise."

That last bit means nothing to me. But I have no other choice but to accept his word.

102

I'M GOING TO BED, **MY FATHER TEXTS ON MY WAY HOME.** We'll talk in the morning.

I'm not sure what to do when I get in. Do I barge into his room and announce it? *Hey, that wife who you thought was dead? Well, she just crashed in the desert on this top-secret government spacecraft that probably has extraterrestrial origins. Oh, and she might be a robot.*

It's like my mind just gives up at a certain point. I crawl into bed and sleep.

103

I WANTED TO GET UP EARLY, BUT I SLEEP IN. AND WHEN I awaken, I pull the covers around me and stay perfectly still for as long as I can. Sunshine pours in thick, right across my bed.

Once, I asked my father what those little specks were, the ones you can see in light rays. He said dust.

And later, I asked my mother. She said they were prayers.

When I reach to touch the light, the specks swirl faster and faster.

104

I SHOWER AND CHANGE. DAD'S WAITING FOR ME AT THE kitchen table. He throws up his arms in exasperation. "What happened?"

I close my eyes. I know Mom said she wanted to tell him, but how can I not right now?

"You were with that boy, weren't you? I knew that kid was trouble, but I didn't say it, porque—"

"Mom's alive." My voice sounds like it belongs to someone else.

He doesn't say anything for a few seconds, but his hands look weak, like he's going to drop that coffee mug any second. I walk over, take it from him, and place it on the table with a clank. He blinks.

"How do you know?" He keeps his voice even, the words slow.

"You're not going to believe it." I shake my head and sit.

"Try me."

I grab my phone and pull up the video of the crash. Noah posted it last night. Dad watches it wordlessly. And then he erupts. "What the hell is this, Sia?"

"We filmed that last night, in the desert." I swallow, even though my mouth is dry. "Mom came out of that thing."

He stares at my phone for a long time, watching the video replay itself. "Stop bullshitting me, Artemisia."

I shake my head, widening my eyes. "I'm not bullshitting you. She's in the safe house right now."

He stands so fast, he almost falls over. "Why didn't you tell me this last night?"

"Mom said she wanted to explain it to you, Papi. I'm sorry. Things were very chaotic—"

"Is she okay? Is she injured?"

I shrug. "She seemed like she might've been concussed. She wouldn't let us take her to the hospital. Probably because of ICE."

"So that's what those people were talking about." Dad's ramming his hand through his hair.

"What people?"

"Last night. Some people came, asking me if anyone had stopped by, if I'd seen anything unusual."

"Dad, that doesn't answer my question. Who were they?"

"I don't know!" He raises his hand like he's confounded. "People. Well-dressed. Two men. And a woman."

I remember the words on the spacecraft. *They're coming.* My hair stands up.

"I'm going to get Dr. Vega," Dad says, throwing a button-down over his T-shirt. "Bring her to the church, check her out. You. Go to her now. Tell her I'll be right there."

"Yeah," I say. "Okay."

105

MOM'S SITTING ON THE PORCH WHEN I PULL UP. SHE'S
wearing one of Mrs. Damas's old wrap dresses. The fabric is put together
in pieces, patchwork, all white with deep blue flowers. The sun's in her
hair like a gold crown. She runs up when I open the car door.

"Sia," she says, choked up, and she's holding me.

Now I'm crying. "We thought you were dead." I can't talk anymore.
My shoulders shake.

We don't move for a long time, not until the sun has glided across
the porch.

106

INSIDE, MRS. DAMAS'S COOKING UP SOMETHING THAT smells like heaven's idea of heaven.

"Oh my God," I say. I'd completely forgotten about food, in general, and my stomach angrily reminds me about that fact.

"Oh, Sia! Hey, there. . . ." Noah's voice fades, probably because he's realized he sounds way too happy. "Good to see you, I mean . . . ," he amends, making his voice gruff. He's got gloves on, and he's chopping away at Scotch bonnet peppers and onions.

I pretend like he's not there at all, even as Mom says good morning. I turn to Mrs. Damas. "Is Rose around?"

Mrs. Damas tenses just a touch, but she hides it expertly. "She says she'll stop by after choir practice at St. Matthew's."

I take it that Rose's forbidden from coming, probably because her dad still thinks the devil crashed a spacecraft into the desert rather than my mother. To give him credit, though, either seems just as likely.

I wonder if Mrs. Damas told him where she was really going this morning.

"Dad's on his way," I say to Mom. "He's bringing Dr. Vega to check you out."

Mom sighs and sits on the couch. There's still a blanket and pillow draped over it, from Noah, I'm guessing. "I'm fine. He doesn't need to do that." Then she smiles that lovestruck smile reserved for and about my dad and I want to groan but I can't. This whole thing is just so, so, *so* weird.

Mrs. Damas puts cups of ginger tea in our hands.

"Gracias," we say in unison. In a matter of minutes, a feast is placed on the table. Eggs cut with peppers and onions, sweet plantains, diced and boiled. Soft bread, sliced and buttered. Like I said, heaven's idea of heaven.

Small talk ensues as Mrs. Damas fills Mom in on Abel and Meena, on how things are with the family. We all avoid the big, fat desert moon in the room, until Noah clears his throat. "Have you guys seen page nineteen of the *Sentinel*?"

Everyone shakes their head. It's an absurd question, really, but then Noah pulls out his laptop and pulls it up. "Unidentified Flying Object Crashes in Desert Off Highway 909." There's a couple of photos, even with details of the script on the side of the craft.

"That one's mine," Noah says, pointing. "I emailed them to Omar, you know? And he sent them to Imani, who wanted nothing to do with them, but then he tried her editor, who was, like, all over it."

"Why did you do this, Noah?" I ask. "What if it alerts . . . *them*?" Whoever the flip *they* are.

"No, this is good," Mom says. She's taken the computer and is looking at it carefully. "Do you think you could contact them again? I'd like to speak with them."

"Why?" I ask. "What good could come of it?"

Mom bites at her lips. "The people who did this to me? They're not going to stop. Not unless someone holds them accountable. And the only way that's going to happen is if we expose what they did. What they're still doing." She grabs my hand. "I have to. I want—need—everyone to hear my story."

I gulp. God. I'm not sure if I'm ready to hear it yet.

"That makes sense," Noah says. "Imani works for the *Sentinel*."

"She's an intern," I correct, but Noah shrugs.

"Still. I bet she has connections with even bigger news outlets. Or at least knows someone who does. And Omar, I mean, he's already asked to come see you. Been texting me about every seven seconds. I'll invite them both."

Before I can protest, Mom nods. "See if they can come today," she says. "The sooner, the better."

107

"NOAH," I SAY. "OUTSIDE, PLEASE."

"What's up?" he asks as he follows me to the porch.

"What the hell is up with you?" I ask. "First of all, putting the video of the crash on the Internet? Then telling Omar about it? All without my permission?"

He blinks. "Sia, this is, like. This is so much bigger than you, no offense. I didn't think I needed to ask first."

"How did it not occur to you?"

He rubs at his temples. "I don't understand the big deal. Look, I mean, even your mom thinks it's a great idea."

"Maybe she's not thinking straight," I say. "Did you not consider that? The first thing she told us, remember, right after a freakin' head injury? She said *they're* coming to get her. How is broadcasting her location going to help?"

"Hey," he says. "We won't broadcast her location, okay? We just— Omar thinks it's a good idea, and I do, too, if we document this. It might protect her. And us."

I take a shaky breath and use every ounce of energy to not cry. "I just can't lose her. Not again, Noah."

He wraps an arm around my waist, but I step away. "Don't touch me."

Noah lowers his eyes, running a hand through his hair. It sticks in every direction, reminding me of Harry Potter. "Why can't we be friends, Sia? Or at least act nicer while all this"—he gestures to the house—"is going on?"

"You lost your chance at *nicer* when you lied to me, Noah. Twice."

"And I said I was sorry, Sia. Jesus." He's rapping one hand on the other. The beat is frantic. He lowers his voice. "I didn't ask for him to be my father, you know. You know me. I'm nothing, *nothing* like him. Or Jeremy."

"That's the thing, Noah. I don't know you. Who knows what else you lied about? Because that's what you are to me now. A liar."

"Sia. There isn't anything else. I promise. I did what I did because I didn't want you to hate me."

"How ironic. Because I hate you *because* of what you did."

He about stumbles when I say *hate*. He looks so hurt, I take a step back when he speaks again. "You seriously aren't going to forgive me? Even after me apologizing, what, how many times by now?"

"I don't know why you think I would forgive you."

"Because that's what you do when you care about someone, Sia! You forgive them for being shitty. Rose forgave you, right?"

"No," I say. "You don't get to bring Rose into this. Not after what you've done."

"Sia, give me a break. Please."

"No." I sound so impassive. So sharp. I feel almost proud of myself. "I can't just forget what you did. All those lies about who you are! Your *father* and *brother*, Noah!"

He hardens his face and turns to me. "So you're saying if I had been up front and honest with you, and told you first thing who my dad was, you would've given me a chance?"

"I—well—I mean, yeah, of course." It's a lie. I can't even hide that it's a lie.

And then Noah smirks. "Right. That's what I thought." He turns like he's going to leave, but he stops, his eyes back on me, hard. "I *am* sorry. I didn't mean to hurt you and I wish I could go back and change everything. But, fuck." He sighs. "All I'm saying is, with everything going on, you could act a little less like a bitch."

I take a step back. "Are you serious right now?" I'm huffing like I've just run a hundred miles. "Did you and Jeremy learn to call girls bitches from your dad? Or is it just genetic?" My voice breaks. I look up at the sky, and damnit, a tear escapes.

"I mean—" Noah looks scared as I wipe at my useless face. "Fuck. Sia. I didn't mean that. I shouldn't have said—I just wanted—"

I make myself sound as hard as I can. Hard like uncarvable stone. "Fuck you, Noah."

Articulate? No. But it gets the message across. Stomping past him, I go back inside.

108

DAD CALLS AFTER MRS. DAMAS LEAVES. HE'D FORGOTTEN
that Dr. Vega works out of town now. She's canceling the rest of her day
and is right behind him.

"I decided to take the 909 back home, see what's still out there,"
he tells me. "Gran error. There's back-to-back trafico, all these people
coming out to see the aliens, I guess. But they cleaned it up, Sia. I mean,
there's nothing out there. Nada."

"But it was *huge*," I say. "Bigger than our house."

"I'm telling you, looking at all these military trucks. Te lo digo, esto
es mas grande que Elvis. Mas grande de Carlos Santana. O incluso
Diego Luna, even."

I scoff. "No way it's bigger than Diego Luna." He laughs. It's good
to hear.

He gets quiet. "Let me talk to her, eh?"

I hand her the phone. "Amor?" She takes it into the room, shuts the
door. I can hear her crying and I can't stand the sound.

"I'll be right back," I tell Noah, my voice sharp.

109

I REMEMBER THE FIRST TIME I LEARNED ABOUT EVOLUTION, in the sixth grade. I ran to my grandmother after school. Finally I had a story for her.

She sat down and listened to me very carefully. About how there was an enormous explosion and all of matter splattered in all directions, until planets and stars formed. And on our planet, there was some great soup with bacteria, all cooking in the ocean like boiled tamales, till they became fish to snakes to elephants to apes to us.

And when I was finished, she looked out the window at all the Joshua trees in her yard. "So that's what they're reaching for," she said. "I always wondered."

The church is in the middle of a sparse Joshua tree forest. I take a slow walk from tree to tree. My fingers run along the shared arms of their stretched hands, beckoning. Beckoning to where we all come from.

110

I'M WITH THE TREES IN THE BACK WHEN NOAH RUNS
over. "Sia. Omar's here." I roll my eyes and stomp past him.

Omar gives me the biggest smile when I walk in. He's in the middle of setting up some camera equipment. "Sia Martinez. My god, your mom. Your mother. Came right out of a real motherfucking UFO, a black motherfucking triangle, no less!"

I guess I should've expected this level of enthusiasm. "Where's Imani?" I ask, glancing around.

"Oh, she's mad at me. Joke's on her, though, because shit got real this time. I mean, it's been real, but, fuck, a real abductee, turns out to be your mom?" He lowers his voice. "She doesn't have green scales, does she? Did you check yet?"

"Sia," Mom says, walking into the room. "Who is this?"

Omar jumps to shake her hand. "Omar Rana. We're gonna get your story all over the map, madam. God, even the Illuminati truthers will have absolutely nothing on this!" He pauses. "Unless you come from the Illuminati, Mrs. Martinez?"

"Do not accuse my mother of taking part in your bullshit, Omar," I say.

"Sia. Dejalo," Mom says. She looks absolutely delighted, for some reason. Is it Omar's winning personality?

"Right, right, I mean no disrespect." He sits across from Mom in the living area. "So what's your objective, Mrs. Martinez? I have about a hundred and sixty questions, but—"

Mom nods, sitting straight. "I want as many people as you can get to see this. To see my story." She glances at me, her eyes dark in the shadows. "I can't think of another way to stop them."

"AFTER WALKING FOR SO MANY DAYS AND NIGHTS I stopped counting them, I fell asleep under this huge moon. I was exhausted. Sunburned, chapped, dry, and thirsty." Mom looks so beautiful, her hair long and silky and swept to one side, the afternoon light through the sheer curtain on her like liquid gold. "And early morning, when it was still dark, I awoke to this blast of light in my face. I thought something had happened to the moon, like a piece of it was falling on me. But it was something else. Round, levitating. Pulsing like it had a heart."

"A spacecraft?" Omar asks. "One of the triangles again? Or, ooh, was it a saucer? Or—"

"Dude," I say. "Let her talk."

"Yes, a craft." Mom takes a breath. "It was round and small. Metallic. Not from space, though."

112

"WAIT A MINUTE," OMAR SAYS. "YOU'RE SAYING THERE'S a branch of government, underground in the desert, that exists solely to perform experiments on immigrants?"

"Yes." Mom nods. "They do it to people no one gives a shit about."

Omar rounds his hand to a fist. "I knew it! I called it three weeks ago." He turns to Noah. "Didn't I write about—"

"Omar. This isn't anywhere close to alien babies in Denver. Stop." Christ, I am ready to punch this asshole.

"It's okay," Mom says. When I give her a look, she half-smiles. "It's kind of nice to meet someone with . . . energy about this." She waves her hand.

"What kind of experiments were they?" Noah asks. He's holding his phone, live-streaming on social media or something.

Mom bites her lip and glances down. She lifts her head, determined. "I'll show you."

"JESUS CHRIST ON A STICK," OMAR GASPS. "DO THAT again."

Mom's sitting in the wooden folding chair, and she points to a blue coffee mug in the kitchen. "The cup."

Then there's a fast wind that flies at us, throwing my sideswept bangs in my face. It lasts two seconds, this blur. I mean, I just blink and Mom's back in the chair, the cup in her palms, facing the camera. When she frowns, I can see where her wrinkles have deepened.

"Did you get that?" Noah asks Omar, whose eyes are about to pop out of his head. "Play it back. In slow motion."

Everyone but Mom crowds around the camera screen. As he slows it down, we see Mom, stepping up, taking careful steps to the kitchen. When she returns to the frame, she's got the coffee mug in her hands. I can even read the script on it. It says, *All I need today is a little bit of coffee and a whole lot of JESUS.*

She sits slowly, deliberately, as though she were just a regular woman in Starbucks, getting her afternoon kick.

114

"SUPER SPEED," OMAR SAYS. "BARELY DETECTABLE with the human eye." He and Noah are jotting down notes as fast as they can. I scoff. Nerds.

"I can go faster than that," Mom says. "But I wanted you to sense it some."

Omar blinks slowly, then snaps back into paranoid theorist–mode. "Is there anything else? Flight? Oh, what about laser beams that shoot out of your eyes? Or, ooh, ooh, do you have any new birthmarks in the shape of crop circles? Or—" I give him one menacing look and the words sort of fall away from his open mouth.

Mom hesitates and Noah speaks. "Fast healing. Sia and I saw it, after the crash."

And now I'm glaring at Noah. Why does he keep jumping in like that? Noah catches my eye and shrinks just a touch. Enough for me to feel the beginnings of guilt. Great.

Omar looks to Mom for confirmation, who nods. "That, too."

"How are these experiments done? I mean—"

"They have scientists that manipulate our genes," Mom says. "I mean, that's what I heard."

"Heard from who?"

"Other people, there. Trapped. Like me."

"And this is all still underground in the desert, right?"

"Yes."

"How would they have heard that information? About the genetic surgery? The other trapped people, I mean?"

Mom sighs. "There was one man who worked there. He was on our side. Or at least acted like it when no one was looking. He told us some things."

"And you believed him?"

"I acted like I did. I think he was telling the truth. He's the one who helped me escape."

"Why did he do that? Didn't he risk, you know, his own life?"

Mom glances down. "He did it because he believed in doing the right thing."

Omar nods. "I bet he had a kick-ass code name."

Mom shrugs, smiling. "I don't know anyone's real names. But he was called River."

"Yes. Definitely a kick-ass code name. Maybe not as cool as Sabertooth, but, River, yeah, can't complain." He scribbles it in his notebook. "What else did River tell you?"

Mom looks directly into Omar's eyes. "He told us that they spliced our DNA with that of extraterrestrial origins." She moves her eyes away, to the noon light that's now orange. "And I was the only one who survived the experiment. So far."

Then she glances at me.

115

OMAR'S MAKING A SQUEAKING NOISE. HE SOUNDS LIKE a mockingbird inside the jaws of a cat. "Did you just say extraterrestrial? She did, didn't she? She said it!"

"Were they the Greys?" Noah asks, his eyes wide.

"No, no," Omar says. "This isn't their style at all, man. I mean, secret experiments on DNA and shit? This is straight from the Reptilian agenda."

"But I thought the government already experimented on the Greys, dude," Noah responds, hitting Omar lightly on the arm. "After Roswell? Right? And their race has been getting revenge on humans ever since!"

"No, no, that was before the Greys went to war with the Rept—"

"Enough!" I say. "We're wasting time."

"Of course. Sorry, Sia," Noah says. I just give him a death glare. *I'm sorry*, he mouths, and I know he's not just talking about his and Omar's gift for running off tangent. *I'm sorry*. This time, he puts a hand on his heart. My mom looks at us with curiosity. Meanwhile, Omar doesn't notice at all.

"No disrespect, Sia," Omar says. "We're just trying to get the story out there."

I drag my eyes away from Noah's. "Talk to my mother, then. Or I'm gonna smash your camera there into little pieces."

"It's fine, Sia," Mom says, laughing. She's totally amused by them and I still don't get it.

Omar flips another page open in his notebook. "Okay, next question." He looks up. "Tell me every detail you know about the experiments. Whether you saw it yourself, or someone just told you, or, ah, they actually did it to you."

Mom nods and sighs. "I don't know much, I'm sorry. I do know they started by harvesting eggs."

"Eggs," Noah repeats.

"Eggs. From women. Girls." Mom is looking off into the distance now, her eyes glistening like she can't bear to say it, but she has to. "They started by trying to make embryos. But instead, and I never saw this myself, I just heard, but instead, they made monsters."

"Holy shit," I say.

"Holy shit," both Noah and Omar parrot.

"And when that didn't work, they decided, as a sort of last resort, to just inject the healthiest of us with the blood directly. Just to see. I don't think they were expecting it to work. At all. And it didn't. It mostly didn't."

"Except with you," Omar says.

Mom nods, and then a tear finally escapes her eyes.

"Let's change the subject," I say. "We can talk more about this later."

116

"OKAY, MS. LENA." OMAR'S TURNED THE PAGE IN HIS notebook again. "So you just happened to crash in front of Sia's Jeep? 'Cause I thought that was coincidental."

"No, no. I knew she was there."

"How?"

Mom shrugs. "Superpowers."

Omar, predictably, asks about three hundred more questions. After an hour, I have to pace in the kitchen as they talk. My legs need to do something other than sit.

"Who are the *they* you speak of?" Omar asks. "Who's the Big Bad Wolf, Mrs. Martinez?"

"Ultimately? The US government."

"Predictable," I mutter. "What?" I say when Noah gives me a questioning look. "Groups in power have been performing unethical experiments on subjugated peoples since forever. It was the first thing we learned in world history." I huff. "I mean, this whole setup, it's kind of their MO."

"Of course." Noah nods. "So, how long have they been doing the experiments?"

Mom shrugs. "A while. Since the fifties, I heard, but I don't know for sure."

Noah jots it down. "So, like, why have they been experimenting? What's their end goal?"

Mom shrugs again. "Immortality?"

"No," Omar says, and we all turn to him. "What? I just don't think that's it."

"Omar, you don't know more than my mom." I cross my arms. "Considering she's the one who's been abducted and cut up."

"Look, I'm not saying I know from experience. But this, these powers?" He points to Mom. "This is everything the military would want. Think about it." He jumps up, his hands waving in emphasis. "What political power wouldn't want an army of soldiers that move so fast, you can't even see them? Who heal so fast, you can barely hurt them?"

"It just seems, I don't know . . . ," Noah says. "It seems like a huge investment in something that hardly sounds possible."

Omar gives a big laugh. "Hardly sounds possible? Come on, man. She's right there." Mom gives him a tight smile.

"Theoretically, though. Before they knew they could do it. Superpowers? For something as serious as the military to invest in?" I ask. "Noah's got a point."

"I've got three words for you," Omar says, holding a fist up to count. "Project. Center. Lane."

We stare blankly.

"What?" He throws up his hands. "You mean you never heard—"

"Just explain it, man," I say.

He sighs. "Fine. Back in the eighties, the army conducted experiments in human astral projection. Psychic research. No, no, listen to me. This isn't a conspiracy. There are actual records and shit. They wanted to know if we could astrally spy on our enemies."

Noah holds up his phone. "I mean, he's right. There are loads of articles from legitimate sites on it."

I roll my eyes. "Okay, so what? What's that got to do with Mom?"

"I'm just saying that anything that's gonna give the military more power? They will pour their money into it. This country is obsessed with war and shit. I mean, think about that jet they've been working on for the last couple of years. The F-35 Project? The most expensive military project in history? It's considered a failure, and they're still throwing dimes at it."

"I hadn't thought of soldiers," Mom says. "But it makes sense, Sia. From the talk I heard offhand, here and there. Wanting to militarize the police. Keep the 'illegals' out. Things like that."

I groan at Omar's triumphant smile. "Okay, whatever, Omar. This one thing might make sense. But theorizing isn't gonna help us right now. Stay on task, people."

We find out Mom, while maneuvering the craft, shot down a couple satellites to prevent *them* from finding her right when she landed. That she didn't mean to crash, but something malfunctioned in the engine. She mentions weird mechanical-sounding words that get Omar and Noah really excited, taking notes and looking stuff up on their phones.

Then Omar asks, "Why did you escape? After two years, why now?"

Mom looks at me again.

Then the door bursts open and Dad walks in.

All of a sudden, no one exists but him. And though Noah and Omar are eager for more information, they can tell my parents need some privacy. Even the Joshua trees outside could probably feel that blast of lightning between them, lit with arms and tears.

117

DR. VEGA'S NOT FAR BEHIND DAD. OMAR FILMS SOME
of the checkup. "I can't motherfucking believe this," he keeps muttering. And yeah, I guess this does feel straight out of *The X-Files*, doesn't
it? When the doc gets some samples of Mom's blood, Mom says, "I want
Omar and his cousin to be emailed a copy of the results." She looks
at Omar as she gestures to the vials. "Maybe that will be all the proof
you need."

"That sounds amazing, Mrs. Martinez." Omar glances at his phone,
which has been buzzing for the last half hour. "God, my mom's gonna
kill me. Shit. I think I have to go." He begins packing his camera equipment. "But even if those test results prove something? We still need to
connect it to the government, you know?"

Mom frowns. "I was afraid of that."

"Don't worry, Mrs. Martinez!" He touches her shoulder. "I'm sending this straight to my cousin, and she's an intern for the *Sentinel*. She's
gonna help me get everything out there." He doesn't mention that she
tends to just blog about kittens and cupcakes, but whatever. I'm not
gonna burst bubbles. Not again, anyway.

"This is the only way," Mom tells us. "This is the only way to stop them. If this isn't taken seriously, if they're not stopped . . ." She pauses and sighs. "They'll find a way to take me back."

The room feels very cold as Omar leaves.

118

WHEN THINGS ARE QUIET, WE REALIZE WE MISSED lunch. Dad orders some takeout.

"What are you still doing here?" he barks at Noah as he gets off the phone. Noah's face reddens and he begins to stammer, backing away.

"Dejalo, Luis," Mom says gently. "Él es el hijo de Ama DuPont."

"Ama DuPont," Dad repeats, eyeing Noah. "So that mean your padre es . . ."

No one answers. No one needs to. Finally, I speak. "How do you know his mom?"

"We helped her get away from Tim. What was it, Luis? Ten years ago?"

Noah doesn't look surprised. He and Mom must've gone over this.

Dad shakes his head. "Almost thirteen years, Magdalena." He looks at Noah. "How's your mamá doing now?"

Noah lowers his eyes. "Not that great, sir."

"Come on, kid," Dad says after a pause. "Come with me to get the food."

Noah gives me a helpless look, but I dismiss him with a hand. When the door closes, Mom gestures for me to sit by her on the sofa.

She wraps her arms around me and we lean back. She holds me like I'm little again.

"What's going on with you and Noah?"

I sigh. "Mom, can we please talk about anything else?"

"Not yet."

I sigh and she puts her warm palm on mine. Christ. I still can't believe she's here.

"He's not his dad, you know."

I close my eyes for a long time. "Mom, he lied to me about how he was related to them."

"I know."

I blink and stare at her. "How?"

"Noah. He told me. When I woke up, I didn't know where I was. He brought me water and toast. And then just started talking." Mom laughs. "That boy loves to talk, huh?" She tightens her arms around me. "You know, once upon a time, I used to think only bad guys did bad things. But then . . ." She sighs. "I met two people. Good people. And they did some bad, bad things. Because they thought it would save their families. Their people."

"What happened to them?" I whisper.

"They're both still around," Mom says. "But they're both trying to do the right thing, you know? But in really different ways."

"Way to be cryptic, Mom."

Mom laughs. "What Noah did, it was because he didn't want to hurt you. He thought it was the right thing to do at the time."

"But it wasn't."

"No. But we all make mistakes, Sia. We have to remember that we aren't our mistakes. We aren't what people have forced us to do, to be." Her voice is so low, it's almost at a whisper. "No one is all good and no one is all bad. Remember this when the anger feels like it's burning everything inside you. Remember that most of us are just doing what we think is right at the time."

I bite at my lip. "Noah really brought you toast?"

"Mm-hmm. With butter and prickly pear jam."

We're silent for a moment. And I can't help but go back to all the times Noah made me feel really good about myself. *You're fucking gorgeous*, he said, after we first kissed. And how when we got naked in my bed and he didn't expect anything from me at all, how he held me when I cried, and how he spent weeks finding the most perfect poem to give me. The way he attacked Jeremy after Jeremy called me *spic bitch*. The way he sometimes stares at me and forgets what he's saying, like just the sight of me makes him light-headed or something.

And then Mom repeats it. "He's not his father, Sia."

I snort, but I also kind of have goose bumps on my arms, the sort that come when you hear something your whole body knows is true. "You sound just like Abuela."

"You're wearing her rings," she murmurs, touching the turquoise on my fingers.

Shit. "Oh, about that, Mom. I forgot, with everything, to tell you—"

"I know she's dead. She told me, in a dream. When it happened."

I relax back into the cushions. "She kept saying you were still alive. Even a few days ago, she kept coming around to tell me."

"You believe her yet?" Mom's chuckling, but I can't crack a smile.

"Sometimes," I whisper.

119

"I NEED TO GET SOMETHING ON THEM. THE GOVERNMENT,"
Mom says after lunch, softly, like she's just thinking aloud. "I need to
catch them admitting it. Aloud. In the act."

"You should go into hiding while you formulate your plan," Noah
says. "Like that Max from *The X-Files*, who lived in his trailer, you
know?"

"Noah," I say. "Calm down with *The X-Files*."

"No, I need to find something, like, tomorrow," Mom says. "They
know where we are."

"What?" I say, jumping up to look out the window. There's no
X-Files-esque black van or anything like that. "How do you know they
know? I thought you shot the satellite down."

Dad looks alarmed, too. "Amor. There's no way—"

"They've been following you, Luis. They followed you here."

"Well, we should do something," I say. "Go. On the run."

"In a van," Noah supplies, drumming on the kitchen table.

"No," Mom says, shaking her head slowly. "I need to confront them.
One of them in particular. If we could get her to talk . . . and document
the conversation . . . That might be exactly what we need."

120

EARLY AFTERNOON, ROSE BURSTS IN. SHE'S WEARING a teal dress and her hair is in gorgeous, long twists. Are those new? I don't remember them from last night. But then again, last night is just a bullet-shot blur.

"Sia," she shrieks, and we hug for a century.

"I missed you," I say. "So much shit has happened."

"God, you're telling me. First you actually kick McAssHat's ugly butt. Then your mom strolls up in a freakin' unidentified flying object? I thought I had a story when Meena's doctor flirted with Mom . . ." Rose lowers her voice. "And Mom actually flirted back!"

My eyebrows drop. "What? Your mom? As in Maura Damas—"

"Yes, the Maura Damas. And oh my God, Sia, she giggled. Mom. Giggled. It was awful but also kind of cute." Rose leans over my shoulder. "Hey, Lena! Mr. Martinez! Noah!"

"Rose!" Mom and Dad say, while Noah gives an awkward wave.

"We're ordering pizza," I say, stepping aside so she can hug Mom on the couch. "Can you stay?"

"Of course," she says. "Dad got an emergency call to fix the organ at St. Matthew's. I've got hours, baby."

121

"DON'T WE NEED A PLAN, MAGDALENA? FOR WHEN they come?" Dad's already got a pen and pencil out to take notes.

"Why don't you guys attend the church service?" Rose says, grabbing another slice of pepperoni. "No one's going to attack you with Jesus on the cross watching."

"They don't really want to attack. They . . ." She sighs. "They want me alive. Me and Sia."

"Me?!" I say at the same time Noah and Dad say my name. "What do they want to do with me?"

"We share the same blood," Mom says. "They want to know if they can replicate the experiment."

All of a sudden, I can hear the crickets singing outside. They sound like they're the size of nebulas. I push my pizza aside.

"We're not letting them take her," Noah says.

I roll my eyes at Noah's superhero act and turn to Mom. "What happened to all those people? The ones that failed the experiment."

"They passed away."

"I know, I know, but how?"

Mom shakes her head. "I can't bear to say it. Fue horrible."

"We're not letting them take her," Noah says, this time more loudly. He stands. "We've got to get away. Go on the run. Hide."

I grimace. "Sit down, Captain America. Jesus."

"They can't harm you if they can't find you," Dad says and Noah gives me a look of triumph as he gets back in the chair.

"They can't *not* find us, Luis. It's the government. They've got satellites, cameras, drones. Guns, bombs—"

"But if they can't find you, Lena?" Dad, for the first time, sounds angry at Mom.

"This is too big to run from. Luis. Look at me. We couldn't even keep me away from ICE. How are we gonna hide from the whole military?"

Rose looks as horrified as the rest of us, but she shakes her head and stands. "You know what? Let's not think about this for a little while. Lena, you're back. I mean, we thought you were gone. And I mean, *gone*, but you're back." She pulls out her phone and sets it to some dance radio. "We should celebrate. No, scratch that. We *need* to celebrate."

122

CELIA CRUZ IS SINGING IN A WINE GLASS VIA ROSE'S
phone. Mom and Dad are dancing la salsa, and it's kind of embarrassing, but also, I missed this. Them, laughing, together. Mom's hair is down in long waves, swirling around like Spanish moss when Dad turns her in his arms. Their skin the same exact shade of brown, always reminding me of smooth hazelwood.

If you look closely, there's only one thing off. My dad's hand on hers is so tight, like he's afraid to let go.

123

"SIA," ROSE TELLS ME, GRABBING MY ARM. "SAMARA'S here."

"Really?" I say. "You told her about—"

"Not about, you know, everything. But I told her I was at the safe house, and she just kinda showed up?"

"Um." I bite my lips and furrow my brow at the excited look on Rose's face. "I didn't realize you two were on the 'come uninvited' level of friendship."

"Sia."

I nod. "Alright. Invite her in. It's a party, right?"

"Yes, yes it is." She smiles, her eyes lit up like lanterns.

I smile back. "Just make sure she doesn't tell."

"You know it!" She whips around.

"Rose." I stop her as she reaches for the door. "I really am sorry." Tears are making my eyes sting. "I should've believed you from the beginning. Not him. I *was* a crappy friend."

Rose throws her arms around me. "I'm sorry, too, Sia. I should've talked to you when I felt hurt, instead of also being a crappy friend." She wipes at her eyes. "You know, my mom told me about everything

Noah's done. Hitting Jeremy, taking care of your mom, making sure Omar has access to all the evidence so we can bring down the bad guys. He's a good guy, Sia."

"He is." And I surprise myself by agreeing so quickly, but then I brush the feeling away. "And Samara is amazing. I like her a lot."

Rose gives me the biggest grin. "She is amazing."

I grin right back. "So are you two official—"

But Dad and Mom twirl near us and Rose puts her hand on my mouth. "Later." She winks and goes to let Sam in.

124

ROSE HUGS SAMARA FOR A LONG TIME. AND THEN SAM reaches for me. "Sorry for being such a bitch to you at the diner," I say.

"Don't worry about it," she responds, and then her eyes are back on Rose and now they're dancing, too, alongside my parents. Sam's got on this long, cerulean top, and her hair is in a mermaid braid. Her skin is darker than Rose's, and warmer, too, like copper. Their clothes look like pieces of sea glass, glimmering smooth and soft.

After a couple songs, I sneak onto the porch just in time to see Noah return with my Jeep. His hair's wet and he's got a fresh change of clothes on—a green-checkered button-down and khakis.

"Hey," he says.

"Hey."

He has a seat next to me on the bench.

"So no black vans followed you around?"

He shook his head. "None at all. But what's weird is they've closed all the streets that lead out of town. They're doing searches of vehicles. It's a nightmare for traffic, according to the radio."

"They're probably looking for her," I say, and he hums in agreement. I frown and decide to change the subject. "Your dad was out?"

He nods. "Yeah, his schedule's been pretty much the same for weeks now. Jeremy was home, though. But he never left his room. I think he had a girl over."

"Ew," I say, trying to imagine who would stoop so low. It's not hard, though. As much as I would rather eat a raw cactus than admit it, Jeremy isn't hideous, with his running back shape, gold hair, eyes the color of lapis. The ultimate proof that a book's cover can hide a heart made of cockroaches. Plus, a lot of girls find the whole aggressive and racist thing attractive, I guess.

"I think it might've been McKenna," Noah says.

"Really? That's too bad." And I mean it.

We sit for a few minutes, swinging. The sun's long set, but there's still the shadow of turquoise on that side of the sky.

I turn to Noah. I really should stop speaking to him, since okay, despite being a good guy, he's an ass for what he did, but I can't help it. I'm still a little freaked out about everything. And, though I'll admit it to no one, I feel a bit lonely. Shaking my head, I take a breath. "You remember, yesterday, when you said you thought Mom was a robot or something?"

"Yeah?"

"You still feel that way?"

He shrugs. "Nah. I mean, she seems legit to me. Why?"

I shake my head. "I mean, I know it's her. It's definitely her. But she's different, you know?"

"She's been through a lot, Sia. Even having her whole, like, genetic makeup rewired. It makes sense that she isn't quite the same."

I nod slowly. "What do you think Mom meant when she said they cut her blood with alien blood?"

Noah purses his lips. "I mean, I think she meant it literally. Even though she can't say for sure, because it was just a rumor or something, right?"

"Yeah." I take a long breath. "It just seems so unbelievable."

"You mean, unbelievable like when yesterday, your mom showed up in a spaceship? With fucking superpowers?"

I tilt my head and say, "Touché." After a few seconds, I groan. "The crickets are so freaking loud out here."

Noah pauses. "Yeah, you're right. I didn't even notice."

I snort. "What's wrong with your ears, man? Bugs are louder than the church choir."

"Oh, I don't know." He chuckles. "They're just in the background. Soothing, you know? Like a babbling brook or something."

"You can't compare that to a brook. No way."

"Well, I think it works." I'm still shaking my head as he continues. "A long time ago, I read in one of my mom's yoga magazines about this person who recorded cricket songs. And, for some reason, they decided to play them in slow motion. And you know what they sounded like, all stretched out like that?"

I raise my eyebrows.

"Chanting."

"Chanting?"

"Like Gregorian chanting."

We listen for a few moments. All of a sudden, the crickets sound a little different. They sound like they're telling tales.

I begin to wonder if there's a secret world hidden in everything, like words in the whine of mosquitoes or myths in the hums of bees or even ancient tales in the microscopic mumbles of water bears. Sounds we find ridiculously annoying, but on a level we can't sense, they somehow hold the whole universe together.

125

"SIA?"

My eyes are still closed, and I'm listening to the cricket chants. I open them and blink when I see that Noah has moved right next to me.

"Are we—are we friends again?" His eyes look so dark right now. They look like the deepest brown inside the rings of a tiger's eye stone.

I think about what Rose said—that Noah's a good guy. And how I agreed so quickly, like my body knew the truth of his worthiness when my mind refused.

But I guess I don't answer quick enough because he says, "I'm sorry. I shouldn't push, I know. But I wanted to say I'm so sorry for saying you acted like a bitch. You were acting totally normal considering the, ah, circumstances. If I were you, I'm not sure I'd ever speak to me again." He's tapping his hands on the cedar of the bench. I wonder if he even realizes he's doing it. "I really like you, Sia. You're strong, and smart, and, you know, the prettiest—" And he puts a hand over his eyes. "God, I sound like such an asshole, don't I?"

Nothing is as it seems, is it? Not even a son of the sheriff. My mother's words ring in my ears. *No one is all good. No one is all bad.*

I grab Noah's hand and he stops whatever train of thought was going to pour out next. And I put my leg over his, until I'm straddling him.

"Fuck," he whispers. His eyes are so intense, I feel almost naked. And then I let myself do what I've been wanting to since yesterday. I press my lips against the bruises on his face, his jaw. They're black and blotched like spilled ink.

"Thank you for hitting Jeremy," I whisper. "And for helping me and my mom." And Noah swallows, his Adam's apple bobbing, and he nods emphatically, and this time I kiss him on the lips.

126

THE FRONT DOOR OPENS WAY TOO SOON. I JUMP OFF Noah and leap onto the porch like a prima ballerina. Rose and Sam step out. "My dad's on his way home," Rose says.

"Yeah, and my mom wants me to pick her up something for dinner, so I have to head out, too," Samara says.

I lean over to give them hugs.

"When do I get details?" I whisper to Rose, raising my eyebrows toward Samara. Her cheeks pinken.

"Shut up," she says, smacking my shoulder.

I give her another hug. "Seriously, when do I get details, Rose?"

She hits me again. "Later."

"See you tomorrow?"

Rose nods. "I'll stop by after church. You know, depending on *them*." She places her hand on my shoulder. "Promise me you'll be careful, Sia."

I nod. "Of course."

She and Sam hold hands as they walk to their cars. I feel so giddy for Rose, I clasp my hands together and smile like I'm not just like Saint Christopher right now, the weight of the whole universe on my back.

127

I'VE READ MAGIC STORIES MY WHOLE LIFE, AND I'LL tell anyone, one of the creepiest creatures someone thought up is the leshii. The name's supposed to mean "man of the forest," but this isn't like any man—or human for that matter—I've ever met.

The leshii can take the form of anyone on Earth, but it'll go for someone you love. Someone you're missing, someone your heart is aching to see. Just to get close to you.

And then? Then it steals you away, marries you if you're a woman, maybe tickles you to death if you're a guy.

The stories say you can always tell if it's the leshii if you look closely enough.

The thing has no shadow.

128

INSIDE, I ASK MOM TO REMIND ME OF THE KEY PLAYERS in our plan.

"So, the guys who came to see Dad, they're, what? Voldemort? Regular old Death Eaters?"

Mom wrinkles her nose. "Death Eaters, I guess."

"So, like, who's Voldemort?" Noah asks.

"The whole thing," Mom replies. "The system, the people who thought it was a good idea to cut up immigrants for God knows what."

Dad's leaning against the wall, cup of coffee in hand. "You sure you don't want to leave, Lena?"

"I can't think of anywhere we can hide, Luis. They're fucking everywhere. I mean it." She sighs. "We've been over this."

Noah clears his throat. "What if Sia and I go, though? Just to keep her safe."

"No way," I say, shaking my head. "I'm not leaving."

"I wish you could take her somewhere," Mom says, giving Noah a sad smile. "But, Sia. You need to stay near me. I'm—" She lifts up her arms, showing the scars from what they did to her. "What I can do now . . . I can keep her safe. All of us."

"You know how to kick ass, too?" Noah asks.

Dad chuckles. "That's how Lena and I met, you know. At a capoeira competition in Vegas."

"Did you guys fight?"

Dad points to his nose, which leans ever so slightly to the left. "I used to be pretty, like her. Pero she messed me up big time."

"Oh, callate," Mom says, wrapping her arms around his waist. He puts one around her shoulders and kisses her head.

Behind them, I line their shadows with my eyes. Yes, there are two. And they're whole.

129

"ALL THIS TIME, I KEEP HEARING, 'THEY'RE COMING, they're coming,'" I say as everyone gets ready for bed. "And now, they know where we are. So why haven't they come already?"

Mom looks at me for a while. "They're making plans, Sia. These people—" She coughs on the word. "They're calculating. They've blocked off all the roads, hoping we'll just drive up into their hands. That would be easier for them." She sighs. "They're giving us until tomorrow. When they come, it will be a little bit more on our terms. Our territory. And there will only be the couple of them, at least, at first. To talk." She makes air quotations at *talk*.

"How do you know they'll be here tomorrow?"

She's finished braiding her hair. She wraps it around her head a couple of times, pinning it into place. "Porque tu abuela me dijo."

Despite all the times I've found Abuela's meddlesome ways annoying as hell, I'm impressed. We've got the dead on our side. That's gotta mean something.

130

THE SAFE HOUSE IS OLD. IT CREAKS LIKE A CRANKY elderly man all around me as I stretch in the pullout bed we set up in the office. I pull a knit emerald throw blanket up to my chin. There's a light rap at the door.

"Come in," I say. Noah pushes through.

"So, you must not be that scared of my dad," I say. "After that stern talking-to about keeping your skinny culo on the couch."

Noah smiles sheepishly. "Not really. I'm freakin' terrified, actually. But." He glances back and lowers his voice. "I think your parents are, like, catching up." He raises his eyebrows, turning back to me.

I grimace. "Ew. God. Disgusting."

"And they're getting loud."

"Shit, Noah! I don't need any more details, okay?" I sigh. "Fine, come in. It's early, anyway."

We sit on the edge of the crappy cot. I've got the blanket wrapped around my legs. "You know," Noah says. "It's totally normal, and expected, even, for your mom and dad to be eager to—"

"Noah! No! We're not talking about that anymore. Or ever again, okay? Jesus."

"Right. Sorry." He claps his hands on his knees, the beat dulled by his flannel pajama bottoms. And then he smiles at me so big, my stomach flutters a little. "Have you read that poem yet?"

I shake my head. "I haven't felt the need to. Sorry."

He nods.

More silence ensues.

I turn to him. "Why do you like to write poetry, anyway?"

He stops tapping his legs. "Hmm." Then he shifts his whole body to face me. "Well, it's hard to say. Well, no, it's not that hard. But you're going to think I'm, like, ridiculous or something."

I shake my head. "I won't."

He bites both his lips, and when he releases them, they're a pretty shade of pink. "There are some things you can't just explain normally, with normal words. Like, you know how sage smells really strong when it gets wet? But what I just said now, that description of it, doesn't even begin to cover that experience of smelling wet desert sage."

I shake my head. "I don't get it."

"Here." He leaves the room and returns with a notebook, shutting the door gently behind him. "Sounds like they're still . . . you know."

"Noah," I warn.

"Okay, okay," he says, flipping open the book. He begins to read. "Sage after rain is a woman, rising in smoke, draped in ice green, warm and sweet to touch." He shrugs. "It's a first draft and totally crappy but—"

"No," I say, touching his arm. He looks down at my fingers. "I like that. That's—that's exactly what it's like. Smelling wet sage. I didn't realize it until now."

Then he smiles, eyes crinkled, dimples all out. His lips still pretty pink.

131

I BEND MY LEGS, ONE OVER EACH SIDE OF HIS WAIST, as I kiss him. He puts his hands on my hips, his fingers in the elastic waistband of my black boyshorts.

I bite his bottom lip as I pull back. "Noah." I gesture to his hands. "There's no way you're as scared of my father as you act."

He smiles. "I am. I just. I just want to touch you more." He drops his hands to my thighs. "Is it okay?"

I look at his eyes, at the bits of green and gold and bronze in them. "Yes."

He kisses me again, slipping his hand into my boyshorts.

132

PEOPLE CALL THIS *COMING* **AND I THINK IT WORKS. IT**
feels like I dissolve into a new creation, one I don't get a good enough
look at before I *come* back, here, on my bed, where I collapse on Noah.
It seems to take forever to get me there, but he doesn't care at all, and he
happily threads his fingers through my hair afterward.

After I catch my breath, I run my hand over him, over the pajamas.
He stiffens.

"Is this okay?" I say softly.

He nods and groans when I do it again. He puts his hand on mine.
"Sia, I don't want you to do this just because I—I mean, you don't have
to, okay? I won't be mad at all."

I tug his pants low, staring at his face as his breathing gets even more
labored. "I want to," I say. "I'm not going to look at it, okay? But—" I
grab him and he's so hot and so hard.

His eyes roll back and he snaps them back on me. "You're sure? I
mean. You're absolutely sure?"

"Yes." I grip even tighter and his whole body twitches. "Tell me how
you like this. Okay?"

But thirty seconds in, my body freezes and I want to scream. Not at Noah, not at his arms or hips or heat, but at myself for being such a fuck-up, and at Justin, wherever the flip he is now, for fucking me up to start with.

Before I can say anything about it, Noah tugs my hand away.

"It's okay," he says, pulling me to his chest. "It's okay, it's okay. It's okay."

133

I PUT MY HAND ON NOAH'S RIBS TO PUSH MYSELF UP,
and he winces. "What's wrong with you?" I ask. "What happened to your—"

"It's from when Jeremy hit me," Noah says quickly. Too quickly.

He lets me lift his shirt and I gasp. A constellation of bruises are gathered on his torso. Fresh ones. "These aren't from Jeremy. I was there. He only hit your face."

Noah says nothing. He's trembling.

"It was your dad, wasn't it?"

Noah doesn't respond. He doesn't need to.

"Does your mom know?"

He shakes his head.

"Let me take photos. For her lawyer. For her case, Noah."

Noah nods slowly. We make short work of it. The getting his shirt off, the lighting. I kind of want to vomit when I get close-ups of the purple and blue and black. There's even a handprint. I want to wipe it all away. Like it's paint.

I'm tearing up when we're done. "Shit, Noah."

He shrugs and lies back down. "You know, it's so weird, but I don't hate him. Because while he was doing it, he was saying things like, *You think this is bad? You should've seen my daddy on a Tuesday night. You think this is bad? You're not going to the hospital over this.* And I just felt bad for him. Afterward, he cried, Sia. And went in his room, slammed the door. And I couldn't help but feel bad for him." Noah looks right in my eyes. "How shitty, you know, to become the person you hate? And then have no idea how to stop."

"He could stop," I say. "We all have choices in who we are."

"Yeah," Noah says. "I know. And I'm not saying he's been a great dad afterward or anything. I mean, I've been living in my car pretty much since." Noah closes his eyes. "I just wish he would change. Because you're right. He could. But he won't." And then Noah wipes his cheeks where they're all wet now.

And now I'm the one holding him. I hold him and I kiss him. I kiss every bruise on his chest and belly and hips until he's shivering. I want to make him feel good, like he's done for me a thousand times, so I run my hands all over, and after whispering *are you sure* a dozen times, he holds my hand still where he's the hardest, over his clothes, and I run my fist up and down and down and up. And afterward, when he's cleaned up and so relaxed, almost boneless, really, I hold him some more. My arms are still tight around him when I fall asleep.

134

WHEN I WAKE UP, NOAH'S GONE, BACK ON THE LIVING
room sofa, I guess. The light reaching through the window is so deep
it's purple, and the edges of it are soft like fur. I throw my arm down,
picking up yesterday's jeans off the floor. I pluck a piece of paper from
the back pocket. Noah's handwriting is blocky and small, but I can read
it alright, even in these shadows.

135

Sia,

I know I said I'd find you a poem, but I hope it's okay that I wrote you one instead.

Noah

Blue

You told me the universe came from a woman
who longed for touch. And I think that beginning
was blue. Blue like the wild violet of an ocean
filled with the most mysterious things. Blue
because blue was the color of the whole desert
when we touched that night. Blue
because that night felt like another beginning,
like the sea became a desert and the desert
became a sea. Blue because a new blue
universe came from me falling for you.

136

I WISH NOAH WERE HERE NOW SO I COULD KISS AND kiss and kiss him. Instead I reread the poem until I feel like he is here, in my arms again, my head on his shoulder. . . . *the sea became a desert and the desert / became a sea.* The words lull me back to a rainstorm sleep.

137

ROSE COMES INTO THE ROOM WHEN THE LIGHT IS BRIGHT, singing something about Sleeping Beauty.

"No," I grumble, putting a pillow on my head.

"My mom had me bring over breakfast, Sia, and if you're not fast enough, Noah's gonna finish off the plantains."

I force my torso upright. "He wouldn't do that to me."

"Well, if he doesn't, that UFO boy might."

I lean back against the back of the sofa part of the cot. "Shit, I just got dizzy." And then her words hit me. "Shit, Omar's here?"

"Yep." She hands me a coffee from our favorite shop. It's wonderfully warm.

"Toasted coconut?" I ask.

"Always." She smiles. "Omar's weird, huh?"

I snort. "You're telling me."

"He totally hit on me when he walked in."

"No!"

"Yes. He did. Asked me if I wanted to be taken out of this world." She laughs and claps her hands.

"Really?" I grimace. "You shut that down, though, right?"

"Of course."

She's perched on the edge of the mattress, wearing a bronze jumpsuit, long-sleeved and tied with a sash.

"Is that one of your mom's seventies outfits?"

"Nah. I made this while we were staying with Meena and the kids."

"Holy cow, Rose. You're amazing. And that looks amazing on you."

"You like it?" She stands and twirls, her twists up in a ponytail and swinging along with her.

I nod and give her a half smile. "How's Samara?"

She immediately plops down on the bed again. "She's—" Rose breaks into a smile. "She's, you know. Smart. Funny. Sweet."

"She a good kisser?"

"Shh," Rose hisses, looking around. "We've only done it once, okay? But God Almighty." She leans back on the bed with her hand on her head. "Sia. I felt it in my heels, my toes, the tips of my fingers! It was so . . ." She sighs and angles her face my way. "Is that what it's like with Noah?"

I take a sip of coffee and smile. "Yes. It's just like that."

138

MRS. DAMAS SENT SOME OUTFITS FOR ME AND MOM along with the food. Well, Dad, too, but he refuses to wear Cruz Damas's casual wear of Hawaiian short-sleeved button downs and cargo shorts. I actually don't mind such a dad-ish wardrobe for Dad, but Luis Martinez prefers to dress like a lumberjack on any given day. He insists he's good with several sprays of Febreze on his flannels and jeans, which, ew, Dad, come on, but whatever.

When I finally sit down to breakfast, I'm wearing high-waisted, huge-belled gray corduroys and a burnt orange button-down that I tuck in. Mom's in an olive dress, one that reaches her toes, with large pockets sewn at the chest and hips. She takes a long look at me and Rose with a grin. "We look like Charlie's Angels."

"Ugh," Rose says. "I hate that show."

"Really?" Mom asks. "Why?"

I make a face. "Uh, it's the most sexist thing we've ever watched?"

Mom groans. "God, I haven't seen one in forever. I don't remember that."

I roll my eyes. "Rose forced us to watch YouTube clips so she could sketch their outfits."

"Well, in my defense, their style was always slammin'."

At that moment, Dad walks in. "Ah," he says, chuckling. "Charlie's Angels, eh?"

"That's what I said." Mom laughs.

"You two need a better reference," I say, rolling my eyes, when the scent of desert lavender and oak envelopes the room. It's so fast and sharp it cuts into me, and from the looks of it, Mom's freaked out, too.

"Mom?" I say, looking at her wide eyes.

"Kids, to la iglesia," she says, grabbing a hammer. "Abuela says they're here."

139

ROSE, NOAH, AND I RUSH OUT THE DOOR, TOWARD THE
church.

"Hold up," Omar says right behind us. "Wait for me!"

People are pouring out the front, saying their farewells to the priest.
We push through the side door.

Before I walk inside, I glance back at the safe house. The front driveway is filled with black vans. They look like beasts.

140

THE ACOUSTICS IN THE CHURCH AMPLIFY THE SOUNDS
of our scamper. I glance around as we go. There's only one old lady in a
black mantilla praying up front. I turn and follow Rose and Noah to the
staircase in the back, which leads to the sound room.

"What's the plan?" Omar asks before I can ascend.

I turn to tell him to shut up, but then someone calls my name. Noah
stops mid-flight and looks at me. "Just go," I whisper. "You, too, Omar. It's
probably Andreah Lopez." She's the only woman I know who wears a veil
to church. "Let me tell her to get outta here before all hell breaks loose."
Noah and Omar nod and I turn around and walk through the threshold.

Shit. The woman is not Andreah Lopez. Shit, shit, shit. It's the
creeper lady from the diner.

This can't be good.

"Sia?" the silver-haired woman repeats, walking toward me.

I feel my grandmother's presence at my side. *No la dejes que se acerque
a ti.* Don't let her get close. I almost feel Abuela's breath on my ear and
I suppress a shiver at her words.

"Do I know you?" I take a step back.

She shakes her head. "No, no, I wouldn't say so. But I know an awful
lot about you."

"From spying on me and my friends?"

She smiles. "Not quite."

There's something totally off about this woman and I can't touch it yet. She stops, tilting her head slowly, assessing me. She wears a form-fitting pantsuit the color of champagne, which looks incredible with her cool umber complexion. On any other day, I'd be complimenting her style, bringing Rose out to see this lady's outfit, but right now, I'm just creeped the shit out.

"You look exactly like your mother," she says, smiling almost sadly. It's something I've heard exactly one thousand times before, but there's something deeper in her voice, like she's talking about someone else, someone who's brought her nothing but heartache.

But just like that, though, she's left memory lane. Her eyes narrow and she walks toward me, her hips swinging.

"I'm sure you've heard the whole story by now." Her voice is lovely, in all honesty. She'd be a soprano in the choir. "The big, bad government, abducting illegal residents, performing torturous experiments, all for some hateful end." She sighs and has a seat in the pew, crossing a slim leg. "And I'm supposed to tell you, no, they're not. They're saving them from a gruesome desert death. They're curing diseases." She looks off into the distance. "Does it really matter, though?" She stares at me and waits.

"You're asking me if it matters whether people are being tortured or cured?"

She gives me a smile. "Do you know how many people your mother killed to get here?" She makes air quotations at the word *mother*. "To get to you? And all for nothing. Pity, really."

"You don't sound very sorry at all." My hands clasp around the only weaponlike object that's near me, the iron incense holder hung on the wall.

rugs. "Ah, you're right. I stopped giving a damn a long time
t your lot." She pats her silvery waves with her hand as she
erself to standing. "Thousands," she announces, arms stretched
theatrically. "That's how many people failed the experiment. One. That's
how many didn't."

"Zero," I respond, swinging the metal in my hands. "That's how
many fucks I give about your shitty monologue."

Before I can finish, before I can even blink, the woman is at my side,
traveling all of thirty feet in a fraction of a second. The only indication
of any movement at all is the wind that hits my hair. And her hand at
my throat.

"I was so close," she says, and there are tears in her eyes as I choke
in her grasp. "I was so close to it being over. All of it. The waiting,
the experiments. But then Magdalena Martinez had to come along. So
strong. So pretty." As she speaks, I grab her, chop at her, lunge, and kick.
I try to swing the iron at her head, but she's too fucking fast, and I'm
wheezing, my eyes wide on her as I wave my arms like an octopus. "And
that human out there? The one who looks just like her with her long,
golden hair, her dreamy brown eyes?" She snarls as her grip tightens.
"That's not even your mother, Sia. That's not even—"

There's a clank as Rose snaps the woman in the head with a bronze crucifix. She goes flying, letting go of my neck, and I fall to the ground coughing,
glancing up in time to see Rose drop-kick her into the pews. The woman's
unmoving. After a few seconds, Rose turns to me. "You good, Sia?"

I nod, clearing my throat. "Thanks, Rose," I say. My voice sounds
cracked open.

"Thanks be to Jesus," Rose says as she lifts the crucifix back up and
places it on the wall.

141

"SIA!" NOAH COMES RUNNING DOWN THE STAIRS AND reaches me. "God," he says, putting the tips of his fingers on my neck.

Omar's just behind him. "Who the hell was that?"

"No idea," I mutter. My voice feels like it's made of broken asphalt.

"Please tell me you got it to work," Rose says to Noah, walking up, keeping her eyes on the woman's body.

"I think so. But they, Sia, when we got there, they'd already been around. They freaking fried the surveillance system. Everything is toast, except for one old camera. I hooked up the adapter to the older monitor, we started recording somewhere between her, you know, admitting she doesn't care about people living or not and trying to choke you to death." He exhales, his breathing hurried. "God, I'm so glad you're okay. And Rose," he says, turning around. "Remind me to never cross you."

"I wouldn't mind crossing her," Omar mutters, scribbling notes.

I grab his notebook and slam it shut. "Hey!" he yelps.

"You don't get to be pervy," I say, shoving his papers into his chest. "Especially with what we're going through right now. Got it?"

"Yeah, yeah, okay. Sorry," he says to Rose, who ignores him.

"Did you get the footage, Noah?" Rose's eyes are still on the woman.

Noah gives a half shrug. "I put it, if we did get it, I put the file on my flash drive. I'll have to check it later."

The doors of the church are thrown open, and two well-suited men are flung inside, followed by my parents.

"Just say it," Dad screams. "Say that there's been nonconsensual experimentation on people out there."

"We keep telling you," the blond one says, on the floor, his arms out. His nose is bloodied. "We were only told to apprehend and recover."

The dark-haired man stands, buttoning his jacket. "You!" my dad says, turning to him. "I know you know something."

"What I know, Mr. Martinez, is that you and your wife have assaulted a dozen or so agents of the United States. I'm within legal bounds to arrest you immediately."

"Oh, yeah? How are you gonna do that? She's taken your guns, your—" He's cut off by the gasp of my mother, who stares at the silver-haired woman.

"We need to get out of here, Luis," Mom says. Her face is pale and her eyes are wild.

"What is it?" Dad looks around. "What happened here?"

"Who is she?" Rose asks Mom, pointing at the woman.

"That's—" Mom pauses. "You know how I said there's no single Voldemort? Well, I changed my mind. Her right there, she's Voldemort." She looks up at us, raw fear in her eyes. "Which means we've got to *move*. Ahora."

142

WE'RE UP FRONT WHEN ROSE PULLS UP WITH ONE OF
the teal choir vans. "Ladies and gents," she says, rolling down the window. "Take a seat, will you?"

We run up, Noah's hand in mine. Omar takes the front seat, my dad hops in the way back. Mom and I scramble into the middle. As Noah pulls off his backpack, we hear a yell. I turn and see Cruz Damas walking up, his fist in the air.

"What do you think you're doing, Rose Sarah Damas?" he yells. "You get out of that car right now, or so help me God . . ."

Rose is frozen, but her brown eyes meet mine for a split second. "You don't have to do this," I tell her. "You could give me the keys."

She shakes her head. "I'm not staying." She repeats it for Mr. Damas. "I'm not staying, Daddy. God wants us to love our neighbors as ourselves? That's what I'm doing." We're all inside now and she hits the gas. When we pass him, he's jumping up and down, screaming, the veins on his head bulging. I give him a cheerful wave.

143

"NO OFFENSE, LENA," ROSE SAYS AS SHE TURNS TO THE highway, "but that woman wasn't quite on Voldemort level. Didn't take much to knock her out, I mean."

"It didn't take much for her to just about wring my neck, either," I say, putting my hand on my throbbing throat.

"The government—those scientists—drugged her for years. She must still be weak." Mom twirls a lock of hair in her hand, something she's always done when she's thinking. "But that one in particular, she's—" Mom pauses, closing her eyes as if in prayer. "She's dangerous. I can't believe they let her out." She glances at my neck. "And she's getting desperate, from the looks of it."

"What do you mean? What the hell is she?" I say as we slow. Up ahead, there's a line of cars.

Mom bites her lip. "I don't know if you'd believe me, m'ija. But she's not—she's not like us."

"Mom. Explain. Please. I mean, she attacked me. I have a right to know."

And of course, this is when Omar has to butt in with his highly necessary commentary. "She's a Nordic, isn't she? The blonde lady? I knew it, I knew from the second she went superspeed like you! I mean, 'cause of the light hair, I thought she might've been a Flatwoods monster at first, but she's way too hot for that. She's gotta be from the fucking Pleiades. The Pleiades, you hear that Noah?"

"Sorry to interrupt," Noah says. "Because, yeah, I really do want to hear more about the Pleiades. But up there? That security checkpoint is even tighter than TSA. They'll search the vehicle. For sure."

I narrow my eyes at all the men in SWAT team uniforms, holding massive guns. "What the hell are they playing at? I thought they wanted you alive, Mom."

"They do," Mom says. But even she sounds unsure.

Rose clears her throat. "Guys, do you want me to turn around, or—"

"No." Mom crawls over the console, nudging Noah to the side so she can sit by me. "I'm gonna do something when we get close. No one panic, okay?"

"What the fuck are you doing, Lena?" Dad says, his hand on her shoulder.

"You won't see us for a few seconds. But act normal." She turns to me. "You ready, mamita?"

144

I HAVE NEVER WONDERED WHAT IT'S LIKE TO BE A shadow. Before today, I might have thought it was like becoming a piece of paper, all flattened and weightless, getting knocked around by even the gentlest wind.

But as Mom grabs my hand, we, suddenly, are nothing like flesh or paper. We become liquid, spilled across the car seats.

It's like I've become everything I'm not. And as I sense the fabric of the seat I'm poured upon, I know there are universes in each and every stitch.

I'm vaguely aware of Rose telling the officer that she's driving us out to practice at St. Matthew's. I know his eyes reach over the space where we were, where there is nothing but the back seat, all a shade darker now. He opens the back, moves some equipment around with the barrel of his gun next to my father. He slams the door shut with a nod and lets us go.

145

WHEN WE SLAP BACK TO OUR BODIES, I FEEL LIKE I'M
going to vomit. I take deep breaths and count the cacti out the window
until the sensation passes.

Mom's worse off. Her skin is gray and she's hyperventilating.

"Lena, what do you need?" My dad's hands are all over her.

"Water," my mom says with a whisper.

We search the car, come up with a half-full plastic bottle. Mom
downs it and requests more.

"Holy fucking shit," Omar says. "You went into invisibility mode
and I didn't even have my phone out! Can you do that again, Mrs.
Martinez?"

"Look, kid," Dad says. "I get that Lena wants you to document
this. But you need to shut the hell up and help me find more water.
Now."

Omar gulps, nodding, and they check under the car seats. Pero nada.

Mom still looks sick, weak, and wilted in Dad's arms.

"We'll hit the gas station in about ten minutes," Rose says.

146

WHEN ROSE AND I FIRST HAD MILKSHAKES AT MAUDE'S by ourselves, no parents, I looked around and whispered, "We're the only brown people here."

Rose looked at me very carefully before responding, "Sia. You and I are very different shades of brown."

When we got our licenses for the first time, I started to see what she meant. Rose gets pulled over three times more often than I do when we're just trying to make our way to school. Once, when taking a walk in downtown Phoenix, a rotted-cigar-smelling seventy-year-old man grabbed her ass and growled, "Not bad for a negro."

Yeah, I know all that shit went down with my mom and the McGhees and I've been called *spic* and *razorback* and *wetback* a lot. But when Rose and I split up at stores, she's the one who's followed.

That's precisely what happens when she and I make our way through the gas station, grabbing water and protein bars and fruit and chips. The tall bald man at the register jumps up and breathes down her neck the whole time. And you know what? I just can't take this crap right now.

"Can I help you with something?" I ask him.

He blinks at me and sort of slows his walk. "You all find what you're looking for?"

"We're fine. We don't need assistance or a chaperone. Got it?"

The man stares, openmouthed.

"Sia," Rose warns beneath her breath.

The bells to the front door chime before I can respond. I turn. It's Omar.

"Do they have any Twizzlers?" he asks.

I shrug, keeping Racist Raymond in my peripheral vision. "I don't know. Find them yourself." I turn and furrow my brow. The clerk's stopped stalking Rose, but now his eyes are narrowed right on Omar. The veins in his neck look like puffy state lines.

The clerk marches right up to Omar and shoves him with a pink, pale hand to the shoulder.

"What the hell!" Omar yells.

"We don't have any Twizzlers and especially not for you." The man takes two long steps toward Omar, until Omar can probably smell his nasty Red Bull breath.

"That's not really an answer, man," Omar says, wringing his hands.

"God in heaven," Rose murmurs behind me. The man pushes Omar until he's right on the front door.

"You can't just push a kid around like that!" I say. "Stop touching him."

"There," the man says, ignoring me, pointing at a piece of paper taped to the window. NO SERVICE FOR TERRORIST, it reads. Seriously. Whoever wrote it couldn't even be bothered to make it grammatically correct.

"I'm an American citizen," Omar says. Even from here, I can tell he's shaking. "I was born here."

"You all think you're gonna change us. Change America. Well, you're not. So get out before I grab the revolver behind my—"

"Jesus Christ!" I yell. "Leave him alone!"

Now Racist Raymond turns to me.

"Get out," I tell Omar, but he shakes his head emphatically.

"You need to go, too," the man says. "Before I call ICE on your pretty ass."

"Oh, for fuck's sake." I try to make my voice hard, but he's getting closer. I close my eyes, searching for a prayer. Which saint is the one for teenagers who can't get a fucking break thanks to old, pathetic assholes like this guy?

But there's a crash and I jump back.

Omar's kicked the jerk's knees from behind, and now the man thrashes on the ground.

But Rose kicks him back down as he tries to get up. "Come on, Sia," she screams. "We gotta move!"

We all run for the door, our arms full of unpaid merchandise. And, unwise as it may be, I actually stop for a split second to grab a jumbo pack of Twizzlers on the way out. I mean, what the hell.

I flash both middle fingers at the store as we leap into the van.

147

"WHERE ARE WE GOING?" ROSE ASKS WHEN WE GET back in. Her voice is still at a scream.

"What happened?" Dad asks, but now I see Racist Raymond stomping out with his revolver.

"Rose, just go!" I yell.

She slams on the gas and we're back on the road, a cloud of dust behind us.

"Keep going this way, Rose," Dad says. "We're going to Liana's."

"Abuela's?" I say. Mom's gulping water as she nods. I settle back in my seat and she takes my hand. "Makes sense," I say. I'm still breathless.

"Sia. What the hell just happened?" Dad asks again.

I lean back, still catching my breath. Noah puts a hand on mine. Finally, I turn toward Dad. "The same old fucking shit."

148

BEFORE I CAN FINISH THE STORY, OMAR DENOTATES.
He was shaking so much, I thought he'd, like, need to punch at the walls
and chairs with his fists, maybe yell. But no. He erupts with tears. The
kind that you're so freakin' furious you can't hold in. I'm very familiar
with the sort. He swipes at his face so hard to wipe them away, it's like
he's slapping himself.

My mother cautiously, slowly, leans into him, hand on his shoulder,
the same shoulder that old white man had pushed. And Omar melts
into her, his whole body convulsing.

"They're the reason," Omar chokes, "my mom can't even go to the
grocery store without being called a terrorist. And she's a veteran, man!
Fought her ass off in Afghanistan."

I put my hand on his, my fingertips resting on his nails. His skin is
so smooth.

"People suck," I say. "All of them."

He gives me a half smile. Chin lined with tears. And red, red eyes.

149

WHEN RUMORS CAME OUT THAT MIGRANT CHILDREN were being taken from their mamis, their papis, put in cages like zoo animals, with no windows, and, for days at a time, no food, the white people couldn't believe it. I guess when your skin is light enough, you get to cast the benefit of the doubt like a spell or something. I bet it helps them sleep easy at night, that white witchcraft.

We knew better. We knew because we have cousins and mamis and tíos and abuelos and amigos who picked tomatoes and strawberries and avocados, who were chained or sprayed with things that made their babies come out without their jaw bones. Beaten, raped, treated worse than perros. We knew those white people never, ever gave a shit about us or our children. We knew better.

And as I watch the crisp line of sand and sky, I think about those babies on the border, locked up, dreaming about Mami's milk, crying so hard they can't breathe. And all the people out there, defending it. Saying those bebitos are getting what they deserve.

I don't know what it's gonna take to make them care about brown people if they treat brown babies like that, you know?

Sometimes I imagine the return of Jesus. Imagine the look on their faces when they see his skin, browner than juniper and drift-wood and hot summer sandstorms. The day they realize God looks more like us is the day they become atheists, one by one, as though they ever believed in the love of Christ to start with.

150

"GOOD GOD," ROSE SAYS. "THERE'S A COP BEHIND US."

We all whip our heads around, jumping when we hear that little beep-beep of a siren.

"Calm down," Dad says. "Just act normal, Rose."

I've know Rose's dad has made a point to tell her a hundred times what to do if a cop pulls her over. This is how I know, deep down, that he does love her. I can hear his commands now. Put the license and registration on the dash, hands on the wheel, high, so they can be seen from the window. Move slowly. Make your voice nice and gentle. There might be more, but I kind of tune Cruz Damas out after about four minutes, no matter the topic. Dad has said similar warnings to me, along with the command, *Don't ever let the police hear you speak Spanish. No matter how brown they look.*

Despite all those lectures, Rose seems completely freaked now. "What do I do?"

"Pull over." Dad's holding Mom against him, covering her face.

"I bet that asswipe at the store called them," Omar mutters.

We're parked now. I glance up—Rose's hands are high. Everything is on the dash. I'm glad she's got her wits back.

"Mom," I say. "Can you make us like shadows again?"

"I can't, m'ija. I'm too weak." She coughs and sips water. "They didn't just give me powers, you know. They messed me up."

"With the experiments?" Dad looks so worried, I want to hug him.

Mom shrugs. "Well, the experiments didn't exactly end when it turned out I was a success."

"Jesus Christ," Noah says, whipping his face toward us. His skin is green. "It's my dad."

151

SHERIFF MCGHEE WALKS AS THOUGH HE'S THE MASTER

of the universe—legs widened, stride slow, shoulders back. I don't get it. He looks like a hairless pug, with the same depth of vocabulary. What's all that confidence for?

He leans on his hip in front of Rose's window and lifts his aviators. "I got a call about a disturbance at the Silverline Mini-Mart gas station." He narrows his eyes in the sun. "The owner said he was assaulted by a couple of, uh—" He glances at Rose again. "License and registration."

As she slides the items toward him, slowly, just like her papi told her, McGhee scans the van. His eyes widen over my father. And then they bug the fuck out over Noah.

"What the hell are you doing here, son?" McGhee snarls. "Out. Now."

Noah glances at me, and back. "No."

"Son." The sheriff is all pink now, huffing like the Big Bad Wolf. "Don't you make me get you out. That'll be all sorts of trouble for you . . . and your friends."

"Don't threaten him," Dad says, his jaw so sharp, I feel like he could cut McGhee right up with it if he wanted.

"Keep your mouth shut! Or I'll shut it myself, Martinez."

"Do you beat your other son, too? Or just this one?" Dad holds his stare, and the sheriff actually blinks in surprise. Shit.

"I don't like your tone," McGhee says, his fingers grazing his gun. "You'll be sorry if you don't shut up, I'll tell you that much." He turns to Noah. "Get out. Now."

With shaking hands, Noah unbuckles his seat belt. He reaches for the door handle, but McGhee is already there, tearing it open, grabbing Noah by the neck and pulling him out. He's muttering something like, "Fucking spic lover."

Noah tumbles into the sand. And shit, Sheriff McGhee looks gleeful. He's actually happy about his own son falling on rocks. Straight-up venom right there.

But then the sheriff's gaze falls on my mother. His smile drops as though the sun melts it right off. "Who the hell is that?" he barks.

Mom lifts her head, her hair parting away from her face. "It's me, settler." Then she lunges.

He releases Noah, whose hands are pushing his father at the hips. McGhee's hands, meanwhile, are now on his gun, but Mom kicks him backward before he can whip it out. Thank God.

McGhee scrambles up. "For years I've been blamed for this illegal's death and you've just been hiding here, this whole time? Just like the lazy spic you are."

Dad jumps out just as McGhee pulls Mom down, hard, smashing her face against the rocks. Now the gun is out, and, Jesus, it's pointed right at my mother. "Don't you take another step," he tells my father. "Or I'll blow her brains to bits."

"Put the gun down," I say. My voice is all shards of glass. "Please."

"Get in the car," McGhee yells at Dad. He lowers the gun an inch, shifting its angle just a touch, just enough. Because then he's convulsing, screeching like an owl. He collapses. And Noah stands behind him, taser in hand.

Mom's up, kicking the gun away, brushing the sand off the blood on her face. Dad's already on her, hands on her hair, her chin, her back.

Noah lifts his finger from the trigger, and McGhee starts screaming. "You'll pay for that, you fucking piece of—"

There's an audible slap as Dad punches McGhee right on the temple. The sheriff's hands fall limp to the ground.

We say nothing for a moment. Everyone's breathing heavy.

"Is—is he dead?" Omar asks.

"No. Just knocked him out," Mom responds. "Noah. Luis. Put him in his car."

"Should leave him out here to rot?" Dad says, and Noah grunts in agreement.

"Now," Mom says. And they carry the sheriff away. Like the shit that he is.

152

WHEN WE'RE BACK ON THE ROAD, I CAN'T STOP MY hands from trembling. I feel like my skin is trying to run, crawl, be somewhere else. Somewhere where mothers don't get guns pointed at their heads, where the police actually want us to live, to be safe. I lean into Noah and I want to cry. I want to so bad, but instead, I count the arms of the saguaros outside. Some of them bloom, their white flowers like crowns. Like a thousand bones in the sand and sun.

153

WE'RE ALL SILENT FOR ABOUT TEN MINUTES AS WE drive farther into nowhere.

"Is everyone okay?" Dad asks. It's kind of a ridiculous question. 'Cause none of us are. Not at all. But everyone sort of hums back at him in the affirmative. Noah's tapping on his kneecaps, increasing the speed until his hands blear.

"You okay?" I finally say, even though Dad just asked. I slip a hand into his, slowing them down.

He stares at me before glancing at Mom. "Uh—well. Yeah." He nods. "Actually, this might be weird timing, but I was wondering if it was okay to ask—what the heck just happened, when you two, like, disappeared?"

"Invisibility mode," Omar says. He's still sniffling.

"Yeah, Lena," Rose says, eyeing us in the rearview mirror. "Scared me half to death with that."

I wonder if it's weird that it doesn't even seem all that weird of an event to me. I'd nearly forgotten it, even. I turn to Mom, who looks worlds better. She smiles lazily at my Dad, who's touching her hair. "What was that, Mom? You, like, made me . . . empty."

She takes a breath. "For a very short period of time, I can become a shadow. I can do it to objects, people." She glances at Dad. "Knocks the wind out of me, though."

"You didn't tell us about that one," Noah says. "How come?"

Mom glances out her window. Outside, the sun pierces my eyes so badly, it hurts. I look back at her.

"I don't want *them* to know everything. It will make them do drastic things. And they're already getting desperate." She puts her fingertips on my neck. "It's possible, likely even, that they will see the interview since you put it on social media."

"Do you think that was enough?" Rose asks. "That white-haired woman's confession."

"That woman," Mom says, drawing out the word slowly. "Her name is Katia. I thought details from her mouth would work, until I remembered . . ." She bites her lips. "God, I'm such a fool. I don't know if there's any records of her anywhere. Birth certificate, social, W-2 forms. If not, we're in trouble. They'll just say they don't know who she is."

"Should've let me beat it out of those assholes," Dad grumbles.

"That would look worse," Mom says. "Then they'd say they were tortured into lying. No. We gotta do this a different way."

"Which way?" I ask.

Mom looks back out the window. "I'm praying on it, m'ija."

154

AFTER A BIT, ROSE TURNS TO A DIRT ROAD SO infrequently used, it just looks like part of the desert. She slows, the van bouncing over rocks and divots. After about three and a half miles, we see a tin trailer nestled in a spot of Joshua and juniper trees.

"Can't believe you didn't sell that piece of crap," Mom murmurs to my father.

"No one wanted it," he laughs, but that's not true. I begged Dad to leave it, to leave everything as it was, because when I turn seventy-five, I'm going to move into it and live just like my grandmother did, with handkerchiefs tied in my hair while wearing long, embroidered dresses, coaxing things to grow in the desert that were never meant to.

Rose pulls up, turning the van off. A cloud of dust pops up as we each get out, the soles of our shoes scraping rocks that point out like teeth.

"Your grandma lives here?" Noah asks, his eyes squinting in the white sunlight.

"Lived. She died last year."

"Oh," Noah says, his nose scrunched. "I thought you said she, like, puts freshener in your car. Like she was still actively doing that."

"She still visits us. She always brings that perfume when she does."

"Huh." Noah's brow stays furrowed when we walk inside Abuela's house.

Inside, everything is untouched. Braids of garlic and peppers hang over the tiny gas stove. Pillows surround a low round table next to the kitchen—the "dining room." Bouquets of herbs swing from the living room roof, tied in twine. Candles line every windowsill—Guadalupes, Madre Marias, Jesus Cristos, saints dotted between them.

"Someone's been here," Noah says, pointing at the dining table. On its center, a tiny cup holds a little water for the handful of desert sunflower. Mom's favorite.

"It's Abuela," I say. "She put that out for Mom."

Mom approaches the table, sitting on one of the cushions. She touches the gold petals, and tears river her face. "I miss her. I wish she were here."

Then I feel Abuela all around us.

Spirit language is different from ours. It's uncivilized. But I know what she's saying, and Mom does, too.

I'm here.

155

"OKAY, HERE WE ARE." MOM'S MIXED SOME OF Abuela's dried comfrey, all boiled up, with cocoa butter, and she rubs it into my neck. I wince. Earlier, in the bathroom, I'd gotten a good look at what that Katia did to me. The spots on each side correspond with her skinny fingers. It makes me hate her. Not that I was fond of her to begin with.

That's not even your mother, she'd said.

I watch Mom closely. Everything looks right. Her high cheekbones, her sunset-gold eyes. The lines in her neck, the scars on her knuckles. Even the way she curses Katia as she slathers the foul-smelling balm on my throat.

"Oi," Rose says, walking in with our gas station bags. "You think we could get that fire pit in the back going again?"

"I don't know about staying out, Rose. Might not be safe," Dad says.

"What about the wood-burning stove? I really need to roast these marshmallows, Mr. Martinez. We've been through a lot, you know, and I believe stress-eating is in order."

Dad gives her a long smile. He's always been fond of Rose, since we were little. "Don't see why not." Dad stands. "I'll see if there's any wood in the shed. Noah, come. Omar, you too. Help."

Omar nods. "No problem."

Noah jerks his head up. "Uh—sure. Okay, Mr. Martinez." He jumps up, snapping his fingers, and follows them out.

Rose snorts when the door slams shut. "Is Noah always that nervous?"

"Only around Dad," I respond.

"You make him nervous, too, Sia." Mom raises an eyebrow.

My cheeks heat up before I can stop them. "That's 'cause he's a weird kid."

"Mm-hmm." Mom eyes the pink on my cheeks as she wipes her hands on a towel.

"Oh, please," Rose says, plopping down next to me. "You can't even call him your boyfriend yet?"

"Well. We—" I groan, putting my hands on my head. "We haven't even talked about it, okay?"

"But you've done a lot more than talking," Rose responds and I widen my eyes at her, silently telling her to please, kindly, shut it in front of my mother.

"You're being careful, aren't you, Sia?" Mom asks, hands on her hips.

I groan again, even louder. "I can't believe I'm having this conversation right now."

"You didn't answer the question."

"We haven't—you know—done that, okay? Nothing to be careful over."

"Good." Mom wraps up the ointment in Tupperware. "Because you can't get pregnant until you get your PhD."

"Dad reminded me of that very thoroughly only last week."

"Muy bien. Let's see how the boys are doing, shall we?"

156

"I'M TELLING YOU," NOAH SAYS, PEERING INSIDE THE ancient oven. "I saw it on, like, this survival in the wilderness site. The fire will burn three hours longer if we build it upside down. Right, Omar?"

Omar shrugs. "I guess? Traps the heat and all. But I dunno why we need it to burn for three hours, though, man. For some marshmallows?"

"Exactly." Rose scoffs. "It's going to take three hours just to set it up at the rate you're going."

Mom smiles at me over their scuffle. I can't help it; I grin immediately. She's perched on one of Abuela's sun-faded folding chairs, right in front of the biggest window. Her hair's so close to the color of a distant boulder, it looks as though that rock might be her mother, not Abuela.

I frown for a moment and turn, walking out the door toward Dad, who's restacking the mess of wood near the shed at the side of the trailer. I can't even call it firewood, really. It's just a bunch of branches Abuela picked up on her long evening walks. There's a ton of it, all twisted and gnarled and pointy, giving Dad a hard time.

"Hey," I say.

Dad jerks his head up, blinking. "Ah, mamita. You scared me."

"Sorry."

I hand him one of the twigs near my feet and clear my throat. "So. It's been a wild couple of days, hasn't it?"

Dad grunts something like "Sí" as he snaps one of the branches on his knee. After placing the wood in the rack, he chuckles. "That's putting it mildly, I think."

His eyes don't really go along with his smile. Like he's witnessed the return of Jesus or something, and it's been a lot more stressful than everyone thought it'd be.

I clear my throat. "So, Mom. She seems the same to you, right?"

Dad stops mid-stack, but returns to it a split second later. "¿Que quieres decir?"

I shrug. "I mean, like, she acts the same, talks the same, remembers things all the same. Right?"

Now he just looks at me, so still that I can see the smoke of the kitchen fire in his pupils.

"It's her." He says it firmly, as though he's angry. But then his expression softens and he reaches out, pulling me in his arms.

"You shouldn't be going through all this shit," he says into my hair. "Dios. You're only seventeen."

I don't know what to say. So I just hug him tight in return, willing my eyes to swallow back more tears than there are stars.

157

I ALMOST RUN INTO NOAH BACK INSIDE. "HEY," HE SAYS, wrapping his enormous hands around my hips, steadying me. "You alright?"

"I'm fine," I say, draping my own hands over his. It's amazing. With how chaotic everything's been? Noah still makes my breath a little short.

"What are you smiling about?" I ask, reaching up to lightly touch his dimple.

"We're in a trailer."

I furrow my brow. "So what?"

"We're in a trailer, on the run from top secret government officials?" When I give a blank stare, he widens his eyes. "Just like Max! From *The X-Files?*"

"Oh my God." I hit his arm lightly. "You are such a nerd!"

"Well, I have it on good authority that you're into nerds." He smiles and I flush.

As I walk to the kitchen, his hand in mine, I can't help but frown a bit. I mean, am I the only one who remembers that episode properly? From the beginning, Max knows too much.

And they kill him.

158

"GOD, I LOVE THE SMELL OF BURNING JUNIPER," MOM says, poking a marshmallow with a stick.

"It gives the marshmallows an interesting flavor," Rose muses.

We're all huddled in the kitchen, having just finished a hearty meal of protein bars and potato chips. Now we're onto dessert. I drop my juniper stick—I've only ever been able to handle maybe two roasted marshmallows in a row, at best—and glance beyond the rose-embroidered curtains. The big rocks on the horizon are pulling the sun down, but there's still plenty of light. More important, there are no black vehicles in any direction.

I sit back against Noah and he puts an arm around my waist. Dad clears his throat and Noah drops it, sliding his hand to my back. I just roll my eyes.

"Uh, Mrs. Martinez," Noah says, his voice wobbly. "I've got some questions, if you don't mind." I give him a sideways glance. Will he and Omar ever let up with the questions?

"Me, too!" Omar says, whipping his notebook out. Noah beams and I roll my eyes. Apparently not.

"Sure." Mom smiles before popping a charred marshmallow into her mouth.

But then, with all my judgments, I'm the one asking the first one. "Mom, you said the experiments didn't end after you. That they messed you up. Made you weak. How? What did they do to you?"

Mom swallows. She looks so sad, and I instantly regret saying it. "You don't have to—"

"No," she says. "I want you to know." She nods and closes her eyes. "Uh, well. The first thing that alerted them to something different with me was I didn't die. My organs didn't reject the injection. They didn't stop working, one by one." Dad reaches over and grabs her hand as she continues. "So the first thing they did was hurt me."

"Hurt you?" Dad sounds murderous.

"Broke a few bones. Sliced a few knives in. And the next day or next hour, I'd be healed. After that, they threw me out of two stories. Then four. Then seven. Just to see if I'd make it." Mom shrugs. "I did, barely. And then someone, the ringleader. I forget his name now. It starts with an *A.*" Mom shudders and I get the feeling that she remembers his name exactly, that she just doesn't want to say it. "He got the idea to put me in a warehouse. Huge. They made it up like a jungle."

"And then?" Omar is at the edge of his seat.

"And then they hunted me." Mom slides another marshmallow onto the stick. "That was actually clever of them. It's how they found out about most of what I can do." She looks at me. "The instinct to survive is so strong. Especially when you're doing it for who you love." Mom holds my hand now. "Anyway, that's the story. And I'm a mess now."

"We're going to make them pay," Dad grumbles.

"No," Mom says. "We're going to survive. And we're going to be better, Luis. You hear? Better." She glances at Omar. "So, what else did you want to know?"

159

"THE TECHNOLOGY LOOKS LIKE OUR IDEA OF FUTURISTIC,"
Mom says, leaning back. "But the machinery is . . ." She chuckles,
throwing up her hands like she still can't believe it. "The spacecraft, it's
almost as though it's sentient. It connects to the engineer's motivations,
emotions, thoughts."

"So, it's organic? Biological?" Noah's taking notes in his green notebook, just like he was this morning. Like it's the middle of earth and
space class.

"Not necessarily. At least, not that I could recognize. But you do
need to share their DNA to control the craft. That's why I could. That's
one of the reasons they want to make more of me." She glances at me,
at my legs and feet and hands. Dad's holding her hand in his lap with
both of his.

Noah clears his throat. "Your turn, Sabertooth."

Omar paces, his own notebook in hand. He can only take about two
steps back and forth, it's so cramped, but that doesn't stop him. "Mrs.
Martinez, do you know who killed JFK?"

We all just stare at one another for a good few seconds.

"Right!" Noah jumps in, snapping a couple times. "And who was the Umbrella Man next to JFK? That's what I'd like to know."

"Man, who cares about Umbrella Man?" Omar's waving a hand for emphasis. "So he gave the signal, so what? Badge Man's the one who actually shot him."

"No, that's the thing. Umbrella Man's umbrella had a dart gun in it. That's how Badge Man was able to shoot him to begin with!"

"Fellas," Dad grunts. "Stick with the point, please."

"This is on the point!" Omar raises his eyebrows. "They say Kennedy was about to go public about the alien invasion when he was offed."

"I don't know anything about that, boys," Mom says, smiling. "Sorry."

"Ah, okay." Noah can't hide his disappointment as he glances down at his notes. "So, uhh . . . why did we spot the craft so frequently before you crashed?"

"Well, my plan was to land it wherever Sia was. Especially in the desert, where I could do it without the risk of hurting anyone. But they hadn't fixed it properly. They thought they had, but . . ." She pauses. "That's the thing. That craft I crashed? It was Katia's only way back."

"Hold on," Rose says, pulling her marshmallow back from the flames. "You're saying that woman was an alien?"

Mom nods.

"I told you that, Rose," Omar says. "She's a Nordic, remember?"

Rose ignores him. "You hear that, Sia? I kicked real alien butt."

But my mind is elsewhere. "How did you know I was out there? In the desert?"

Mom smiles. "You know how."

And just like that, my grandmother has a seat between me and

Mom, her red rose skirt rippling in the breeze slicing through windows. She's always been the dramatic one of us.

And now I get why Mom didn't want to tell Omar how she knew where I was. Aliens, government conspiracies, secret experiments. That's all unbelievable enough as it is. No need to add meddling dead abuelas to the mix.

160

ABUELA ALWAYS SAID THERE'S A HIDDEN WORLD INSIDE of this one. That the world we normally encounter is the world of the mind, and it's filled with problems and worries and measurements. But then there's the world of the body. The world where we remember that we are animals, with our instincts whole and accessible, where our nails are claws, our hair, fur, and our hands and feet, padded paws that touch and walk and crawl.

The world of our animal bodies tends to come when we are on the edges of cliffs. When there's a clear pathway between us and death and we've got nothing of this life left but this moment, this breath, the coppery sand beneath our clawed feet.

But it can also happen at the most simple, everyday moments, too. My grandmother said the mind-world split open every time she pushed out a baby and every time she washed the dishes, her nails in water, the sunlight pouring through her windows like milk.

She also said el mundo oculto comes just before an answered prayer or to warn of danger ahead.

As Mom and Noah continue to talk, with Dad and Rose cracking jokes in between, I notice that the flames of the oven fire are so beautiful.

They look like people, dancing, with lilac at their cores. And then I notice that I'm noticing it, that there's nothing but me and a fire, like maybe I am this fire. And I snap out of it quickly, looking at all the windows.

And there, right in the center of indigo-ink clouds, a couple of blue lights appear.

161

WE'RE ALL GATHERED OUTSIDE NOW, WATCHING THE
spacecraft get closer and closer, its blue lights like beams in the foggy sky.

"Get inside," Mom says, standing. "The four of you." Dad pulls a handgun from his pocket.

"Why do you have that?" I say. "They'll shoot you first the second they see it. Jesus!"

"No si los consigo primero," he growls and I roll my eyes.

"Inside," Mom repeats.

"No!" I roll my heels, deepening into the sand.

"Come on, Sia," Rose says. "Don't be ridiculous."

"He's the one being ridiculous with that gun," I yell, loudly enough for my father to hear.

"He wants to protect you," Noah says. His voice is low and on my ear. "Let's go in. Watch from the windows."

I groan and stomp toward the house. Omar's eyes are transfixed on the craft and I don't think he's heard a word of anything we've said. I grab his arm and drag him in as I mutter, "Watch from the windows. Watch my parents die, sounds like a great idea."

Inside, Rose, Omar, and Noah press their noses on the glass, but

I can't. Instead, I decide to pray big time. I light all the candles. Saint Teresita, San Juan, La Guadalupe, Mother Maria, Saint Catherine.

"Sia, what are you doing?" Rose asks. "Get over here. The craft, it's landed." Noah's filming it with his cell.

"It's dark," I respond and resume my impromptu ceremony. Saint Fatima, another Guadalupe, Saint Peter, Saint Francis of Assisi, another Madre Maria, and Jesus on the cross. I count them as I go, whispering, please, God, and there's thirty-three in total, the same age of Christ when folks got together to nail his hands and feet to wooden planks.

I never liked that the Church worshipped such a violent act. My grandmother agreed with me, but she said if Christ hadn't suffered, he wouldn't know resurrection. And that's what it's like for us, too, how every shitty thing to happen to us leads us closer to understanding the point of life on Earth. Or elsewhere, apparently.

"It's a man," Rose breathes. "A man's come out of it."

"A human man?" I rush over.

Rose shrugs. "He's hot."

"Rose!"

"What? Just because I'm probably a lesbian doesn't mean I can't appreciate the male form."

"You're a lesbian?" Noah asks, tearing his eyes away from the window.

"Oh, that's why you kept shooting me down," Omar says, nose on the glass. "You should've told me!"

"Yeah, I'm sure that's the only reason she wasn't interested," I say, snorting.

"Shit, I forgot you two were there," Rose says. She sounds worried.

"I mean, I like boys and girls. I just prefer girls. I mean, just, lately, I prefer girls."

"You don't have to explain yourself," I tell Rose. Turning to the guys, I make my voice hard. "No one else can know. And if either of you say anything disgusting about it, I will literally break the window with your face."

"Come on," Omar says. "I'm not going to say shit."

"Sorry, I just—I just didn't know." Noah's hands are up.

"Why does it matter?" I retort and Rose pats my arm.

"It's okay," she whispers. "Look."

Mom's giving the man a hug, which makes me feel relief and unease at the same time. They turn and make their way toward us.

The man's got skin like amber, dark and rich. His hair is thick and black, and he's got a gray-streaked beard. His eyes give a strange silver glow and I get the feeling he can see things he shouldn't. As if on cue, he directs those eyes right on me, holding his stare way too long to be coincidental. A few seconds later, the door opens and all three walk inside.

162

"RIVER," I REPEAT.

The man nods.

Omar jumps up. "Sabertooth," he says, pushing his chest out and squaring his shoulders. He shakes River's hand aggressively. It's like watching a little kid meet Mickey at Disney World.

I shake my head as Omar steps back as though he's making room for a king. "So, what the hell are you doing here, *River*?" I ask.

He smiles, but it's not the patronizing smile most adults offer when I'm bitchy. The smile, it's warm. Which actually makes it more unnerving.

"Well." He takes a breath, glancing around at us. Dad looks even more suspicious than I feel, but everyone else is politely listening. "They let Katia out."

"We know," I say. "She tried to kill me." I gesture to my neck.

"Sia," Mom says in a please-tone-it-down voice.

The man is furrowing his brow at my neck. "I—they released her on the condition that she bring you back, Sia. I don't understand why she'd try—"

"Maybe because I broke the Selkie," Mom says.

Now River looks shocked. "I hadn't heard it was broken."

"What the fuck is a Selkie?" Dad asks.

"That spacecraft I crashed. I'm sorry," she says to River, her fingertips grazing his hand. Now Dad stares at River like he's planning on tearing his limbs apart.

Mom turns back to us. "River and Katia. They're not . . . from here. Earth."

Now we all whip our heads to River. I mean, him? He's an alien?

There's a prolonged squeaking noise from Omar's direction. "Are you serious?" he whispers.

"You look pretty human to me," Rose finally says.

River laughs. "That's because, in a way, I am human."

"Human, just like the Nordics. I called that! I called that shit!" Omar looks as though he might break into a dance.

Dad's not amused. "What does it matter that the ship broke?"

"It was their only way back home." Mom looks guilty.

River shakes his head. "Look, Lena." My dad bristles at her name on his lips but River just continues. "You know that I never believed we were ever going back. Craft fixed or not—they weren't going to let us go. Ever. But Katia was different."

"She's a mother," Mom says, her voice soft. "Mothers don't give up hope easily."

River seems like he wants to say something, but he stands and looks out the window. "So Katia knows there's no way back now. Not for decades, which is probably how long it'll take to repair the ship."

"It was totaled," Mom says. "Might take even longer than that."

"She was on her last leg of sanity as it was."

"She was fucking out of her mind," Noah says. "What? She was. You were there, Rose. Omar. Sia."

"She was," Rose agrees.

"She's not using her Nordic powers to help humanity at this point," Omar adds. "Must be a traitor, huh?"

Mom sighs. "She also seems to have at least one ability returned. Speed, at least."

"Speed?" River raises an eyebrow.

"You know. Time."

"Time?" Noah asks.

Omar pumps his fists. "Time travel. I knew it! I knew it, Christ on a cracker, I knew it." And now he's actually dancing.

"Look," I say, standing up. "What does this all mean? Will someone explain? You," I say pointing to River. "Explain it. Now. Like I'm five freaking years old."

He gives a half smile. "Explain what?"

"The whole damn story. From the beginning."

163

"HUMANS ON EARTH, AS YOU KNOW THEM, ANYHOW— or as you know yourselves, yes?—arrived thousands of years ago.

"There are so many things we don't know for sure. The exact time of arrival, for one. We don't know why they left our home planet. Moon, I mean." There's pain in his face as he says this.

"A moon on the Pleiades?" Noah asks.

River smiles. "Not quite."

Omar jumps up. "You mean you're not Nordic?!"

River shakes his head. "I'm not certain what you mean by that."

"That's okay," Omar says. "That's fine. Should've known, the Nordics look like the Aryan race. You all are too brown for that. But I think you might still be Nordic, you know. It's the only species that makes sense to me. The one of them that looks human."

I roll my eyes. "Omar, calm down. Please." I turn to River. "So humans left the home moon and what? Migrated here, to Earth?"

River nods. "We don't know why they didn't develop . . . abilities like us." River glances at Mom, and my father tightens his hand around hers.

I take a breath. "What's this got to do with the woman who wants to kill me?"

River nods, glancing down. "Our . . . race has been studying the Earth and its inhabitants for a while. Keeping an eye on our cousins."

"But you were shot down," Mom says.

"Yes. We weren't expecting such an explosion of war technology our last go." He sighs. "Once our feet touched the Earth, we were tranquilized. Couldn't access our powers anymore. Though your government officials had seen enough of our abilities—healing, shadow work—to begin making their greedy plans."

Mom gestures to River's arm, which frames a dozen scars. "They kept you all inebriated for years, right?"

River nods, leaning against a wall, crossing a leg. "Decades."

"So you were captured by the government," Omar says slowly. "Kept as prisoners. Just like the Greys after Roswell, right? Experimented on. Forced to perform experiments."

"Yes." River nods. "About sums it up."

"So there are Greys. You just admitted, the Greys exist, right?" Noah's holding his breath.

River shakes his head. "I haven't personally encountered these Greys you speak of."

"Come on!" Omar slices the air with a fist.

"Relax," Noah murmurs. "Just because he hasn't seen them—"

"Doesn't mean they're not there. I know, I know, man."

"So what now?" Dad barks. "What do we need to know to save Lena and Sia?"

River glances down. "They'll stop at nothing to get them."

"Unless we expose them," Mom says.

I think about brown babies in cages. I don't say it, but I don't know. I don't know if people will care about experiments on immigrants enough to stop anything.

"Katia has . . . ," Mom begins. She's focused on River. "She's getting desperate." It's the second time I've heard Mom describe Katia that way, and each time, her tone makes it seem like it could be the worst thing we're dealing with.

"Yes." River's voice is deep and silky.

"I destroyed your only way back." Mom's eyes are teary.

River looks down again. "Yes."

164

ALMOST EVERY MEXICAN KID HAS HEARD THE TALE OF
La Llorona. My grandmother used to tell it to me so I wouldn't play
alone outside after dark.

La Llorona was a beautiful woman with hair as long and black as
desert shadows. She caught the eye of a wealthy hidalgo and bore him
two sons. She cooked him tamales from the maíz she plucked from her
own gardens and made him huevos con salsa from the eggs of her hand-
raised hens. But he still left her for another woman. A nobler woman.
A whiter, richer woman.

La Llorona blacked out from grief, and when she awoke, her children were missing. She searched all over for them, especially by the river
they loved to play in. She only found a few items—a shoe, a carved toy
horse. But not her babies.

When La Llorona died, she went to heaven, where Saint Peter told
her she could only enter the Kingdom if she found her sons.

And so to this day, the spirit of La Llorona wanders the riverbanks
and cacti forests, looking for her bebitos. She especially hides in the night
and in the shadows, where her dark hair cannot be seen. She howls sometimes, in that black of night, and it makes everyone's blood run like ice.

And now, I wonder if La Llorona thinks she can get her babies back by capturing me and Mami.

La Katia now roams the desert roads, looking for us. Looking for her way back to heaven.

165

OMAR'S PHONE RINGS, SHATTERING THE SILENCE AFTER
River finishes speaking. "Oh, it's Imani," he says. "She's probably gonna
yell at me some more, but wait till she hears all this!" He waves a hand
at River. "Be right back."

Rose is laying in my lap, her hands on her face. "Holy smokes, you
guys. My gone-to-church-five-days-a-week-since-I-was-three-days-old
brain cannot handle this. It is literally sizzling in my skull."

"Thank God your dad's not around," I say.

"Right? Like, this would convince him, beyond any doubt, that this
is the devil's work. Like, we are aliens? God Almighty. Jesus, Mary, and
Joseph."

"Alright, so you helped Lena escape," Dad says, clearly not impressed
by Rose's fall from grace. "What's your plan now? Hmm? Did you make
another deal? You here to take her back?"

River shakes his head.

"He wouldn't," Mom says.

"How do you know? I don't trust—"

"But I do, amor. I trust him."

Dad looks like someone made him taste old pennies.

River stands. "They actually were going to force me to . . . participate in your retrieval. Yours and Sia's. But . . ." He pauses. "There was a lot of chaos when the photos of the crash leaked. So much so that I was able to escape in a tiburón."

"Ah," Mom says.

"A who?" Rose asks, pushing herself upright.

"We made small versions of our ship. Called them tiburones," River says. "For the government's use. The only problem is . . ."

"No one can man it unless they've got the powers," Mom finishes.

River nods. "The tiburones only obey me and Katia, and presumably you. We've tried a lot of scenarios with some of the military pilots. Pods won't even hover if they're just the co-engineer."

Mom snorts. "Trillions of dollars," she says, "and the tiburones won't even go for them."

River smiles sadly, and I can see something like pain in his eyes when he looks at Mom, at her head on my dad's shoulder, their hands intertwined.

"How'd you know we'd be out here?" Dad asks gruffly.

River shrugs. "Heard a lot about Liana's place when I was caring for Lena."

"Caring." Dad gives a bitter laugh. "You call poking her, cutting up her spine and blood, you call that caring?"

"Luis," Mom says, but we're interrupted by the door flying open.

"Hey, guys," Omar says. "Imani says she doesn't believe me. Again. Which is bullshit. Predictable bullshit, but bullshit all the same."

"How are we going to get this information out there if our one legit connection doesn't believe us?" Rose asks.

"Jesus, Omar," I say. "What did you tell her, that my mom is green and scaly?"

"Obviously not," Omar says. "Though did you happen to check for—? Okay, sorry, sorry. No, I told her the truth." He lifts his hands. "That I just watched a member of the Nordic alien race land a saucer-type UFO right in front of my eyes."

"Yeah, that sounds completely logical," Dad mutters, but the hairs on the back of my neck are prickling.

"What a minute," I say, standing. I turn to River. "You have a spacecraft."

"Yes." His eyes bore into me and I swear, I feel like he can read my brain, which is disturbing. But, no, focus, Sia. You're onto something, here. "How fast can it go?"

River inhales. "It can cover about a hundred and twenty miles in seven seconds."

"What?" Noah's mouth has dropped open. "But you can't take that back to your home planet?"

"It's too small," Mom says. "It'd be like taking a Smart car into the Grand Canyon. Doesn't have that kind of power."

"Wait, wait," I say, holding a hand up. "Remember what Imani said, Noah, when you asked her what it'd take? For her to believe in all this shit?"

Noah grins. "She said to land a spacecraft in front of the newspaper headquarters. Then she'll talk."

I bring a hand to my forehead. "How could something like that not make international news?"

We pause for a moment.

"Imani's there right now," Omar says, checking his watch. "Wrapping up a meeting with the other bloggers. We gotta catch her soon, though. Tonight's family game night, and she gets to my house early. She's competitive."

We all look at one another.

"Yes," Mom says, standing. "We need as many witnesses as we can get."

166

"WAIT," I SAY, LIGHTLY TOUCHING RIVER'S ARM AS everyone heads out. "I want to talk to you."

"Yo no quiero que ella habla con ese pendejo," Dad retorts.

Mom places her hand on his shoulder. "She can ask him questions. She's got a right."

"Solo, Lena?"

I huff. "Dad. Please."

"Artemisia, you don't know—"

"Five minutes," Mom says. "Five, Luis."

He grumbles, giving River a hard look as they leave the trailer. Before the door shuts, I hear Omar saying something like, "Hey, I have a lot of questions, too. I get five minutes with him next!"

River seems unaffected by my father's murderous stare. His silver eyes are directed on the candles, his arms crossed.

Jesus, Rose was right. River is beautiful. But his beauty is refined in such a way that my instincts are sharp around him. Like I know he's not quite human. Or not the sort of human I'm used to.

I decide to blow out all the candles in an attempt to feel less jumpy. "I have a question," I say between huffs of breath over Saint Andrew and Saint Diego.

"Sure."

I'm tired of puffing, so I start to pinch the flames instead. "Why did the experiment work on my mom? After killing so many. Why?"

He glances at my face before watching my hands on the candles. His eyes are still sort of glowing. They look like a pair of gray moons.

"Because I love her."

"Wow," I say, pausing between candles. I was definitely not expecting the most cliché possible explanation. But then my stomach tightens. "If that's true, that makes you a total assface. You know that, right? Like, you didn't have it in you to love anyone else, though? Knowing they were gonna die? Knowing love could save them?"

River's gaze is so intense, I wonder if he can see the inside of my brain. "Is that something you all can do?" He furrows his brow. "You can make yourself fall in love with someone?"

There is no hint of sarcasm in his voice. Just curiosity. "Uh—I—" But my mind whirls too much to respond coherently.

Did Mom ever love him back? When she thought she was stuck there? When she thought she'd never see Dad or me again? Don't people fall in love in extraordinary circumstances all the time? It's 'cause the emotions are high and we naturally seek comfort in each other. Well, we Earth humans, anyway.

I clear my throat and decide to ignore his question. "So, that's her, right? That's my mom, Magdalena Martinez. No robot or alien shape-shifter or . . ."

He tilts his head. "Why are you asking me this?"

"Something Katia said. That she wasn't my mom. Wasn't real or something."

"Ah."

I'm down to the last three candles. "Well? You gonna answer my question or . . ."

He looks out the window. I'm on the last candle, Saint Kateri. And I'm not snuffing it till he speaks.

"Yes," he finally says. "It's her."

Dad bangs on the door. I pinch the flame, and we are all dark, all except for River's pale moon eyes.

167

I'M NOT SURE WHAT I'M EXPECTING WHEN I FOLLOW
Dad and River into the tiburón. From the outside, it's a smoother and
rounder version of what Mom crashed in the desert . . . fuck, was that
only a few days ago? Why has it seemed like a whole life has happened
since then?

Inside, I give a low gasp. I can't help it. Streams of what looks like
sunlight come through the ceiling in thick chunks. "Concentrated
moonlight," River explains when I run my hands over it. It's just after
sunset outside, but in here, it feels like late afternoon. It jars me.

The walls are made of metal, but the metal contains textures, like
wood grain, and they're constantly changing. Symbols appear here and
there, just like the ones on Mom's ship.

There are no buttons, no soundboard-looking system. There are
seats, but they look like bean bags made of molten metal and they're
just tossed about randomly. Noah's already in one, taking notes. The
metal shifts under him as he adjusts and leans back. Like it knows where
he's going to go.

"Amazing, isn't it?" Rose whispers to me when I touch a spiral on
the wall.

When I lift my hand, there's an indentation of my fingerprint. "I'd even go so far as to say fucking incredible," I whisper back.

Rose laughs. "I agree."

Omar's walking around, talking into his phone like it's a walkie-talkie. "You're not going to believe this," he says into it. "We got localized clay tech, we got sentient tech, we got a written alien language. I'm about to take photos. Over." He lifts his phone when I raise an eyebrow at him. "Keeping my associates updated," he explains.

"Are we ready?" River asks.

"Don't we need seat belts or something?" Rose asks.

River laughs. "Not quite. The ship will provide them if we need them."

"Exactly, Rose," Omar says. "The ship will provide them if we need them."

River bites at his lips as though trying not to laugh. "Right now, just enjoy the ride, okay?"

"Hear that, everyone?!" Omar says. "Enjoy the ride!"

"You can have a seat," River tells him and Omar nods so hard, he looks like a bobblehead or something. "I'm about to mark the craft."

I hear Dad scoff under his breath behind me. I wonder if he'll punch River before this shit is over. Or worse.

River puts his hands on the wall, pressing in to make deep marks. Then he has a seat near Noah.

Suddenly, the metal evaporates. It just fades away like it was a phantom all along. The only indications that it was ever there are the lines of moonlight streaming in all around us. I can still make out the shape of the tiburón thanks to the light lines, but my stomach flip-flops as we lift up into the air without the visual of even a floor beneath us. I catch Noah's wide eyes and he grins at me, pulling his phone out.

168

I IMAGINE SOME UPBEAT ANTHEM SONG PLAYING WHEN we descend from the tiburón, us looking cool and desert-weathered and mysterious, especially because we're walking out of a fucking *spaceship*. People gather all around us, many running up from a distance, and they've all got their cell phones out. I glance up at the windows of the *Sentinel*. Now they're packed with silhouettes.

"Oh, Imani," Omar says into his phone in a singsong tone. "Did you look out your office windows yet? Onto the main street? What? Just, just look okay? Now, please. I'll wait. . . . No, it's not a projection. I didn't just project a UFO on the streets! How out of it do you think I am?" He scoffs. "It's real! You said you'd believe if we landed a—you know what, just meet us downstairs. Then you'll see." He hangs up. "She just called me the boy who cried sabertooth, you believe that? Don't know what I ever did to her that she'd treat me this way."

"One of God's great mysteries," Rose mutters in my ear and I snort.

But in the lobby, Imani's arms are crossed and she has an eyebrow raised. "So. Not a projection, huh?"

"I told you! It's real!" Omar says, jumping with glee. He looks about four years old.

Mom's next to me, slipping my hand into hers. "I love these things," she says wistfully. "I hope the tech leaks and our cars and planes can be like this."

The ride is smooth and I'm without words as we glide toward the last orange hint of the sunset. Below us, the shadows of the desert take on their blue-black ink. Some of them move. I recognize a pair of hares before they become tiny, gray blurs on the landscape.

"We're going pretty slow," Dad says with a scowl.

"Just wanted you to see how pretty it is." River's voice is smooth and soft. "We can speed it up."

He closes his eyes and leans back on the seat. The ship gives a little growl and Rose grabs my free hand. I glance at Omar, who's mouth has been wide open for the last five minutes. Noah grins, recording on his cell.

There's a lurch, then the feeling like I'm compressing into a tiny ball. It's like the world out there is also, somehow, inside me.

Is this what the universe was like when it all began? When all of matter sought itself out, so tight and so close that it exploded and made whole new worlds, one after the other like empanadas pulled from the oil, crisp and ready to eat?

The ball that is my body jumps and slowly unravels. When I open my eyes, we're hovering over a street in downtown Phoenix. I can tell because the main *Sentinel* building is a quarter mile ahead, its name glowing in white. Silhouettes of people line some of the windows.

"You want to make headlines, right?" River asks Mom, who nods, the corners of her lips curling into a smile. River grins back. "Let's make an entrance, then, shall we?"

The last thing I hear before we really speed up is Dad grumbling something like, "Fool thinks he's Captain Fucking America."

"Okay," she says slowly. "Fine. So it's real. What's the plan? Who are the players? I see Noah and, Sia, was it?" We nod.

"This is Sia's dad," Noah says, stepping up. "Biologist and capoeira master."

"Luis," my dad mutters, his voice all gruff.

Omar jumps in front of Noah, practically tripping Imani, who scowls. "And this," Omar says, pointing, "is her mom, smokin' hot Mexican lady, abducted over two years ago in the desert. That makes her an honest-to-God abductee. Also classified as a close encounter of the third kind. The third kind, Imani!"

"Actually," Noah says, "we're all having a close encounter of the third kind right now." He gestures to River, whose arms are crossed, his moon eyes glinting in amusement. "'Cause that's the kind when there's one of them actually present . . ."

"Shit, you're right, man! Imani, stop rolling your eyes and listen! That fellow's code name is River, which could be a little better, you know, it's not quite on the Sabertooth level, but he's actually"—Omar lowers his voice—"alien."

Although we've landed a UFO right in front of her, practically, this seems to stretch Imani's limitations. Arms still crossed, she gives River a long once-over. "I'm at a loss, Omar. There are no green scales, no big eyes."

"I know! It's confusing, isn't it, especially because I've almost elimi-nated the possibility of the Nordic—"

"You know what, Omar?" I say. "This is great and all, but, Imani? The government has been experimenting on my mother without her consent. We get proof out there, and quick. Because they're on their way to get her. Right now."

Something about the tone of my voice, or maybe the hardness of our eyes, who knows, but something makes Imani uncross her arms and straighten her back. "Why don't we go upstairs. This way." She points us to the elevators. "They're with me," she calls to the security guards who surround us as we approach.

"Christopher's gonna give you that position when you graduate, after today," Omar says. "You wait."

She gives Omar a small smile. "Sure he will." She shrugs. "I mean, I'm just assisting folks who claim to know—and be—aliens into the newsroom. What could go wrong?"

169

"JESUS CHRIST, IMANI." A TALL, GRAY-HAIRED FELLOW RUNS
to us as soon as we hit the newsroom. "What the fuck have you done?"

She barely looks at him. "Hello, Christopher."

"I just got a call that I need to evacuate the building immediately, or
else there will be casualties, thanks to some group of young criminals. Is
this them? You just brought them right into the office?"

Imani stares for a moment. "Really? You really got a call like that?"
She shakes her head. "Omar, I can't believe you might be right about this."

"I told you, I freaking told you!"

"Imani," the man says, warning in his voice.

She just gestures to him. "Everyone, this is Christopher. The assistant editor."

He doesn't look at us. "What's your grand plan, Imani? Trying to get
us all killed?"

Imani raises an eyebrow. "I'm trying to get the truth out there, Chris.
Which is my job, if you'll recall."

"Okay, okay." The guy throws up his hands. "You do whatever you
want with them. But I'm washing my hands of this bullshit." He turns
and stomps away, calling, "We'll see how high your horse is when *they*
arrive, Clarke."

170

IMANI'S INTERVIEWING MOM AND RIVER FIRST, WITH Noah by their side, taking notes, showing their previous interviews from his phone. And, of course, Omar is front and center, interjecting with his super-grounded-sounding commentary. I sit with Rose on a bench we find in the newsroom.

"Oh my God." A golden-haired, dark-skinned woman walks up and stares at Imani, Mom, and River through the window. "That's that lady who was deported down south a couple years back, isn't it?"

"Really?" A redheaded woman walks up, holding a paintbrush for some reason. "You remember that?"

"Yeah, I mean. She had a daughter."

The redhead makes a face like this doesn't explain anything.

"That part of the state, you know, Caraway, Pastila. It's rough for people of color. God, last time I was there, at a gas station on the 99, I got called the N-word. And once, I got a flat right next to Rangestown, and not one, but two trucks went out of their way to splash mud on me before someone stopped to help."

Redhead's got a sour look now, like someone's forced her to drink piss. "Well," she says with a huff. "I lived in Pastila for many, many years and I've *never* met a racist there." She gives a half shrug, crossing her arms. "Roberta, when you focus on the negative things in life, you miss out on all the kindness people have to offer." She lifts her head and walks away.

Rose and I glance at each other. Both our jaws have dropped.

Roberta sees and shakes her head. "It's nothing new," she tells us, walking away.

171

"THANK YOU FOR BEING HERE," I SAY TO ROSE.

"You're my best friend," she says simply.

"HEY," NOAH WHISPERS. I TURN AS HE GESTURES FOR me to follow. I glance at the room with Mom and Imani. Looks like Omar has taken over the interviewing process. Typical.

"Be right back," I tell Rose.

"What is it?" I say as he ushers me into what looks like a supply closet.

When he turns to me, his cheeks are pink. "I just." He places a hand on my waist. "I just haven't gotten to kiss you in too long."

I can't bite back my grin. "We kissed last night."

He gives me a half smile. "Like I said, too long."

173

KISSING NOAH IS LIKE MY WHOLE BODY GETTING TOO close to some exquisite lightning storm. I know that sounds ridiculous, but it's the only thing I can think of that's even close. Goosebumps glide along my back, and I shiver as he sucks in my bottom lip. And when I do the same to him, he gasps and presses his hips into me. And I feel him, hard on my belly, and I really think that one day, I'll be okay with it. With every part of his firm and freckled body. 'Cause I push my hips back and it feels good, right now, just like this. It only feels good.

THERE'S A MUFFLED SOUND PENETRATING THE WINDOWS, like a bullhorn. Someone opens a window.

"I repeat, each occupant of this illegal aircraft must exit the building with both hands up, or we will force entry."

I run and see what looks like dozens of SWAT cars and unmarked black vans and SUVs piling up down the street. They've drawn yellow caution tape on each side of our building, where folks have gathered, phones extended.

"We have a basement that connects to our neighboring buildings," Imani says, putting a hand on my arm. "Used to deliver mail that way, back in the day."

I hardly hear her. My grandmother is in front of me, obscuring Imani's face. "Ella está en el edificio," she whispers. Then she's gone.

Mom's face pales. "Katia." She turns to Imani, my father, Noah, and Rose. "I just need five minutes alone with Sia. You all, go through the basement."

"I'm not leaving," my dad growls.

Noah shakes his head. "We can't. We can't leave you here."

Rose crosses her arms. "Looks like you're stuck with us."

Mom closes her eyes, as if in prayer. She opens them and spots River. "Don't let her kill anyone."

"Don't worry, Mrs. Martinez," Omar says. "We won't."

River nods over Omar's head. "You know I can't hold her back too long. She's probably at her wit's end right about now, and you know what that means."

Before he's even finished speaking, Mom wraps her arms around Dad. "Te amo," she says, as though it's torn from her. She grabs my hand and pulls me into an office.

The last thing I see before I shut the door is River staring at me with those moon eyes. Like he knows something.

175

WE'RE IN SOME OFFICE. SMALL, WITH A DESK SQUEEZED in. It's dark except for the occasional spotlight leaking through the window. When I look back at Mom she's got a pained expression on her face. "This is something I need to do, Sia."

She holds a knife.

176

"KATIA KEPT TELLING ME THAT YOU'RE NOT MY MOM," I say, my voice shaking. "I didn't believe her until now. My mother would never do this to me."

"Sia." She's crying. "I don't want to. But I know what they'll do with you once they get you. They'll torture you so bad, you'll want to die. Then they might actually do it. Kill you."

"This isn't gonna help. Your plan is outrageous." I back up until my shoulders hit the wall. "How do you know this is even gonna work?" I gesture to the glint of metal on the blade. It shakes.

"The powers. They're viral. They're in la sangre."

I close my eyes, my chest heaving. There's some absurdly loud yelling outside the door. "How do you know this is gonna work?"

She grabs my hand and when I look up, her eyes are right in front of mine. "Because however much River loves me, I love you *whole universes* more."

I snap my hand away. "Whole universes, huh? If that were true, we wouldn't be in this situation in the first place, Mom. If you hadn't walked the fucking desert by your fucking self—" I can hardly breathe, so I take a second and just choke in air. "If you really loved us—" Again, a choke.

The paths of our lives are cut, no, *stabbed* with shouldn't haves. And at every point, there's someone to blame. Sheriff McGhee. Our entire racist fucking country and its immigration system. But right now, I am pointing a finger right at my mother's face. And she's crying.

"It was reckless," she says. "I was so desperate to be with you again, I didn't think anything could stop me." She scoffs. "Mami did it with me when I was a baby. I didn't think it'd be that bad." And she laughs and then cries again.

"Abuela was a bruja." I'm wiping my eyes, too. "Remember, she could make the sky break open with a swish of her knife."

"I remember." And she looks in my eyes. "I'm sorry."

I want to be mad at her for a hundred thousand years. But the fact is, I thought she was dead. And instead, she's right in front of me, warm, beautiful, even with red-rimmed eyes and a snotty nose. A week ago I would've crossed the whole Sonoran alone just to be able to hug her again. So I get it. I can't pretend I don't.

And that's what I do now, I wrap my arms around her and hug her as hard as I can. She sobs into my hair. And then I step back, holding my arm toward the knife, like an offering.

177

SHE ROLLS UP MY SLEEVE AND NICKS ME AT THE TOP OF
my forearm. "I'm sorry," she whispers again. She cuts her fingers and
drips her blood onto mine.

We stare at my arm for a few seconds. "Do you feel anything?"
she asks.

I swallow. "It feels tingly."

"Good," she says. She looks like she wants to bawl again, but instead,
she holds my hand.

178

"YOU KNOW HOW I SPEED UP REAL FAST?" SHE SAYS.
I can barely hear her through all the banging and yelling outside the
door. We jump when there's a shot.

My hands shake and she wraps her arms around me. "I want you to
remember this. It's not that I'm faster. It's that everyone else is *slower*."

"I don't understand," I whisper.

She holds me tighter. "We can control time, m'ija."

179

THE DOOR BURSTS OPEN AND THERE IS KATIA, ALL
elegance in a white suit with a long jacket. She smiles. "Aha."

180

KATIA LUNGES FOR ME, HAND ARCHING TOWARD MY throat again, but Mom jumps between us. "Sweet Magdalena," Katia hisses. "Always in my way." She grabs a large picture frame off the wall and knocks my mother in the head—all so fast, it's a blur. I'm not sure if I even saw what I saw.

And then Mom flings the frame right back at Katia, broken glass scattering like beetles.

"Sia, run!" Mom screams.

Katia lifts a desk and hurls it at Mom, who kicks it right back.

I look around. There. A terra-cotta pot holds a cotton candy–pink amaryllis. I lift the whole thing and fling it right at Katia, who's in the middle of a freakin' roundhouse kick.

A six-inch clay pot. What's that gonna do to a woman who can lift an office desk with the tips of her fingers? I'm not expecting much.

But when it hits her, she *flies* back. I mean, Katia slams to the floor and slides as though I'd just tossed a fifty-pound kettlebell into her belly.

Katia rolls her legs and kicks up to standing with nothing but ease. But the way she looks at me. Like I'm the biggest platter of arroz con pollo. Like she's starving.

"Well, done, Lena," she says, her eyes still on me. "A blood transfer by a, what, a pocket knife? A little brute. But I'm not going to complain. You've just made my job very easy."

"You will not touch her," Mom yells, and her body melts until there's just the shadow of her, stretched across the floor, curling around Katia. When Mom returns, there's a humming noise. Apparently coming back to the land of the living makes you part of a bee swarm for just a moment.

She grabs Katia by the waist and hurls her against the wall. When Katia lands, she doesn't move. We wait a few moments. There's nothing but the sounds of our breaths. My eyes are still on Katia, but she doesn't look like she's even breathing. I resist the urge to run over and kick her.

Mom doubles over, coughing.

"Mami," I say.

She holds her hand up. "Sia, leave. Please. Go now."

She can't even look at me. Her skin is pale. "Mom, I'm not—"

But we're interrupted with a chuckle. Katia performs another flawless kip-up and lets her laugh end with a sigh. "Shadow work, Lena? You know you're way too weak for that."

Too fast for me to make anything out, Mom and Katia run toward each other. Their bodies are just pieces of smoke, their edges all faded and fast.

And then they stop.

"Oh my God." I stumble backward.

181

THIS. THIS IS CLEAR AS THE FULL MOON ON A DRY
desert night: Katia, shoving the gun at my mother's head. Mom,
half-conscious, glancing at me. "I love—" she begins.

Katia pulls the trigger.

My mouth is wide open, my eyes are wide open, I'm clawing the
carpet to get to her, my mami, my moon, my mamá, my everything.

But she is empty. Nothing moves but her blood into the carpet.

"Take her," Katia says. Black-clothed men grab me and I scream.
They drag me out of the room.

"They killed her," I choke. My voice sounds so far away and I don't
even know who I'm talking to. "They killed her."

I hear my father yelling, telling them to let me go. I see Noah, under
a table, cell phone out. "They killed her. They killed her."

I can only whisper it now. And it's like I can't stop.

They killed her, they killed her, they killed her.

182

DAD'S FACE IS BONE-WHITE. A SOUND COMES OUT OF him I've never heard before, like he's being strangled from the inside. And then he narrows his eyes and tightens his jaw and I know in that moment, his rage has been pulled over the grief like a cloak.

He tosses his head back and I swear I can hear the crunch of the SWAT guy's nose behind him. "Fuck!" the man yells, but before he can move, blink, breathe, Dad's tossed him over his shoulder, pulling the man's gun into his own arms.

"Which one of you killed my wife?!" The gun waves wildly in Dad's hands.

"Sir," another man says, his gun aimed at my father. "Put the weapon down."

"What for? So you can kill me? Kill my daughter, these children? I don't think so, fucker."

"Aw," a cool voice rings behind me. I clench my hands.

"It was her," I say, flinging my head in Katia's direction. "She shot Mami."

Dad points the gun at Katia.

"Don't, Mr. Martinez!" Rose shifts her shoulders under the arms of the SWAT jerk behind her. "That's your soul. What she did, that's between her and God, what you're doing—"

"Ah, a believer." Katia smiles. "I've always liked those the best."

I blink and Katia is on Dad, the gun now in her hands. She smacks his face with it and blood flies. She steps back with a smile on her face.

"No!" I scream.

Omar's struggling in some other bastard's grip, right next to Rose. "What do you mean by that? You like believers? What does that mean?" His face is pale and sweat dots his temples.

"Omar," Rose hisses. "Now is not the time."

"Oh," he says, "now is the perfect time! That Nordic alien just killed Sia's mom, right? Well, she has to explain herself! Nordics are pledged to honor and protect humans! Ever since Roosevelt sold us out to the Greys back in the late thirties!"

"Oh, one of those believers!" Katia approaches Omar, who shrinks back. "I changed my mind. Actually, you're my favorite sort." She shakes her head, narrowing her eyes. "So much more absurd than the rest."

"Absurd?" Omar huffs, but then he widens his eyes. "You just killed someone! A really nice lady, okay? For no reason! And you're calling me—"

He's cut off as Katia bops him on the head. Omar now hangs limp in the officer's hands.

"Omar!" Rose screams. "Omar!"

A blur of redwood and taupe whirls in front of her. My eyes adjust when it stops, and River's hands are on Katia's gun, swiping it away. "Not again, Katia," he says.

Her eyes widen for a moment, but then she pulls her mouth into a hard line. She lifts her head and straightens her jacket. "I thought I threw you out the window, River."

Before she's finished her sentence, River becomes a blur again, and it's so hard to keep track of what the hell is happening. A whine and a buzz later, all the guns are piled behind River, unreachable, and each SWAT team member is knocked out on the ground.

"Go," he tells us. "Now!"

"Come on!" Dad tosses Omar on his shoulder and we all follow.

River flings Katia against the wall, and as we run out, I glance back at them, fighting so fast they're clouds, men in black around them like the ravens that dot the sky.

183

"WHERE ARE WE GOING?" I YELL.

"Down." I turn and see Imani running alongside us. She speeds ahead of Dad, which is like its own freakin' superpower to me in those high heels. "This way." We follow down a labyrinth of hallways, until we reach a massive cargo elevator. She slams her fist on the button.

"Go to the basement," she says as she ushers us in. "When you get there, run along the red stripe, following the exit signs. The door for Edman's will take you to the grocer's next door. From there, you can make it to the street."

A pounding noise begins and gets louder. She glances back. "You take care of Omar, you hear? I'm going to stall them."

"With what?" Noah says, his breath hard.

She gives us a strained smile. "Live-ass footage."

The doors close on the image of Imani Clarke running toward the chaos in her gorgeous red stilettos.

184

WHEN THE ELEVATOR DOORS OPEN, WE'RE HIT WITH
warm, musky air. We run out, Rose grabbing me as we go.

"Are you okay?"

I shake my head.

She nods, squeezing my forearm before letting go.

The exit signs are so dim I wonder when this place was last inspected. Not for long, though. Mostly I just run.

The door to the grocer's is right there, or I hope it is. I mean, there's a sign on it with a cornucopia filled with pumpkins.

"What's going on?" Omar grumbles. "Are you an alien? Damn, an alien that lifts. Hey, do me a favor, though. Put me down."

Dad and Noah help Omar until he's standing upright. "We gotta move," Dad barks. Before we reach the door, though, a dark blur darts in front of it.

"What the—" Rose begins, but before she finishes, River is here, crouched, hands on his knees, looking like he might hurl.

"Not that way," he chokes out. "They're waiting for you."

"Then where are we supposed to go?" My voice echoes, the anger heightened.

"My car is right next to a grate." He points behind us. "We could get—"

"No." My father's voice shakes. "I don't trust you. You got my wife killed. Now you're trying to get my daughter—"

"Not me," River says, shaking his head, straightening his spine. "Katia—she's—she's lost it."

"Imani told us this is the only way out," Noah says.

"I know another."

"Yeah?" Dad says, stomping around Rose. "And I know you. You wanted my wife and now you want my daughter. I'm not letting another person I love—" His voice breaks.

"You have to listen to me! They're just on the other side of that door. We need to go—" River grabs my arm, pulling me backward, but he stops, releasing me. "You're bleeding." He stares at the stain on my sleeve.

"Yeah, what of it?" Rose asks. "We're all bleeding."

"She did it, didn't she?" River's eyes won't leave mine now. "Lena. She turned you."

"Whoa!" Omar says. He seems wide awake now. "What's 'turned' mean?" His eyes get huge as realization falls over him. "No way, Sia. No fucking way. She, like, marked you? Did she give you the green scales? What about crop circle tattoos?" He examines my arm with his fingers.

"Shut up, Omar," I say, snapping my hand back.

"What's—what are they talking about, Sia?" Noah asks.

"Mom, she. Before she. Before they." I take a breath, closing my eyes. "She put some of her blood in me."

River mutters words I don't understand under his breath. He grabs my hand again. "Now we've *really* got to get you out of here."

"Let her go, hombre." There's the sound of a metal clink. I turn and Dad's hands are out, his gun pointed right at River's temple.

"Mr. Martinez," Rose hisses.

"Dad, for the love of—" I huff. "Put that thing away."

"Open the door, Artemisia."

"That's where they are." River's hands are up. "They're waiting for you, Sia."

"Open the door, Artemisia."

"Dad, what if he's right?"

River moves impossibly fast to grab my father's gun, but it's like he's weakened or something. My father kicks him and River hits the ground. "OPEN THE DOOR—"

"Christ! Fine!" I push on the metal bar of the door.

There, Katia smiles.

"Sia," she says. "Good to see you."

185

MY GRANDMOTHER ALWAYS SAID WHEN WE EXPERIENCE trauma, our soul fills with espanto, or terror. And that espanto makes your soul split into pieces and run away to hide.

I think that's what's happening to me right now. My whole soul shatters into a hundred parts, handfuls that scatter into the roads and bushes and desert like kangaroo mice.

I'm not even there when they wrestle my father and Rose, Noah, and Omar away, slamming them against the ground with dull thuds. It's like I'm in a bubble when Katia snarls at Noah and says, "You were warned via email to stay away from reporters, weren't you? But you couldn't listen. And now you'll have to pay."

Noah's grunts of pain snap me back. As though I breathe in all the pieces of my soul for just a minute, just for him. "Stop it!" I scream and she kicks at Noah's belly.

She turns and does the same to Omar. "How were we supposed to know that email was from you?" he squawks. "What kind of alien sends a threat by email, huh? Do you know how much spam—" He coughs as she kicks him so hard he rolls back.

"Jesus Christ, stop it." I can't make my voice any louder without it breaking. "Stop!" Katia just smiles and turns back to Noah.

186

WHEN NOAH PASSES OUT, HIS HEAD GOING LIMP ON the asphalt, I feel it again—espanto. The thick exhale of my soul, breaking into parts, running away. Perhaps for good. Who knows. Who cares.

I barely feel the black-clothed arms yank me up the stairs and into the night air. After a long while of nothing, I glance up and am not quite surprised to see I'm actually inside one of the black cars.

I'm not sure if anything will ever really surprise me again.

KATIA CLIMBS IN, LEANS BACK, AND LETS OUT A LONG sigh. "Well, I'm getting in trouble for that unfortunate incident with Magdalena." She frowns, and her eyes, they look like agony. After a split second, though, she smiles. "Thank goodness for daughters, eh?"

Some guys jump in the front and start the car, slamming on the gas. Katia pops open a black box connected to the console. Bottles of water and cans of soda and tea are inside.

"Care for a refreshment?" she asks.

I shake my head.

"Well," she says, shrugging and grabbing a can. "Help yourself whenever. We've got a bit of a drive."

188

MY MOTHER HAS BEEN MURDERED. AGAIN.

"THERE'S NO NEED TO CRY," KATIA SAYS.

"Because she's not real?" My voice screeches like an owl.

"Precisely."

"What the fuck do you mean by that, anyway?"

Katia looks out the window. There are tiny village lights in the distance and I briefly wish I could send a Patronus to someone, anyone for help.

"There were rumors . . ." She says it in a low voice.

My God. She's been telling me my mother's not real because of a fucking rumor?!

I snarl. "Didn't you cry when you realized you'd never see your children again?"

She snaps her head back toward me, her eyes hard. "Don't speak about my children. You know nothing."

"I know what it's like to have something I love taken from me. I know what it's like to be used. And so do you, Katia. And now you're doing the same shit to me."

Her hand is on my throat now. A wheezing noise escapes my lips. She grits her teeth. "You. Know. Nothing."

190

MY GRANDMOTHER SLIPS INSIDE THE CAR, BRINGING smells of herbs and prickly pear. Katia looks around, her eyes narrowed, but her grip on my throat doesn't loosen.

"I've got nothing left," she says, bringing her eyes back to mine. "I've got nothing left. Your mother took everything from me. My ship. My spouse. Why not return the favor?"

The man in the passenger side turns, his gun cocked to Katia. "We were instructed to bring the specimen in ideal condition."

Katia rolls her eyes. "You're aiming a gun? At me? At me." She laughs, and, faster than I can process, reaches over and knocks the man out. It sounds like she hits him on the head with his own gun. I try the door in the chaos. No surprise: it's locked.

She glares at the driver through the rearview mirror. "Do you share the same sentiment as your partner?"

The man gives a swift, firm shake of his head.

Katia smiles. "Good." She turns to me, her hand returning to my throat. "Now. Where were we?"

REMEMBER, MY GRANDMOTHER WHISPERS TO ME. *TIME*.

192

KATIA'S SQUEEZING MY NECK SO HARD, I FEEL LIKE MY eyes are bulging. Through stinging tears, I somehow see the clock on the dashboard. It's 8:58 and I will it to slow the fuck *down*.

That's not time, my grandmother says. I feel her hand on my head. *This is.* She gestures all around me.

She must mean something about . . . perception? But it's so hard to just *think*. I look at Katia, at the spots of blue in her dark eyes, at the tears that line her face, mirroring mine. Each tear has a quarter moon in it. In the front, our driver has turned up the radio. It's playing "The Chain" by Fleetwood Mac, right on that deep, drawling guitar solo.

And then, all around us, the cacti shiver and shimmy, like a thousand-armed wind just ran through the desert. Just beyond Katia, one drops, reaching a hand out toward me. I can almost hear its prickly voice.

Care to dance?

KATIA SAYS SOMETHING, BUT I CAN SCARCELY UNDERSTAND
because the words come out thick like molasses. She's—she's *slow*.
Slower than the migrations of stones across the desert.

I grab her hand from my neck and punch her ugly, beautiful neck as
hard as I can. She flings back against her door, her head rattling on the
window. But the impact is slow going, absurdly idle, her head on the
plexiglass mimicking a calm, dull drum beat.

I grab the seat for leverage and lean back, kicking my own door. It
opens with such fluid ease that I realize my superpowers must include
Buffy strength.

Though we're going something like ninety, I step out of the car as if
it were parked.

As though our beefy driver slowed down just so the desert can welcome me not as a captive, but as a warrior.

I take a breath, staring into the wide sky with its black silt on one
side, a line of peach on the other, and in the middle, the quarter moon.
I pause, listening to the crickets.

They sound like the chants of men. The deep of their voices echo
with long hums in this ancient, earthly church.

194

THE CAR SCREECHES AND STOPS WITHIN A FEW DOZEN feet, all still in slow motion. Katia climbs out of the side with the broken door, her eyes on mine immediately. I idly touch my neck. It should hurt like a bitch, but oddly enough, it doesn't. I remember how my mom's arm lacerations healed in a few hours. But that gets me thinking about my mom, and I cough, suppressing the urge to throw up.

When I glance up again, Katia's moving at normal speed. She raises an eyebrow and smiles.

I already have my arms up, hands in fists, when she's close. No matter. She slings one right at my cheekbone, too fast, and I fly into the sand.

I push up immediately, ignoring the ringing in my ears. "Is everyone from your planet a bitch? Or just you?"

She just smirks at me. As though anything about this is humorous.

I LAND ON THE SAND FOR THE FIFTH OR SIXTH TIME, ON my shoulder this go. "Christ," I groan.

Katia's on me, giving my hip a good kick. I roll a few times, getting about another pound of sand in my hair.

I stand, but my back is to her. I can't bring myself to care all that much right this second. Everything hurts too much.

I face the moon and I wonder if its light can see my mother's body now, in that office in Phoenix. If it can touch the blood running down her face. And if it does, maybe it can connect the blood on my head and shoulder and arm with her somehow. Maybe right now, I'm cradling my mother's face as I hold my hands to the moonlight.

The crickets' chants are louder, like a thousand spirits surrounding me, giving me strength. They hold their candles out to me, each flame a star in the black silk sky, just like I've done with them a hundred times.

Before Katia grabs me, I see my abuela in the desert, her hair lined in silver.

Katia feels so light. Like the skins of garlic and onions.

I bend my legs and flip her over. Something crunches and she moans. Her hips twitch and she looks at me. She's not cocky anymore.

She looks frightened.

196

I'VE ALWAYS THOUGHT IT'D BE DIFFICULT TO KILL someone, but when I remember the blast of the gun and Mami crumbling to the floor, when I remember the deep black of her blood on the shitty gray carpet? I find it's rather easy.

My fingers are on her throat and she's gasping with a high-pitched whine.

My hands are impossibly strong. They're carved from desert boulders, like they were made for this woman—this fucking *thing's* neck.

I tighten my grip until I hear my grandmother.

No.

ONCE, DURING OUR HERB-GATHERING WALKS, ABUELA took me really far out. Like, five or more whole miles out of the way of our normal path. After my feet felt like they'd been rubbed raw, she let me take a break next to some boulders.

"Mira," she said after a minute.

I dragged my feet over to where she pointed. There, just beyond her finger, black paintings adorned the stone wall. Animals, men, triangles, and lines.

"Holy crap," I said. "Are those real?"

Abuela was running her fingertips above the edges of each image, somehow seeing them perfect with her eyes still closed. "Sí."

I swallowed. "Who made them? The ancestors?"

"Not our ancestors."

Right. Abuela was always going on about how our people were from jungles and jaguars and that's why we'd never feel at home in the desert. It wasn't in our blood.

"What happened to them?"

"Their descendants are here, Sia." Abuela shrugs. "But a lot of them, lost."

"Lost how?"

"Gringos."

It was one word, but it explained everything. A wave of rage went over me, and I kicked at the boulder to try to get it out. "Why do people have so much hate about everything? Where did all that racism come from, anyway?"

Abuela shrugged. "They believe in the cruelest god, Artemisia. What else can we expect?"

198

I RELEASE HER THROAT WITH A SHARP INHALE OF AIR.

Before I can finish the thought, Katia's up, faster than I can make out. She slams a kick into my head and, once again, I'm digging an outline of my body into the sand.

199

"GODS," SHE SAYS, STANDING, HER SILHOUETTE COVER-
ing the moon. "You're even more foolish than your mother is."

"Was," I say with a cough.

"I beg your—"

"Was," I say. "'Cause you killed her, you murderer."

Her eyes glint. "Let me earn that name twice, then." This time, her kick is to my stomach.

200

I DON'T KNOW WHAT IT IS WITH THIS WOMAN AND necks, but she's got her hands on mine again, hell-bent on asphyxiation.

I'm stronger now. I can feel it in the tingle in my hands and feet and bones and jaw.

But not strong enough to push her back. Not strong enough to outlive this monster.

Dozens of SUVs lumber on the road, right toward us. It distracts her just enough. Enough for me to pull her hand away just a touch. I look right into her eyes and say, "What would your children say if they could see you now?"

201

I DON'T THINK SHE EXPECTS THAT, 'CAUSE HER JAW
drops a little. Maybe she thought I would call her a bitch or a murderer
again. I don't know.

And I sure as hell don't expect for her hands to pull away from me,
all gentle. For her to fall to the sand, a choke of a sob leaving her lips.

202

I DON'T GET TO WONDER ABOUT HER REACTION FOR long, because we are then surrounded by headlights. They cut into dusk like machetes.

Her hand returns to my arm, tightening so hard I wince.

"Come on," she says, pushing me toward the cars.

203

"THIS IS MAGDALENA MARTINEZ'S DAUGHTER," SHE yells out to the armed silhouettes. "She has been turned. And it is a success. She can alter time, expand her strength."

A man approaches. In the car lights, I can see how sharply pressed his tweed suit is, like he'd just picked it up from the dry cleaner's. "Katia. What are you doing?" He smiles, but it comes off as more of a grimace. "Release the girl's neck." I hadn't realized her hand was back to my throat. Maybe it's 'cause I'm in too much pain.

"Not until you let me go. I want out, Armando."

"Katia." The man sighs. His hair is dark, his skin tawny. "We've been over this. We have to be able to replicate the experiment. You have to teach us how."

"You have my notes! You have my records, my videos! You have my everything. And you said once we're successful—"

"Successful with duplication." The man gets closer, close enough for me to make out the pale morning blue of his eyes. "Many times over, ideally."

"No." Katia's hand tightens around my neck and I groan. Shit, that woman has a hell of a grip. "I've done my end of the deal. I want access to the Selkie parts. I want a team to repair it. I'm going to go home."

The man bites his lips. "Katia, do you hear yourself? The Selkie is in several hundred pieces. There's no way—"

I can feel her fingers pressing into my spine. "For fuck's sake!" I rip her hand away. "They're not going to give you what you want. Ever. I've been listening for two seconds and even I can see that."

"Ready," the man murmurs into his forearm. We hear the clicking of guns pointed our way. "Sia. Step away from Katia. Slowly."

I can't. I mean, I know Katia has been bad news. But weirdly enough, this guy seems worse. Maybe it's the way he says my name. Like he's known me—or about me—for a long while.

"Aim," the man says. Shiny glints of gun barrels now point right at us.

Katia grabs my hand.

We melt into the orange night just before the shots.

204

I'M SMOOTH AND DARK ALL ACROSS THE DESERT, HAND in hand with La Llorona. We are nothing but shadows, and we should be the only humanoids here under a swirl of stars, but we're not. Figures stop to let us pass—women who are part saguaro, men who have tails like wolves, mice with the eyes of children. I wonder if this land—the shadow land—is also where myths live. Or maybe just spirits.

I look for my mother but she isn't here. I wonder if it's because I haven't yet draped her body with yellow roses, haven't had a chance to sprinkle holy water over the wounds.

I ache for my father and Rose and Noah. I pray for them.

They're okay, the spirits say.

When we reach the city of lights, Katia releases me.

205

"I'M NEVER GONNA SEE MY BABIES AGAIN." KATIA'S voice breaks like she might cry, but she settles for looking up. Like this black sky might give her a glimpse of who she's looking for. "I'm never gonna see them again."

I stand, praying to God she doesn't lose her shit on me. And something weird happens. As soon as I see her as, God, I don't know, a *human*, I can feel her pain. I know it sounds so ridiculous, but her emotions, they spin off her body in waves and breezes and I stumble in the thick of it. It *burns*.

Jesus, I can't take anymore. I jump back.

How can someone feel like that and survive?

After a minute, I catch my breath. "Why—why haven't your people come looking for you?" I swallow. "You came on a routine check, right? They should've come to find you by now."

Katia closes her eyes and her shoulders drop, like my questions put the weight of moons and universes on her back. "They don't know we're here." A tear drips off her chin into the sand. "They'll never know."

I stare for a few moments. "But River said—he said you just came here to check on us. Humans. Your cousins."

She looks right in my eyes. "River lied."

206

"WHAT DO YOU MEAN HE LIED?" I SAY. "I—WE—MY mother *believed* him. He said he loved her. But he lied? To her?"

Katia closes her eyes as she brushes dust off her white blazer. It's fruitless. The only way to get that amount of sand off will be to burn the thing. Much like my hair, likely. "We didn't come to check anything. We came because we were attacked. And when we consulted the ancestors—for the last time, because the colonizers destroyed our connection—they said Earth was our only hope." She smirks. "No explanations. No plans. Just one ambiguous line."

She opens her eyes and looks at the last bits of sunset on the horizon. It's deep orange. Almost red. "River and I took a ship—the Selkie. I didn't want to leave them." Tears fill her eyes again. "My daughters. But he said we'd all die, anyway, if no one tried.

"We were spouses back then. I trusted him."

She inhales. It sounds painful. "I don't know what we expected when we got here. But we were reckless to think we'd get any answers. Reckless to think we wouldn't be in danger."

"You got caught," I say. "So River was right about that. Drugged. Forced to—"

"Forced to fix the ship. Forced to make humans like us. When we got your mother? When I heard she could talk to her dead mother, just like we did to our ancestors? I had a feeling she was a key." Now Katia can't keep the tears in. "River went on about love, how it made the experiment successful. I didn't pay much attention to that. Him and his wishful thinking." She slid her boot along the ground. "But she was. Magdalena was the key. I was so happy. So elated. Finally I was going to have my chance to go home." Katia gets real close to me, enough to make me much more nervous. I hold my breath. "But when she took the ship, she took the only thing I was living for." She wipes her tears, smearing terra-cotta dust on her cheek. Fire returns to her gaze and she stares at me, her eyes dark and hard. "She destroyed my only chance to see my daughters again."

I take a step back and exhale. "Okay, River lied, whatever. But the fact that you won't see your children—that's not my fault. That's not my mom's fault." My voice is hoarse and I cough.

Katia's response is so low, I hardly hear it over the wind. "I know."

I swallow and think maybe I should change the subject. "What was that guy gonna do back there? Kill us?"

She shakes her head. "Those were tranquilizer guns." Her voice is numb; her eyes are back down toward the earth. "We would've woken up in a lab tomorrow. Maybe the day after. Maybe we wouldn't have been woken up at all. Just poked and sliced and diced until they got what they wanted."

I nod. "Well." I'm not sure what to say. Do I thank her for saving me from that? Do I thank the woman who just killed my Mom? A wave of nausea passes over me and I cough. Instead of responding, I look around. "Where are we?" I stare at a tall building. It's made of polished marble and there's a gargoyle carved onto the top. Or maybe that's just another spirit.

"That student," she says. "Imani Clarke. Sixteenth floor. Door A."

I gape at her. "What?"

"Here." Katia grabs something from her pocket and hands it to me. "What's this?"

Katia stares at me for a beat. "It's what you've been looking for."

I turn the slice of gold in my hands. "What is it, a memory stick?"

"Yes."

"I've never seen one this fancy."

Katia almost smiles. "It's filled with fifty years of files. Reports. There might even be names for the ones who went missing. Or at least photos."

My grip tightens around the object. "Why are you doing this?"

She stares up at the sky for a moment before returning her gaze to mine. "The only reason I haven't done this before is because I thought there was this chance, however microscopic, that they'd let me go." She looks up and I follow her gaze to one yellow star. "Anyway, if I'm gonna stick around, I may as well watch them burn while I'm at it." She glances back at me. "Take your shadow inside. At least until you get in the elevator. They'll see you otherwise."

She turns.

"Wait," I say. "Where are you going? We might need your testimony or something!"

She looks back at me. "I'm sorry, Artemisia. About everything." Then she fades.

I follow the shadow of La Llorona with my eyes until it disappears into the street.

207

MAMI IS DEAD.

Mami is dead *again*.

Fuck.

I almost laugh, but I weep instead, all over this beautiful, olive green carpet. I hear the creak of the door but don't look up.

"Sia?"

Imani bends down, leveling her face with mine. "I was just about to leave for the hospital when I heard you. Christ, Sia. Are you—"

"Hospital?" I say. "Is my dad there? Rose? Noah?"

She nods. "Omar, too."

I exhale, long and hard. "Here," I say, handing her the USB. "It's got everything. *Everything.*"

She takes a long breath. "Come on, Sia. Come inside."

208

I WAIT UNTIL THE FULL MOON TO SCATTER MOM'S
ashes. Dad's in the passenger side of my car, the urn in his lap.

I pull up to Adam and Eve, their arms rising like serpents.

When I park, we both say nothing for a long while. The only thing
that speaks is the wind, whistling into the corners of my windows.

Dad clears his throat. "You ready?"

I nod.

"'Ta bien," he says, which is ridiculous 'cause there's nothing good
about this, and even though I know it's a figure of speech, I roll my eyes
anyway.

I sit between the cacti. Dad stands next to me.

"Should we say something?" he asks.

I close my eyes and two tears cool my cheeks. "I don't know what to say."

Dad drops next to me. His arms are around my shoulders. "Me
either, m'ija."

"Then let's just say nothing," I say. "Like the dark of la tierra."

Dad nods, releasing me. "Tell me that one again. I don't remember it."

I grab the urn, cradling it in my arms. "Abuela told me it just once.
I'm not sure it's right, but—" I take a breath. "Once there was a girl who
wanted to know her one true path. And she thought the best way was

to ask the sun, since the sun sees almost everything. The sun told her, *I have never seen your path.*

"Then she went to the sky. The sky told her, *I have never seen your path.*

"Then the girl spotted a serpent. And she said to the serpent, *Please help me. I need to know my one true path and you must know about paths, since you make them wherever you go.*

"The serpent said, *Yes. If you want to know your truthful path, go to the moon.*

"The moon told the girl, *Go to the big boulder when the sky is black.*"

"New moon black?" Dad asks.

"Yeah. And the girl went to the boulder when the sky was black like coffee. And there she met the spirits of Silence and Darkness. And they taught her that the most precious things, like paths that are true, can only be seen in shadows. In the dark and in the quiet. Like a seed in the black earth." I close my eyes. "And when the sliver of moon returned the next night, her light shone on the girl's footsteps, where she had walked away on her path." I sigh and focus on the sand beneath me, sparkling in the sunset's glow. "The weird thing, though, was there were tons of true paths for her. They were all spread out, long and lined like snakes. Her true path right then was just the one she'd chosen."

"What does it mean?" Dad says after a bit.

I bite both my lips and glance at him. I mean, it's got so many meanings. Like, there is no one true path. Or have some damn patience when you make a big decision. Eventually, though, I settle for: "I think it means that good things happen in the darkest places. Even though we can't see them. Or hear them."

Even if it feels like nothing good could ever happen again.

209

I POUR THE ASHES GENTLY. I SEE ANOTHER HAND HELPING
me, and when I look up, I catch a vision of my grandmother.

The wind picks up, and we watch the ashes glide into the desert, swirling like spirits.

210

TU MAMÁ, MY GRANDMOTHER WHISPERS.

"Yes?" I say.

Ella vive.

I shake my head in a chuckle. "You've got to be joking, Abuela." When there's no response, I continue. "We just poured her ashes into the desert. Like, that just happened literally ten minutes ago, you old bat!"

Only silence greets me. Silence and darkness, as thick clouds pass over the moon.

211

"SO, YEAH," NOAH SAYS, DRUMMING HIS HANDS ON the podium. "People have been using the moon for hundreds of years—for mapping and directions. And farming. And counting time."

"Can you repeat that last one, Mr. DuPont?" Mr. Woods asks. "Couldn't hear it with the, ah—" He gestures to Noah's hands.

"Huh?" Noah asks, his drumming even louder.

I grab his arms and still them. "Oh," Noah says, his cheeks pink.

I smirk and shake my head. "We've been using the moon to count time for thousands of years."

"Ah, yes, of course." Mr. Woods stands. "Does that conclude your argument?"

"Uh, we've got a little extra information," Noah says, running through his notecards.

"A little conspiracy theory. None of which is true," I add. "It's just for fun."

"Photographs of the moon," Noah says. "Have shown structures. Like buildings, maybe. To some people."

The photo on the screen behind us contains little blurs on a white landscape that honestly could just be specks on the camera lens.

"And some folks say it's hollow and moonpeople live underground." I click the computer on the podium and the picture shifts to a cartoon of little green men wandering moon craters.

"But those aliens are above ground," says Thomas Windor.

"It's just a cartoon." I shrug. "Not, like, evidence."

"Also." Noah peers at his cards. "Some people say there's a whole alien civilization on the moon's far side. Which isn't dark." He lifts a finger. "That's just a myth. And, uh . . . that's about it." He lifts his head up.

"Well done." Mr. Woods smiles. "Questions, anyone?"

Chana Moore lifts her hand. "So, like, did aliens actually land in Phoenix? I mean, that ship-thing looked totally cosmic."

I expect someone to laugh at her, but as I gaze at the class, everyone's attention is as sharp as a sword. And they're all looking at me.

I glance at Noah. His eyes are wide.

"Um," I say, looking back at the class. "All the papers say it's an advanced military craft. You know, one that was a secret."

"My dad was in the Air Force." Thomas crosses his arms. "He says he's never seen anything like that thing in his life. Not even in his dreams."

"Um." Noah stares at me.

"And all those interviews with the *Sentinel* interns," Chana adds. "They all say there was this woman who, like, ran and moved so fast, she covered a quarter of a mile in a just a second—"

"And what about that insider, what was his name? Sabertooth? What about his social media feeds!" Thomas looks at me. "Sia, everyone says it looked like it was your mom on there, before it was taken d—"

"That's enough," Mr. Woods says. "As fascinating as these conspiracy theories sound, it's important to remember that's all they are. Theories."

He nods at Noah and me. "Thank you for your presentation, Mr. DuPont and Miss Martinez."

Everyone claps as we return to our seats.

Rose places a hand on my back, but I barely feel it.

212

"REMIND ME," NOAH SAYS WHEN WE'RE AT MY LOCKER.
"Why aren't we telling anyone? About, you know. *The X-Files* stuff." He whispers the last bit.

"Because they've covered that part up, Noah. Remember? No one's going to believe it. Not anymore."

"I know but . . . Thomas believes it." He glances down. "Chana, too, I think."

I shake my head. "No one can know, Noah." I frown. "Otherwise I'll end up just like my mom was. Chained to an operating table, sedated. Or worse. And the last thing I need is everyone knowing what a freak I am, anyway."

He shakes his head. "Sia, you're not—" But he stops. He runs his arm around my waist, pulling me in. "I know," he murmurs instead. "I'm sorry."

I want to cry, but I push the tears all the way down into my belly. Tonight, in bed, when I can see the moon at the corner of my window, rays of white light breaking through the clouds. I'll cry then.

For now, I lean my head against Noah's chest, listening to the steady beat of his heart.

213

I'M WAITING FOR ROSE ON THE FRONT STEPS WHEN Jeremy walks by. He stares at me for a half second before scowling and stomping away.

A piece of paper falls from the folder in his hands. I watch it float to the ground like a white feather, and I stand and reach for it. It's trig homework.

I almost laugh, because freaking Jeremy McGhee and I actually have something in common. Mathematic negligence.

"Jeremy."

He pushes the door and walks inside.

I catch it before it shuts. "Jeremy."

He turns. "What the fuck do you want, Martinez?"

I know I should expect this from him, but his anger. It stuns me every time. My gaze drops to the top of his shirt, where one button is undone. A piece of the fabric bends back, revealing a black bruise.

Jeremy looks down. He gives me a death glare as he tucks his folder under his arm and aggressively buttons his shirt. "I said, what the fuck—"

"Here." I shove the paper at his chest. "You dropped this."

He swallows, staring. I watch the bob of his Adam's apple so I don't have to look at his face.

"Oh." He takes it into his free hand, the tips of our fingers grazing for one second. In that moment, I wonder about where hate comes from. If it was passed to Jeremy by the fists of his father, and maybe Sheriff McGhee's father did the same to him, all down the line until we reach the murder of Abel. Until we reach to when God told Adam and Eve they deserved to suffer.

None of us are all good and none of us are all bad. Like my mom said. All I wanted to do was label the sheriff a murderer and get on with my life, but he didn't actually kill Mom, you know? And I keep thinking about what Noah told me, that Sheriff McGhee cried after hitting him. That's gotta mean some little speck of soul is still left in there somewhere. And even Jeremy, who went to court, he could've lied about his dad's abuse, but he didn't. He told the truth. And that's what helped Noah's mom win her case.

Jeremy stares into my eyes and turns without a word.

And when I turn around, I don't feel angry. Not at him, not at anyone. I wonder if this was what Mom was telling me, about being better. I think it might be.

214

"I CAN'T BELIEVE YOU'RE LEAVING ME," ROSE SAYS, collapsing on my bed with a theatrical flourish.

I open one of my dresser drawers and pick up a bundle of clothing. Depositing it into a box, I look at her, still reclined, wearing a lavender dress and looking, for all intents and purposes, like a woman in the middle of a *W* photo shoot. "I thought you were gonna help me pack."

She gives me a look. "I'm protesting."

I shake my head and throw open another drawer. "It's not what I want, Rose. It's just, after everything that's happened . . ." I don't get specific. I don't say, having lost Mom again, living someplace where everything reminds me of her . . . it feels like being constantly stabbed in the gut with dull knives. Instead, I add, "We just can't stay anymore."

Rose sighs. "I get it, Sia. I do." And raises an eyebrow. "So . . . no one knows about . . . you know. Your superpowers." She whispers the last bit.

I shrug. "Armando, that head honcho. He knows. And probably a bunch of other head honchos and shit. But ever since the whole experimentation program's been exposed, they've been kinda busy, testifying and all that."

"You're not afraid, though? That they'll come and find you?"

I think of the way I can slip into a shadow, all flat and dark. I don't even get sick afterward anymore. And of how I kicked open a locked car door as though it were made of paper. And then I think of what they did to all those innocent people. To my mom. "I think they should be more afraid of me."

"Heck yes, they should." Rose nods, then brightens. "In all the chaos, I forgot to tell you, I had dinner with Dad last week."

I straighten my back. "Oh? How was it?"

Rose half smiles. "It—well, it was kind of awkward. At first. Okay, it was awkward, like, the whole time. But he apologized, Sia. For giving me such a hard time with my clothes and stuff, and he said he was proud of me, for everything. From my good grades to being a good friend and good Christian." Her eyes are a little shiny.

"Wow."

"Yeah."

"That's, like. A miracle, huh?"

Rose nods. "It is, isn't it?"

We're silent for a moment as I think about Cruz Damas and how he really does love Rose, and how maybe we're all doing the best we can and the best we know how at the time, but we all make mistakes. And the beauty of it is we can fix them, you know? Just by being humble, by saying sorry, by showing our love.

Rose clears her throat. "Well, you're coming over this evening, right? Mom's cooking you a farewell dinner."

"Crap," I say. "I was supposed to go out with Noah, but there's no way I'm missing your mom's dinner."

"Bring Noah."

I look up. "Really? You're mom's not—"

Rose shrugs. "She's different now that she's kicked Dad out. I know you've been too busy to visit, but trust me. I don't think she'll mind."

I nod slowly. "Okay. Sure. I'll call and see if he's game." I go back to shoving my clothes in boxes. "Will Sam be there?"

"She can't. Her dad's going to be in town and he's taking her out." Rose stops my hands. "Shit, Sia. I already miss the heck out of you. How are we going to get through senior year apart, huh?"

Now Rose is crying for real, and so am I, and we hug for so long, my hands go numb, but we just keep holding each other until we're okay again. I've known this since the sixth grade: if you hug your best friend long enough, everything almost feels okay again, even if just for a little while.

215

I PASS A MOUNTAIN OF BROWN BOXES ON MY WAY TO the backyard.

I hadn't wanted to see what's become of my garden after weeks of neglect. But now I have to. To say goodbye, at least.

Predictably, the corn is brittle and half-dead. I run my fingers through its papery leaves.

"I'm sorry," I whisper.

But my hand catches on something big—a husk. I peel it back and gasp.

There, a hundred perfect, plump kernels. Red like our blood, the blood that goes back and back until we meet our antepasados de maíz.

It makes me feel like I can keep the corn tradition going, in our new home. Maybe I can still make tortillas for Dad. Maybe I can make peace with the kitchen spirits.

I cup the crimson cob like it's the most precious thing I've ever touched.

216

I FIND DAD IN THE OFFICE, STACKING BOOKS. "HEY," I SAY.
"What's up, m'ija?" He doesn't look at me. It's like packing has hypnotized him lately. Sometimes he even forgets to eat.

I clear my throat. "Just wondering if you're, you know. Okay."

He finally looks up and gives me a smile. "'Course I am. Why wouldn't I be?"

Uh, I don't know. Maybe because Mom's dead for the second time and nothing could possibly suck more? Obviously I can't say this. So I lean on the door and gesture to a frame in his hand. It's an embroidery of my name, Artemisia Liana Martinez. Abuela made it when I was born, all in different purples with swirly letters. I've always loved it.

My question is so sudden, I don't even realize it's inside me until it's out. "Why did Mom name me Artemisia?"

Dad blinks. "You mean she never told you?"

I shake my head. All I know is it was Mom's choice.

Dad sits in his office chair, rolling back a little. The light from the window hits the lines on his face so perfectly, I get a premonition of what he'll look like as a viejo. "There's an artist," he begins. "Named Artemisia Gentileschi. She was raped by one of her tutors. And she took him to court. Nothing much happened to the guy, but still. Women didn't just do that stuff back then. Hundreds of years ago."

I shift my weight from one hip to the other as he continues.

"So on our second date, your mom and I went to the Cortaro Museum of Art. And they had an exhibit for this artist's work. Her paintings are vivid. Women who are strong, plotting to murder a wicked man. Women slicing off the heads of men. And your mother, she looked at her self-portrait and said, *I'm going to name my daughter after her.*"

I burst out laughing. I can't help it. "And that didn't scare you?"

And Dad cracks a smile, too. His first since . . . everything. "To be honest, yeah, I was a little scared. But then I forgot all about it until we found out you were a girl. She said, and I'll never forget this, she said she wanted to bless you with that power in your name. The power of a woman who survived and made her own way." He smiles again. "And now I can't imagine you as anything but Artemisia."

I don't know why, but I hug my father then. We just hold each other in the afternoon light coming in like drips of gold across us.

If I could name this moment, it would be Hope. Cheesy, okay, but true. Because despite everything that happened, we talked about Mom and didn't lose it. We laughed. And I know that's what Mom wants for us. And I also know Dad and I, we're going to do okay. Even when we do have to cry because of our broken open hearts. We will always have these memories of Mom. And we will also have each other.

217

"HEY," NOAH SAYS WHEN I WALK UP TO HIS CAR.

"Hey," I say, smiling.

He peers at my house. "Is your dad watching through the window?"

"Probably." I climb in.

"Ah," he says, dropping his hands. "I'll have to kiss you later, then, yeah?"

I nod and buckle my seat belt. "How's your mom?" I say.

"Well, awesome now. She said she's getting us a bigger place." He glances at me. "I told her to please consider Tucson."

I can't even think of something smart-ass to say. I just smile like a clown and finally smack him on the arm. "You did?"

He nods. "No guarantees, but she was open to the idea."

"Well, shit," I say. "That would be really nice."

He grins, flashing that dimple. "It would."

218

"SIA," MRS. DAMAS SAYS, PULLING ME INTO A HUG. I
about drop in shock when she does the same with Noah.

Rose's house is much lighter. It's like Mrs. Damas is keeping the
curtains open a little wider. And also there isn't so much bible crap
crowding everyone's vibe.

Of course, it might also be because Omar was invited to dinner.

"Noah! My dude." He gives Noah a handshake and pats me awk-
wardly on the shoulder. "Sia." He sits back on the sofa. "So." He folds
his hands. "Seen any Reptilians lately?"

"No alien talk!" Rose calls. "Not for dinner." Mrs. Damas pushes us
into the kitchen, where we join Rose at the table.

"Smells good," Noah says.

"It smells incredible," Omar corrects. "I've never tried Haitian food
before and Rose says my life hasn't been worth it as a result."

"It's true," I say.

"Let's say grace." Mrs. Damas clasps her hands together, beckoning
us to do the same.

"Mommy," Rose mutters.

Mrs. Damas ignores her and bows her head. "Thank you, God,

for the earth, for food, and friends." She looks up and reaches for the platanos. "Sia?" She hands me the platter.

"Wow," Rose remarks. "That was really casual."

"I like it," I say.

"Me too." Rose nods.

Mrs. Damas beams at us. "Eat!" she commands.

And we do.

219

NOAH PRESSES HIS LIPS TO MINE ALL GENTLE WHEN HE drops me off.

"I'll see you tomorrow," he says, his voice husky in my ear, a hand at my hip. "To help load up the truck."

I nod and wrap my arms around him, jumping over the console to kiss him deeper.

220

I DON'T GO INSIDE THE HOUSE WHEN NOAH LEAVES.

Instead, I get in my car and head to the highway.

221

I CAN'T HELP BUT THINK ABOUT ALL THE ALTERNATIVE realities spread out before me, the ones Mr. Woods once said may very well exist alongside all of us.

In one universe, the United States welcomes the hungry and the poor. Even the brown hungry and poor.

In another, Tim McGhee is a decent person, or at least decent enough that he doesn't care that Mom is around. And he doesn't call ICE on her. Ever.

And in another universe, Mom stays in Mexico after deportation. Even broke, even hungry, even brokenhearted. Maybe one of those mythic "another ways" would've been opened up by some miracle de Guadalupe. Maybe she'd have gotten a place, even a shack with holes for windows and dirt for floors. Maybe Dad and I could've moved in and I could've gone to the Universidad Autónoma de Chihuahua, and majored in something that would make this fucked-up world better somehow.

Maybe right now, I'd wake up to her in the kitchen, cooking migas with leftover corn tortillas, made from our gemstone maíz. Maybe Dad would've made her that corn kernel jewelry with it, too, plump beads of rose and sun and water at her neck. He'd pour the coffee and we'd all sit down and pray. Not to an old white dude in the sky, but to the great, unnamable mystery that makes seedlings crack open and reach toward the light. That makes the cacti dance when you're not looking.

Jesus Cristo. I need to stop thinking about this shit.

222

I SPOT HIM WHERE THE WORLD BEGINS BEFORE I CAN
even see him. I know that sounds unbelievable, but it's the truth. Maybe it's 'cause we share the same blood now, I don't know, but when River appears in my headlights, I don't even blink.

He's wearing a button-down the color of rust, and, coupled with his ochre pants, he looks like he's a ghost of the desert. Like something risen from the sand itself.

I step out of the car and walk up to him. He's perched near Eve, like he's been examining her.

"This is my spot," I say. "Mine and my mom's and my grandmother's."

He nods. "I know."

I cross my arms. "What are you doing here?"

He glances at the sky, where the sun hovers over the line of distant hills and boulders. "Paying my respects."

I scowl. "She didn't love you, dude. She loved my dad."

He nods again. "I know that, too."

We both stare at the peach horizon line for a while, until the temperature noticeably dips several degrees. I shiver.

He puts his hands in his pockets and approaches me. "If you want, Sia, I can teach you. How to control your abilities."

I scoff. "Why would I want that?"

He shakes his head. "Those officials—they're not going to leave you alone for long. When they come again—and they will—it's best if you know everything."

I nearly shiver again. The way he says *everything*. But then I narrow my eyes. "You lied, though. About visiting Earth to just check on us. And God knows what else. Why the hell should I trust you to tell me anything, much less everything?"

"It wasn't a lie, Sia."

"Oh? What was it, then? An alternative fact?"

He lifts his mouth in a half smile, his eyes on the few stars visible against the inky indigo. "We came to see you on Earth for the first time. So yes, that part was a lie." He sighs. "We weren't even certain you humans were here. But Gods, you were, you are." He looks at me for a moment and sets his eyes at the sky again. "This universe is so much bigger than I could've fathomed."

"Why'd you come?" I'm not interested in his philosophical epiphanies.

"For a myth. A fairy tale." He closes his eyes, like he's in pain. "We were desperate." It's hardly above a whisper. I'm not even sure I heard that part right.

I shake my head and scoff. "Fairy tales? More lies, you mean."

"All those stories have the truth in them somewhere." He looks at me from the corner of his eyes. "Like a seed in the black earth."

I frown and tear my gaze away. Asshole. "What if I don't want you to teach me shit? Because I don't like you? What then?"

He shrugs. "It's up to you." He reaches behind his back and pulls a folded paper from his pocket. "Thought you might be interested in the information on page four." He turns to a white pickup truck.

"Hey," I call. "How do I contact you? If I decide to let a liar tell me more 'truths,' I mean?"

"I'll keep in touch." He gets in the car, revs up the engine. I don't watch him drive away. Instead, I trace a wayward gray cloud with the tip of my finger. Like I can touch it.

223

IN THE JEEP, I LIGHT LA GUADALUPE. THE CANDLE'S SO low, I burn my fingers a couple of times while trying to reach into the glass. Finally, it gets going. I lean back and open the paper.

"Details of Human Experiments," reads the headline. I turn to page four, where there are bullet points summarizing all the nasty little secrets of the mission. Apparently someone's taken the time to comb through the thousands of files that were in that drive Katia gave me.

One of the points is marked with a blue-ink star.

I stare at it and blink. And then I blink again.

Under the header of "Successful Experiments" is *human cloning*.

224

DESERT ROSE AND OAK FILL THE CAR. I INHALE DEEPLY,
letting the scent settle all around and inside me.

Ves, my grandmother whispers. *Ella vive.*

She lives.

ACKNOWLEDGMENTS

Sia Martinez and the Moonlit Beginning of Everything arrived in my life one evening in Tallahassee, Florida. I was taking a walk among the magnolias, the hibiscus, the wisteria. Everything smelling soft, sweet, sticky like honey. The sky was sealike in color. And there, as I took a step on the sidewalk, the idea came: a UFO crash in the desert. I knew the only occupant was Mexican, I knew she was an undocumented immigrant, and I knew she was looking for her daughter. The second image of the book arrived soon after: that daughter, in class, reading a letter to a boy who'd been hateful to her. These were the two scenes that began this whole adventure.

At the time, I was working on my MFA thesis in poetry, I had a baby, and I was preparing to publish my first book of poetry. So I had to wait several months before I could put the pieces together, the connecting words between a girl reading in class to a mother crashing a spacecraft in the desert.

When I finally had the time, I was living in a tiny side-of-the-house apartment in Albany. It was summer, everything was blooming once again, but this time, they were northernly plants I never learned the names of. I just remember colors: white blossoming trees filled with bumblebees, purple gobletlike flowers that emerald-sparkling humming-birds would visit. I took my baby, then fifteen months old, to the park every day. And when we got back, I would nurse him to a nap, and I'd write.

Between those moments and now feels like the most gorgeous dream, with the kindness and support of so many people along the way. My gratitude can't be conveyed enough, but I'm going to try anyway.

To my son, Ansel, who was my constant writing companion. I hope one day you'll read this book and feel proud of your mama. I hope that you'll see exactly what happens when you stick up and make time for your dreams. To my husband, Jordan, who has read all my crappy first drafts and did nothing but encourage me, especially through the times I needed it the most. To my agent, Elizabeth Bewley, for believing in Sia, and me, from day one. Your support, encouragement, ideas, input, and friendship are invaluable to me. And to everyone at Sterling Lord for making me feel at home from the beginning.

To my editor, Jen Ung, for your enthusiasm, cute dog GIFs, and ingenuity in helping to shape *Sia* to be the best it could be. Polishing this manuscript with you has been a joy. To everyone at Simon Pulse for your wondrous kindness and support.

To my very first readers, my sister, Jessica Selby, and friend, Larissa Anne Simpson. Knowing how busy the both of you are and how you still made time to read my draft will always be a gift to me. I'm grateful for all of your feedback, advice, and love.

To my family, for always believing in me: Mom, Dad, Joey, Nana, J. R., and Polo (rest in peace, Welito). To Tod and Tina for everything you've given me and my family, especially the gift of writing time!

To everyone who helped to make *Sia Martinez* its absolute best, including production editor Rebecca Vitkus and copyeditor Carla Benton. I'm so grateful for your marvelous work. And to Laura Eckes and Jeff Östberg, who made the most gorgeous cover I've ever seen. Your art was beyond everything I hoped the cover would be, so much so that I cried upon seeing it for the first (and second, and maybe third) time! I will always treasure it.

To Anne Caston. The seeds of your mentorship are in this manuscript. I will always be grateful for your tender guidance and encouragement.

To my ancestors, whose descendants came to the U.S. as refugees. So much has been lost, but I hope, somehow, my work makes you proud.

To my spiritual guides. You know who you are and I offer you all the pink roses and crepe myrtle blooms in gratitude. I am well because of you.

To all the writers who came before me, who paved the way. I wish I could name you all here, but I'm afraid my list would be endless. Just, thank you for your courage.

And to the writers who are arriving now. *Sia Martinez* started with an idea in a cramped Airbnb, baby in my lap, spiral notebook in my hands. Imagine the worlds you can create at this moment, right where you are. And go make them.

ABOUT THE AUTHOR

Raquel Vasquez Gilliland is a Mexican American poet, novelist, and painter. She received her MFA in poetry from the University of Alaska Anchorage in 2017. She's most inspired by fog and seeds and the lineages of all things. When she's not writing, Raquel tells stories to her plants and they tell her stories back. She lives in Tennessee with her beloved family and mountains. Raquel has published two books of poetry. *Sia Martinez and the Moonlit Beginning of Everything* is her first novel.